Staying Relevant

Names for grandpa on lower front cover
Grandpa- English
Opa – German
Daideó – Gaelic
Papi – Spanish (South America)
阿公 (A-Gong) – Taiwan
爺爺(Yeye) – China
Ojisan - Japan
Nonno - Italain
Lito - Spanish

Additional books by author:

Firehouse Fraternity Oral History Series:
Volume I: Becoming a Firefighter
Volume II: Life Between Alarms
Volume III: Equipment
Volume IV: Responding
Volume V: Riots to Renaissance
Volume VI: Changing the NFD

The Newark Riots: A View from the Firehouse

An Eerie Silence: An Oral History of Newark
Firefighters at the WTC

First Days/First Nights: The Beginnings of Newark
Fire Department Careers

Remembrances of Newark

The Best Job in the World: Learning the Job

Hervey's Boys: New Jersey's First Chinese Community
1870-1886 (And What Happened After That)

Fiction:
The Firebox Stalker
The Hand Life Dealt you
A-zou: A Woman Living in Interesting Times

Children's Fiction:
A Hundred Battles (YA)
A Broken Glass (YA)
Balancing Act (Middle Grade)

Staying Relevant

A Novel of Adjusting to Life After Sixty

Neal Stoffers

Springfield and Hunterdon Publishing
Copyright 2023
www.newarkfireoralhistory.com

Special thanks to Chicago Fire Department Battalion Chief Mike Burns (ret.) for his help with the details of the CFD.

Copyright © 2023 by Neal Stoffers

First Printing: 2023

ISBN: 978-1-970034-36-3

Springfield and Hunterdon Publishing
East Brunswick, NJ 08816-5852

Chapter One

"But Burt- - -You've been with Burt since you graduated."

"Burt's gay Dad. We just roomed together to save money and make it look good. He didn't want to break his parent's heart and I didn't want to break yours."

"Mine? What about your mother?"

"She knows. But now Burt has found someone he wants to commit to, so I'm making room and telling you. I don't want to live a lie anymore, so you need to hear the truth."

Jake Covey stood quietly in front of his daughter in shock. The studio apartment he was helping her move into seemed to fade. He had spent thirty years going into burning buildings, pulling people out, getting knocked down by the heat and the smoke and the buildings collapsing. After the strains, the sprains, the burns, the smoke, the exposure to who knew what to raise this child and her brother, now this?

How much longer did he have? Yeah, some firefighters made it to ninety, but most didn't and some didn't crack sixty. He just had the feeling he was running out of time. Granted he had reached so many of his life goals. After he retired those goals had been whittled down to two. Die before his children and hold at least one grandchild in his arms. Tim seemed to be in no rush to find a wife and start a family. How could his last goal be reached if his son was slow on the draw and his daughter was a lesbian?

Up until now, the biggest challenge was just staying relevant. If you have reached all your goals in life, is what you do pertinent anymore? He wanted to do more than help keep the economy going my spending his pension. He wanted to contribute something. Yes, he was a CPA and that allowed him to be part of the work a day world to the extent he wanted to be, but how to stay relevant in his family's life? If he had a grandchild, there would be a reason to strive for better.

He would be a grandfather and had examples of how to play that role. His role as father to adult children in a changing world was more ambiguous.

"Dad? I really need you to accept me for who I am."

This snapped him out of his stupor. The apartment background came back into focus. He wasn't happy with the balcony and there was too much glass, but that could be covered with curtains. That had been his assessment when he had walked in. It all became trivial to him when Pauli made her confession.

"Pauli, how could I not accept you?" he replied quietly. "I'm your father. I've always told you the only way for you to know how much I love you is for you to have a child of your own."

A look of relief passed over his daughter's face.

Then he muttered to himself, "I guess that's not happening."

She reached out for his hand and reassured him. "I remember how much you've hinted around about grandkids. Don't worry, I want to have a child."

"Doesn't that become problematic now?" he asked. "Who's going to be the father?"

"I'll cross that bridge when I come to it," she replied ending that discussion.

"Do you have someone also or is it only Burt?

"Only Burt, Dad."

"Okay," he sighed. "We can talk while we put this bed together. Your mother only loaned me out for a week, remember. Could you hand me the hammer?"

His mind was racing as he accepted the tool. No use trying to talk her out of her orientation. He had seen more than enough responding to incidents in the middle of Newark to know people had no control over who they found attractive. The price some people paid for being different was frightening. Hide your disappointment, he counseled himself, or she will vanish from your life. Organizing the pieces of the metal frame on the floor, he did a quick change of subject and became the practical dad again.

2

"Isn't this bed a little large for the space you have?"

"Well, yes, but I didn't want to go out and buy a smaller bed until I landed a job."

"And how is the search going?"

"I'm scouring all the job postings on line. Sent out a lot of applications while I was in Oklahoma, but it seemed if I wasn't in Chicago and ready to go, I got passed over."

"A PhD wasn't impressive enough?" Jake asked as he started knocking the bed frame together.

"There's more than one PhD applying to the positions I'm looking at," she replied, pausing each time her father hit the frame. "That's why location is important. In this economy, they need someone now."

Jake stood up after hammering the pieces together. "Let's get the box spring on it," he said, then stepped out of the frame's middle toward the box spring leaning on the wall. "How long have you known?" was his next question. He found he couldn't verbalize the "you are a lesbian" yet, so cut the question short.

"About being a lesbian?" she asked. "Since freshman year of college, although I had some inkling of it in high school."

"And you told your mother when?"

"When Burt committed to Cortney, which is about six months ago."

Grabbing the box spring, the two of them wrestled it into position on the bed frame. As he straightened up, Jake thought back over the past six months. He could see no indication that Johanna was unusually upset. She snapped at his antics on occasion, but after forty years of marriage Jake just let it roll off his back. It must have been a ten-ton weight pressing down on her. Only for their children would his wife keep such a secret. He expected an emotional response when he told her Pauli had informed him.

"Okay, let's attach the headboard before we put the mattress on," Jake

3

suggested before stepping around the frame. That should have been done before the box spring was put down. A simple mistake that told him how upset he really was. Would his daughter pick up on it? Focusing on the task at hand would be the only way to keep a lid on his reaction.

"Are you going to tell your godfather, or should I?" Jake asked.

"Paul already knows."

"Already knows? I'm the only one you didn't tell?"

"He's not a fireman. He's Dr. Nereto," Pauli pointed out. "And can be a lot more reasonable than an over protective father."

"Over protective?" Jake scoffed. "His brother was a fireman."

"Doesn't count. Different attitude."

"You prejudge us."

"I know you."

They both moved toward the headboard that was leaning against the far wall. Dragging it to the frame and positioning it in silence, each was navigating through choppy waters trying to gauge how the other felt.

"Could you hand me the wrenches?" Jake asked.

Pauli reached over to the kitchen counter and picked up the package of wrenches they had purchased that morning in Ace Hardware. Jake had insisted she have the basic tools necessary to do small repairs while living alone. She handed them to him with a small smile.

"Why the grin?"

"Oh, just remembering all you said this morning at Ace," she replied. "Or at least some of it. You threw a lot at me in a short period of time."

"Trying to make up for lost time," he chuckled. "Tim got all the 'repairs to the house' lessons. I never expected you to live alone."

"Now, that's sexist, don't you think?" she teased.

"At least you didn't say misogynistic," he responded. "No, I don't think so.

4

It's practical. The world is engineered by men for men. You ladies have a hard time with tools because of it."

"Well, you didn't seem to have a hard time choosing tools for me. It was simple. Don't get a sixteen-ounce hammer, get a twelve-ounce hammer."

Jake laughed at his daughter's observation. She was right. There was always a way around a tool problem. It was men who insisted on doing the physical work around the house. The women just used words to get things done. They could always use words better than men.

"Don't get too technical here," Jake parried while crouching to bolt the headboard to the frame. "I did fires and do numbers, no philosophic discussions."

"Numbers?" she asked. "You did fires and do taxes, Dad. You don't want to get into a conversation with a mathematician and say you do numbers. As for a philosophic discussion, you're the one who brought up how the world was engineered."

Finishing attaching the headboard Jake stood and pointed at the mattress. They both moved the few steps to where it was leaning. The thought crossed Jake's mind that nothing was really out of reach in this apartment. Studios didn't give you a lot of space, but they were inexpensive which made them ideal for a newly graduated thirty-year-old woman starting her career. Sliding the mattress over, they let it drop onto the box spring and adjusted it.

"There," Pauline sighed. "Now we'll put some things up on the walls and get something to eat." With that she walked over to the boxes they had piled in the hall and pulled out a flag. Then she pushed another box with picture frames into the kitchen/living room area. When she unfurled the flag, Jake didn't recognize its colors. It certainly wasn't the US flag, neither the German nor Irish colors.

"What country does that belong to?" he asked.

"Dad!" Pauli responded in exasperation. "It's the LGBTQ colors."

"The LGBTQ flag?" he asked. "What's that? The rainbow coalition only different?"

"Rainbow coalition?" she laughed. "Well at least you understood LGBTQ even if you don't recognize the flag. I want it to hang over the hallway entrance."

Jake caught himself hesitating. Why advertise it when there was no shortage of wackos in the world. After a second, he came to the conclusion that it was inside her apartment, so no wackos would be able to see it. Problem was Pauli picked up on his studder step. She stopped and turned to him.

"Dad, thanks for trying so hard," she whispered, struggling not to be emotional. "I really appreciate your effort."

Jake reached over to brush a tear from his daughter's cheek. "I just want you to be happy, Pauli. That's the only way I'll be happy."

She gave her dad a weak smile and then walked over to the hallway. "I picture it hanging down from here, kind of like a Japanese restaurant."

Jake chuckled. "You going to take up Asian cooking?"

Chapter Two

"Jake!"

His wife's shout woke Jake from a deep sleep. Johanna always got up early to ride her exercise bike, so she was calling from the spare room. Her urgency pulled him out of bed and propelled him down the hall. He grabbed a pair of sweats on the way.

When he got to the doorway of the spare room, Jo was on her bike pointing at the muted television she had been watching while he slept. There was a breaking news report of the screen: Newark firefighter seriously injured.

"Do you think you know him?" Jo asked.

"It could be a her, but it's possible," Jake answered. "I've been in every firehouse in the city over the past year doing personal taxes or accounting for part-time businesses."

What tour was working last night? Mark O'Brian was the only one from his old crew still on the job. He is a Battalion Chief, so he is not supposed to be stretching lines into buildings anymore. Jake slipped his sweats on while staring at the screen reading the subtitles.

"Could you turn on the sound? I'm awake now."

"As we get more information, we'll inform you," the reporter said before the news switched to the weather.

"What did they say?" he asked still shaking off the sleep.

"That there was a report of a Newark firefighter seriously injured at a fire in the Ironbound section of the city."

Jake could tell from her tone that she was shaken. The tough part of being a fire department wife was getting to know so many of the guys. This was especially true of Jo because guys have always come to their house to have taxes or accounting done. Now she was struggling with this news because it was personal.

"Why did I have to fall for a firefighter?" she asked. Normally this would be said factiously, but now it was with regret.

"You didn't fall for a firefighter," Jake countered halfheartedly, still struggling to come to grips with the news. "You fell for an accounting student."

"Accounting?" she scoffed. "Once a firefighter, always a firefighter. And once a firefighter's wife, always a firefighter's wife."

"I'll reach out to the deputy to see what happened," Jake said purposely ignoring his wife's statement. The phone rang before he reached it. He felt his stomach drop as soon as he saw the caller ID. It was Mark's wife, Jill.

"Jill, how is he?" he asked on the assumption she was calling to tell him something had happened. He heard Jo react in the background.

"I don't know yet," Jill answered. "I'm on my way to UMDNJ right now. Chief Gardiner called me, but he wouldn't say anything other than he's banged up."

Jake reacted slowly. Jill was a strong woman who had been through a few of this type of emergency trip over the years. He was trying to figure out if the Chief calling was good or bad. The first time Mark had been seriously injured the Chief had sent Jake down to tell Jill. That was thirty years ago. Had department procedures changed? Was Mark so badly injured they weren't sure he would make it through the morning and so needed Jill to get to the city quickly? Questions with no answers were all he had right now. Jill needed support, not an inquisition. Deciding they would send someone to inform Jill if it was life threatening, Jake settled on a reassuring tone.

"You're driving, so I'll make this quick," he said. "Jo and I'll hop in the car and meet you at University."

"Brian's driving," Jill told him. "I'm too angry to drive right now."

Brian? Mark's youngest son had just been appointed to the job. Did the department send him? That would change his calculations.

"Brian's driving," he muttered.

8

"Yes, he came back for a five-year high school get together. Then he crashed in his old room."

The relief Jake felt was short lived. The second part of what Jill said registered. She was pissed. No matter what happened, Mark was going to catch hell.

"God, I wish I had followed Jo's example," Jill sighed in a husky voice.

Jake had retired after spending the last year of his career driving Mark. That transfer out of Six Engine had been the result of being caught in a partial collapse that put him in the hospital for a few days and then rehab for a couple of months. Jo had insisted on it. Then when they did away with chief's aides, she demanded he retire.

"We'll meet you at the hospital," Jake assured her. "Then you can talk it out with Jo."

"Thanks Jake," Jill replied. "I'm going to need her shoulder to cry on."

After he hung up the phone, it immediately rang again. Jake saw it was from Mark's firehouse.

"Hello."

"Jake, it's Tom North from Twenty-seven Engine. Did you hear what happened to the Chief?"

Tom was an old friend who had spent years fighting fires in the center of the city with Jake. He had transferred Down Neck after getting promoted to captain. Twenty-seven rode out of the same house as Mark, but Tom was on the tour that was working today. "Tom, I just got off the phone with Jill. She is on the way up to Newark, but could only say he got banged up."

"Banged up?" Tom said with a bitter chuckle. "Jake, he fell through one of those level skylights they have in the new construction. Dropped twenty feet and landed on a concrete floor. Thank God he had a mask on. Landed on the tank which took the brunt of the fall. If he had fallen ten feet to the left or right, he would have landed on machinery. That would have probably killed him. The guys pushed into

9

the building after the roof guys sent a mayday. His PASS alarm was on, so they found him pretty quickly."

"What was he doing on the roof?"

"You know how he is. He had to check it out for himself, make sure the guys were safe up there."

"How banged up is he?"

"He was in pretty bad shape, Jake," was the honest reply. "When EMS rolled him out, he was strapped to a backboard and he wasn't conscious. They seem to think he broke his back."

"I'm on my way up with Jo," Jake said. "Told Jill we would meet her at University."

"Good, I think she's going to need some support."

Jake got Jo up to speed as the two of them prepared to leave. A quick change of clothes, protein bars for breakfast, and out the door. They didn't say anything until the car was on the Turnpike.

"Jill said she wished she had followed your example," Jake said.

"Not the same," Jo said. "The fire department is Mark's life. You're an accountant who liked to play in the firehouse. You had somewhere else to go. He doesn't."

Jake maneuvered the car through traffic at a good clip, hoping his firefighter plates would give him a little leeway with the State Troopers. His thoughts had turned inward and he began blaming himself. It didn't take long for these ideas to force themselves out of his mouth.

"If I were still on the job, maybe I could have prevented it"

A shocked appearance passed over her face for an instant, then she exploded. "Don't even go there! If you were still on the job, you'd be very lonely." Then she got hold of herself and calmly began counseling him.

"Will you listen to yourself. Mark is a professional Battalion Chief. He knows how to operate on a roof. You broke him in. You know that."

"I'm a useless piece of shit is what I know."

Jill reacted negatively. "Useless? You have a thriving CPA business. That's useless?"

"It's not the same," he insisted. "Crunching numbers doesn't have the same immediacy as fighting fires."

She looked up at the roof of the car and then came right back at him. "Jake, you have to accept that you're not twenty-five anymore," she reminded him. "Mark made his decisions. He'd ripped you apart if he heard you now. Let it go, babe."

Jake took a deep breath and exhaled slowly. "That's easier said than done."

Jill didn't accept that and instead continued to push the subject, apparently trying to resolve Jake's doubts before they got to the hospital. "It's a young man's job unless you make chief and you didn't want to do that."

"If he hadn't listened to my reasoning for not studying, maybe he would have sent someone else up there instead. He was an engine man. He had no business on a roof. I should have been there."

"What are you talking about?" she shot back. "First, he was a firefighter, not just an engine man. He knows how to get the roof. And been there? So you would have fallen through the roof? Aren't the scars on your back and your screwed up knee enough? They did away with battalion drivers anyway, so you wouldn't have been there."

"My knee is a non-issue," Jake insisted.

"Non-issue?" Jo said. "You think I don't see you rubbing it when the weather changes? How many ligaments did you tear when your leg went through that hole? You can't even walk on the beach without pain."

"Discomfort."

"Ha! Okay, discomfort, your knee's more of an issue than your back; that's just scarring. Careful in the sun. Ten years from now you'll probably need a knee

11

replacement."

"Thanks for the vote of confidence."

"The truth hurts as much as your knee, sweety."

He knew not to reply as soon as he heard, sweety.

They rode in silence for a few exits before Jill started to reason with him. "Remember the valor awards dinner? I asked him when he was going to retire and he said . . . "

"When it's not fun anymore," Jake answered. "You said he was a sick puppy."

"No, I said you were all sick puppies," she corrected. "I don't think it's fun for him anymore. When you retired, you didn't think it was fun anymore either."

Jake remembered saying that, but it was only half his thoughts. It wasn't fun anymore because she threatened to divorce him if he didn't retire. He thought better of mentioning that.

They passed through the toll plaza as they finished their debate. He guided the car through the exiting traffic and onto Route Seventy-eight. From there they got off at the Clinton Avenue exit. Twenty-minutes later, Jake pulled into the UMDNJ parking lot. There were a couple of rigs and a chief's gig in the lot, as well as a television crew from the local cable news network. Jake hoped they would leave Jill alone. After parking the car, he turned to Jo.

"I don't anticipate talking to Mark," he said. "From what Tom told me, he's probably full of morphine and completely out of it. You get to Jill and I'll try and hold off all the guys who will be pestering her."

"Okay, if Brian is still here, he can carry messages between us," Jill suggested. "We're going to have to eat at some point. Do you think Jill will be up for it?"

"I don't know," he sighed. "The impression I got is she's livid at Mark and herself. Him for being stubborn and herself for not threatening him."

"Promise you won't bring up the useless piece of shit comment?" she asked.

"Jill has enough on her plate right now, she doesn't have to hear that."

"You'll have to call Paul and tell him tonight is off," Jo said as they began walking toward the building.

"Yeah, he'll understand."

"Understand? He'll be upset," Jo snapped. "Understanding is not the issue. Mark was John's captain, right?"

"John was Paul's brother, not his clone. He's going to want to know how he can help and what his injuries are. Then he'll immediately put together a treatment and chiropractic plan that Mark won't do." Jake chuckled.

"From what Tom said, Mark broke his back. Shouldn't he be careful about doing chiropractic adjustments?"

"Paul will do the research. Remember the oath, do no harm."

"Do no harm?" Jo asked. "He's also a Casanova. A lovable Casanova, but a Casanova all the same."

Jake couldn't help but laugh. It was a much-needed respite from the self-criticism he had been engaging in on the ride up.

They stepped into the normal controlled chaos of the UMDNJ emergency room and were quickly directed to the room Mark had been moved to. After explaining to the receptionist their relation to the Battalion Chief just admitted, the two of them made their way through the hospital hallways. Jo had worked this ER for twenty years. Jake was amazed when it didn't bother her that she no longer knew the people who worked here. Firemen may miss the firehouse and their crew after they retire, but nurses didn't seem to miss the ER.

At least Mark wasn't in intensive care, Jake thought as they moved down the hall. When they turned the corner to the hallway leading to Mark's room, there was a group of firefighters quietly talking at the end of the corridor. One of the guys looked up and saw Jake. He said something and the group turned towards Jake and Jo. Everyone there knew Mark and Jake had a long history going back to the "war years" of the 70s and 80s. No matter how irrelevant Jake felt, the

13

immediate respect he received from these guys let him know he was still part of the brotherhood.

"Jake," Tom North called out and walked down the hall to meet them. "Jill's inside with the Chief and the Deputy. He's pretty banged up. Broken vertebrae, broken collar bone, broken ribs. They got him full of morphine right now, so he's not very responsive."

"I understand," Jake replied. They continued down the hall. When they reached the group of guys, his hand was grabbed by all the guys with rough hugs and pats on the back. Jo was greeted with quiet nods of the head from the young guys and gentle hugs from the guys she knew. The uncharacteristic silence of the group told Jake how serious it was. They quickly finished their greetings and stepped into the room. Jill was sitting next to her husband's bed. She stood up when Jake and Jo entered the room. Mark seemed to be sleeping.

"Jake, Jo," she said quietly. "Thank you for coming." Before the two of them could respond, Mark came to life.

"Fucking Covey," was all he could get out.

Jill looked at her husband, seeming unable to decide whether to laugh or cry.

"It figures," she finally said. "Can't say a word to me, but he can curse at you." They all laughed. Then Jo went to give Jill a hug and they both began to cry.

Jake walked over to Mark's side and leaned over to talk quietly into his ear. "You dummy," he said. "You're too old to be up on a roof like that. You're gonna catch hell when you get out of here. We're going to have to sit down and work the numbers for a disability pension, bro. The ladies aren't letting you back in the firehouse."

Mark moved his hand slightly to let Jake know he heard. Jake patted it and stepped back. He needed a little distance for self-control. One negative of getting older was getting more emotional or was that just the result of over forty years of friendship. A friendship that almost ended last night. If he had fallen ten feet in

14

either direction, he would have been killed is what Tom had said. Feeling both irrelevant and emotionally exposed, Jake stepped out of the room for a moment. Chief Gardiner followed him. The companies had left by now, so the hallway was empty.

"Jake, you okay?" the Chief asked. The two of them had come on the job the same day and had worked with each other for decades.

"Yeah Chief," Jake replied. "It's tough, but I have to be there for him and Jill. They're going to need us."

"It's good Jo came," the Chief pointed out. "Jill needs a shoulder to cry on."

"She's a strong woman, Chief," Jake said. "She got Jo through it when I was in that collapse. They're a good team."

"As good as you and Mark were," the Chief laughed.

"Better," he replied, then changed the subject. "Chief, I should have been there. I can't help feeling I let Mark down. If I hadn't retired, maybe I could have given him a heads up and prevented this."

The Chief put his hands on Jake's shoulders and shook him gently. "Jake, there were two alarms on the scene. It was a smokey fire and they needed to assess the roof. What got him hurt was these new style skylights. You couldn't have prevented it any more than the dozens of guys on the scene. Stop beating yourself up. Thank God, he's gonna pull through."

"You sound like my wife," Jake chuckled. "I guess you're right. But I feel like a useless piece of shit. Like there's nothing I can do."

"There is something you can do. You've been through the whole rehab grind. He's going to need support, someone to kick him in the ass when it gets hard. Can't think of a better person for the job than you."

Jake laughed, then sighed.

"Why don't you come back to the firehouse for lunch?" the Chief suggested.

"Thanks Chief, but no. Jo doesn't want to set foot inside a firehouse again.

15

Doesn't like the ambiance, if you know what I mean."

"Is it the smell, the fly strips, or the noise?" the Chief laughed. "My wife hates the noise more than anything else. Even though it's a lot quieter than it was when we had bells."

"You sound like a dinosaur," Jake chuckled. "The young kids don't even know box numbers anymore. Counting bells is well beyond them. The Locution system will give them a print out and tell them the address. No need for nineteenth century technology now."

"You're making me feel old."

"When are you going to retire?"

"Have to go next year," he replied. "Hit the sixty-five-year-old pension limit in March."

"Let me know your last night. I want to be there to support you when they throw you out."

They laughed and shook hands. Then the Chief had to leave. As he walked away, Jake remembered the Chief was one of the youngest guys in their Academy class. The thought time was running out crossed his mind. No matter what Jo or the Chief said, he felt like a useless piece of shit. With that he stepped back into the room vowing to get his friend through this toughest of times. The Chief was right. They had been a hell of a team and they would be again.

It's ironic, he thought, it used to be "We need a ladder in the back. There are people hanging out of the third-floor window!" Now it's going to be, "I know it's hard, but you have to push. You can do it." How far the mighty, or at least the useful, have fallen.

Chapter Three

Jake looked at the caller ID before picking up the phone in his basement office. He chuckled to himself remembering all the prank calls he made as a boy. "Is your refrigerator running? Why don't you go catch it?" Kids these days couldn't get away with that silliness. The caller ID would give them away. The ID said it was Pauli calling. Johanna had warned him to expect this call.

"Jo," he called. "It's Pauli." Something told him his wife was holding back information. Was he being set up by the women in his life? They had been so secretive lately. He picked up the receiver knowing full well that any conversation would be dominated by mother and daughter. All he had to do was grunt occasionally.

"Hello, Pauli."

"Hi Dad, is Mom getting on the line also?"

"Yes, she's been waiting for your call," he answered. "Should be on in a second."

"How's Uncle Mark?" she asked, filling the void.

"He's back up to speed," Jake told her. "It took some doing, but he listened to my advice and went out on the disability pension. Now he's adjusting to retirement. Your Aunt Jill is keeping him honest. Did I tell you what the therapist said when he started working with her?"

"Not that I remember, but that was almost two years ago, wasn't it?"

"Something like that, anyway, she asks him what he did for a living and he tells her he's a firefighter for the past thirty-five years. She looks at him and says, 'You've been on a thirty-five-year adrenaline high. Now you have to come down and work slowly and deliberately.'"

"Ha!" she replied. "Seems she knows something about firemen."

He chuckled at her reaction then leaned back and waited for the show to begin.

17

At least he was in his office and not upstairs. This was a man cave if ever there was one. Walls covered by pictures, some of the family at Union picnics, but most of them were of fires, rigs, and the guys, mostly him and Mark with John showing up on occasion. There were a few plaques on the wall. He called them "at-a-boys". Each received for a rescue of some sort. These days they were given out with ribbons to put on uniforms for grabs that weren't even mentioned when he was in the firehouse. That was a good thing, he thought. The guys put their asses on the line every day. They should get some recognition. The sound of the upstairs phone being picked up snapped him back to reality. All were now present.

"All here?" Pauli asked.

"All here," Johanna replied.

"I've got some news," Pauli began. "As you know, I met someone special last year and we've been talking about our future. Since they passed these new laws about same sex marriages, we were trying to decide if that route was appropriate for us."

Jake was dumbfounded. Jo may have known about this, but it was all new to him. Someone special? Same sex marriage? Appropriate route? What was going on?

"So, what does Liz think you should do?" Jo asked

"Liz? Who is Liz?" Jake spat out, unable to contain himself any longer.

"Elizabeth is my housemate - - - partner - -- love interest," Pauli stuttered.

"Jake, let her finish her news," Jo admonished.

Let her finish her news? His wife was completely unfazed by what their daughter had just said. With a million questions coursing through his mind, Jake shut down and waited patiently hoping everything would come to him if he did.

"As I was saying, Liz and I have been talking about making things more permanent," Pauli continued. "And we came to the conclusion that we would like to formalize our relationship."

18

As Jake listened, the first thought that crossed his mind was how unromantic it all sounded. If he had approached Johanna like that forty years ago, she would have turned him down cold. Pauli made it sound like a business relationship. Making things more permanent. Formalizing their relationship. It sounded like one of his clients before they took on a partner. The next thought was, why go through the trouble? After all, the primary purpose of marriage in the modern age seemed to be to provide a stable environment for children. He decided discretion was the better part of valor and stayed quiet.

"Has Liz spoken with her parents?" Jo asked.

"She's talked with her mom," Pauli explained. "But not with her dad just yet."

What was it about this generation? Jake thought. They talk to mom and leave dad out in the cold. Are fathers that unreasonable? Even though he had decided to be discrete, he couldn't stay quiet any longer.

"You girls seem to have the situation under control," he said a little too sharply.

"I was hesitant to tell you," Jo confessed. "In case it didn't work out."

"Work out?" Jake countered. "Don't you think I deserve some advanced notice?"

"Well, she just wanted the flexibility of establishing a relationship before the pressure of introducing Liz to you. Didn't want any complications."

"Complications?" Jake asked.

"Jake, it's not like she's going to tell you she's pregnant."

Jake heard the last sentence and waited for an explosion from his daughter. He would never get away with such a brash statement. Of course, she wouldn't be pregnant. Pauli has declared herself a lesbian and pregnancy requires a male. Then he remembered the conversation he had with her two years before. Pregnancy was an option, but to call to say she was pregnant without any preliminary discussions would have been a slap in the face.

19

"Could you do me a favor and get me up to speed?" he requested.

"What do you want to know, Dad?" Pauli asked.

"How'd you meet?"

"You won't believe it."

"Try me."

"I was in a club wearing one of those NFD t-shirts you gave me and she approached me. Asked if the t-shirt was for real. I said no, it's from my dad. She said, you're kidding. My dad's a firefighter too."

"Her dad's on the job?"

"Yup. He's a Chicago Battalion Chief."

"And I'm a CPA."

"I know, Dad, no need to be defensive."

"Sorry, you're right." After so many years, he thought he had outgrown the need to explain why he hadn't been promoted. Guess being an in-law was a little different. "Was she wearing a Chicago FD shirt?"

"No, she had a Harry Potter shirt on. So, we talked about Harry Potter, about firefighters, and the World Trade Center."

"The World Trade Center really? What brought that on."

"Her father was there and saw a lot of Newark guys on the pile."

"Maybe I already met him."

"He hasn't mentioned knowing any Newark firefighters." Pauli pointed out.

"Didn't say I knew him, only that I might have met him," Jake answered. "It was kind of crazy there, so you really didn't get to know anyone not in your crew. But anyway, tell me about Liz."

"Liz? Liz is great."

"I hope so, but so was the milkman. Could you be more specific?"

"Give me a chance, Dad," Pauli said. "Liz is smart. You'll like her. She's an accountant, When I told her you're a CPA, she was floored. She's studying for the exam now. We figure after she takes the exam, we'll do it. She's witty, she's sensitive, and she's a great cook."

A great cook? Jake got the feeling if Pauli were a man, he'd be hearing the same description. Was that good or bad? When in uncharted waters, sail cautiously. "So, I'll like her father because he's on the job," Jake chuckled. "And I'll like Liz because she's an accountant. I'm running out of reasons to like people. Why should I like her mother?"

"Because Mom likes her," Pauli laughed. "She has a brother too."

"Have you met him?

"Yeah, he reminds me of Tim."

Reminds her of Tim, Jake thought. That implies the brothers will get along? Sometimes yes and sometimes no. That concern is for another day. She has to live with Liz not her brother. "How far along are you in planning this? We put aside money for your wedding. How does it work with two brides?" Jake asked.

"Dad, I'm thirty-two years old," Pauli reminded him. "You don't have to pay for my wedding. I'm a career girl remember."

All the conversations he had with Johanna over the years passed through his mind. A mother's dream of a big celebration in a large hall after a church wedding with hundreds of guests. That dream seemed to be dying a quiet death. At least his wife was not protesting. There was no telling how she would react later, even though she had been aware of Pauli's plans before the call.

"Have you and your mother discussed this already?" he asked, suspecting that was the reason Johanna was so peaceful.

"Yes, dear," his wife answered. "Not all the details, but the preliminary things."

Not having a groom complicated matters, Jake thought. The wedding is usually in the bride's church. Which bride will get to choose the church? Would they even be able to get married in a church? What about the surname of the couple?

21

He wouldn't dare ask the last question. The church question he felt was legitimate.

"Have you decided on a church?" he asked hoping it wasn't a live wire.

"We've only decided on the location."

"The location?"

"Yes, we decided to get married in Jersey."

"Really?" Jake said involuntarily. "Why Jersey? Not that I'm complaining."

"Well, once you get outside Chicago, folks around here are more conservative," Pauli pointed out. "Liz thinks some of her relatives might balk at attending."

Jake let that sink in for a moment. Jersey is a more forgiving place than Illinois when it comes to the unusual? Outside Chicago, folks are more conservative? He knew more than one conservative Jersey native, but it was true that every county in New Jersey is part of a major metropolitan area. Ben Franklin didn't pity the state for being a barrel tapped at both ends for no reason. North Jersey leaned toward New York City and South Jersey leaned toward the City of Brotherly Love. That's why it's so damn expensive to live here. Lots of college degrees, engineers, scientists, and researchers settled in the state. It's said that education broadens the mind. How much will be seen when the wedding invites go out. He came from a big Irish family with lots of civil servants. Johanna came from German stock with lots of engineers. Pauli was close to cousins on both sides. How many of them knew of her choice? The one cousin who would undoubtedly know was her cousin Pete, the son of Jo's sister Jane. Pete would be there no matter what. Jo and Jane hadn't spoken since their mother passed away two years before.

"Liz's family is going to have to come to Jersey," he thought out loud. "Even if they want, that might be too large a nut to cover."

"She thinks they'll come just to see the Apple," Pauli said. "You know, go see a Broadway show, see the Statue of Liberty, Ellis Island, Times Square . . ."

"The World Trade Center Memorial," Jake added.

"Of course," Pauli replied. "Her dad will take everyone on a walking tour and tell them about his experiences, the Chicago Fire Department view point."

"He said that?" Jake asked. He had never had it in him in all these years to actually go back to Ground Zero and doubted Liz's father would be enthusiastic about reliving that time. As far as Jake was concerned the time had never felt right to chance resurrecting those memories. They were kept in a lock-box deep in the back recesses of his mind, only relived with firefighters on rare occasions. Johanna had never heard the grim stories of those days immediately after the towers came down. Now he was going to meet a brother firefighter who shared the horror of the 9/11 rescue effort. Was he ready to accompany Liz's father and give a tour of the site? Was Liz's father up to it? This was getting more complicated by the minute.

"Dad?"

His daughter's voice snapped him out of his thoughts. "We'll have to see about that," he said.

"You haven't been back yet, have you?" she asked quietly.

"Haven't had a chance, but we're talking about your wedding, aren't we?" With that a dark cloud receded.

"Yes, you asked about a church," Pauli reminded. "I'm doing research on that. There are understanding clergy in Jersey if we want to go that route or we could have a simple civil ceremony."

Jake waited for his wife to react, but heard nothing. It seemed the big church wedding had just died that quiet death. He knew in the end Johanna was only interested in her daughter's happiness. Maybe he wouldn't have to comfort her when they hung up.

"What town hall do you want to get married in?" he asked.

"Haven't done the research yet," she told him. "Newark City Hall would be the most impressive, but I don't know if they allow marriage ceremonies under the rotunda."

23

"I'll ask around," Jake said.

"Thanks Dad."

There was some small talk between mother and daughter after that, but Jake didn't pay attention. When they hung up the phones, he walked upstairs to the kitchen with trepidation. Johanna approached him, wrapped her arms around him, and buried her head into his shoulder quietly crying.

Chapter Four

Jake pulled into the side parking lot of the small firehouse on Springfield Avenue and Hunterdon Street. He had called this building his second home for twenty-five years. Built in 1895, Six Engine had been responding from this street corner for well over a hundred years, excluding a short period when the neighborhood was so burnt out that they moved the company. The structure looked the same, but the neighborhood surrounding it had changed dramatically. Gone were the Hayes Homes, the twelve-story brick housing project that had towered over the two-story firehouse for more than fifty years. Neat two-story townhouses now occupied the area diagonally across the street. Bill and Ted's Sportsman, the bar directly across Springfield Avenue, was gone as were the occasional bullets that would come out of that establishment in the 70s and 80s.

Springfield Avenue's wooden commercial buildings and littered vacant lots had been replaced by a twelve-screen movie theater, an Applebee's restaurant, and a Home Depot. Jake stepped out of his car with his briefcase and made sure to lock it. Some things change more slowly than others. He opened the door to his former home away from home and stepped into the kitchen. Today Jake was here to speak with the Deputy Chief about his side-business accounting and about one of the Chief's friends. A chief in Chicago who might know a Battalion Chief in that city. A Battalion Chief whose daughter was named Elizabeth.

He stepped into an empty firehouse, which was to be expected at eleven in the morning. Mornings were always busy in the firehouse. Cleaning up the place, drills, and in service inspections ate up the time before lunch. The vacant quarters didn't matter to him. If the Deputy's gig was in quarters, his client was upstairs. Walking through the house watch room, Jake noted the company journal. Out of habit, he glanced at it to see if they had any work recently. Reading the entries only heighten his sense of changes on the job. When he was appointed, the man on the watch had to record every alarm that came over the old bell system no matter from what part of the city companies were being dispatched. This had allowed them to know what companies were out of service in case they had to cover for one of those companies. Today's entries were more focused on the company's responses. If they had to cover for another company, dispatch would tell them. Computers now controlled the responses. Back in his day, computers were the province of major corporations, governments, and research universities. They were kept in large airconditioned rooms, but didn't have the memory or power of the smart phone in his pocket. Now computers were ubiquitous. The department used them for dispatching companies, for writing and submitting reports, and for filling out the forms required by the State.

After flipping through a few pages of the journal, Jake moved past the reminders of technology's grip on the modern world. He continued through the door onto the apparatus floor, remembering the kitchen on the day he had arrived. It had been half the size of the room he had just passed through. Then one of the other tours had forgotten to shut off the flame under French fries cooking on the stove when they responded to a three-alarm fire. The kitchen had only been one alarm, but that brought down a wall and doubled the room's size.

On the apparatus floor he was immediately confronted with more change. A large SUV was parked on the side of the floor once used by Six Engine's rig. The station wagons that had been used by chiefs years before were a forgotten footnote. Moving around the Chief's gig, Jake climbed the stairs to the bunkroom on the second floor.

Today he was also a retired firefighter returning to his house to ask a favor of an academy classmate and hopefully get some information that would ease his concerns. Reaching the bunkroom, his senses continued to be assaulted by change. What had once been home was now a foreign country. Strolling past the deputy aide's work station with its own computer, Jake stepped into the Chief's room.

"Jake," Chief Gardiner shouted as he stood up from his desk. "How's Mark doing?"

Jake chuckled at the question. It was not the first query he had anticipated getting, although it probably should have been. The Chief had told him the morning after Mark's fall that Jake would be needed by Mark for the rehab grind. "To give him a kick in the ass when it gets hard." He had done that.

"He's adjusting to retirement," Jake answered. "Rehab wasn't as hard as convincing him that his body couldn't do the job anymore. The firefighter supported him through physical therapy. The accountant led him through the disability pension."

"I told you," the Chief laughed. "You two were a great team in the firehouse and made a great team at rehab and beyond. Have a seat. I've been expecting you to call."

Jake was surprised to hear that. It sounded like there was more on the Chief's mind than accounting. He dropped down into the wooden chair next to the Chief's bunk. "Sounds like you were expecting a call for more than your quarterly estimated taxes."

"Got an email from Chicago. Seems a certain Battalion Chief wanted to know if I knew a firefighter named Jake Covey."

Jake chuckle. He wasn't surprised. The fire service was like a village. Someone seemed to know someone on the job in all the major cities in the country. "What did you tell him?"

"I told him, yeah, I knew you. You're my accountant."

"You didn't."

"Yes, I did. Of course, I didn't stop there. I said you were an LWW kind of guy."

Jake was confused. "What's an LWW?"

"Oh, I never used that term with you? I guess it's something I use when giving

27

a letter of reference. You're a guy someone came trust with their life, their wife, and their wallet.

Jake burst out laughing. "You mean like Mark?"

"Just like Mark. In fact, I thought up the term after that incident at University Hospital."

"What incident?"

"The one with the security guard after the collapse that gave you all those scars on your back."

Jake instantly knew the incident the Chief was talking about. After Six took up from the fire that scarred his back, they stopped at UMDNJ and Mark went in to take Jake's wallet back to the firehouse. A security guard saw Mark take the wallet and stopped him. According to the colorful and probably highly embellished account Jake heard, Mark reacted with an imaginative string of curses before the captain came over to break up the confrontation.

"You trusted him with your life, your wife and your wallet that night," the Chief reminded.

"So, did the email explain why this chief was interested in me?"

"Seems his kid has a love interest named Covey."

Jake hesitated a moment, unsure if the Chief was aware how unusual the couple might be, Then, he jumped right in. There were few topics that were taboo among people who had fought fires together.

"Did he tell you his daughter's love interest was Pauline, not Tim?"

"Well, yes that did come up, but only to prep me in case you showed up asking for a hand. And he wanted to get a feel for your reaction when Pauli came out." The Chief then turned very serious. "Jake, remember what happened to my daughter."

Jake shifted in his seat remembering the tale that had circulated around the firehouse. A marriage made in heaven. The groom was an Ivy League graduate

28

and successful entrepreneur. A man any woman would find attractive. Within a year of the wedding, he had morphed into a hard drinking, wife abusing bastard. It had been a nasty divorce that took her years to get over. Then there was Jo's sister Jane. She had married a newly minted lawyer. He turned into a gambler who blamed all the troubles his addiction created on his wife. "Chief, my attitude is if she's happy, I'm happy."

"You're a wise man, Jake. Now, there's the matter of my quarterly estimated taxes for the business."

Jake put his briefcase on the bunk, opened it, and took out the information for the Chief's landscaping business.

Chapter Five

Jake stood over the stove working julienne sliced peppers in a wok. A skill he picked up in the firehouse from one of the guys whose wife was from Taiwan. It was what he called firehouse Wednesday. He took over the kitchen at least once a week to keep his firehouse cooking skills sharp and his wife happy. The aroma of ginger and garlic mixed with the scent of fried peppers. Jo came into the kitchen just as the phone rang.

"That smells delicious," she commented while reaching for the phone.

"Since I've retired, I've discovered that you feel any food prepared by someone else tastes extra special," he said while shutting the flame.

"Not just anyone, dear," she countered. "By you. I guess I taste the love."

He laughed while she picked up the phone,

"Yes, it is," she replied into the phone. Then she became animated, waving at Jake. "Well, hello, Chief. Yes, he's right here."

Holding her palm over the mouth piece, Jo motioned toward the door leading to Jake's office. "It's Kevin Moore, Elizabeth's father. Go downstairs and pick it up there."

As Jake made his way down the stairs, he heard Jo answering Kevin. "I know. It's just a habit formed over the years. Kevin it is. Jake's going to pick up the other phone."

He reached the phone on his office desk and picked it up. Dinner was apparently going to be a little delayed. "I'm here," he said.

"Good," Jo answered. "How about you introduce yourselves," Jo suggested.

"Firefighter Jake Covey," Jake shouted. "At your service, Chief."

"Please Jake, I just told Jo there's no need for a title. Just call me Kevin."

"Got it, Kevin," Jake agreed. "So, I'm not going to ask why you're calling. We can start with did you speak with Chief Gardiner's buddy?"

30

"Yes, I did," Kevin laughed. "And he said Chief Gardiner said you were a --- now let me get this straight, An LWW kind of guy." They both laughed, but Jo was quiet.

"Don't feel bad," Jake said. "I hadn't heard the term until the other day when I went to help the Chief with his taxes and ask for a favor."

"What's an LWW," Jo interjected.

The sound of another phone being picked up interrupted the conversation.

"That would be my wife Kate," Kevin told them.

"Hello all," Kate said in a cheery voice.

"Hello, Kate," Jo replied. "We were just talking about what an LWW is."

"Yes, I thought so," Kate laughed. "Kevin has been holding back. He said it's something only firemen could understand."

"Oh, you have one of those husbands, too," Jo laughed.

"Okay, ladies," Jake interjected. "All will be made clear now. An LWW is someone you can trust with your life, your wife, and your wallet." He had to hold the phone away from his ear because of the vocal reaction to his explanation.

"Seriously, only a fireman can understand," Kate playfully scolded her husband. "Any fireman's wife has that down pat."

"Jake, where did the Chief come up with that?" Jo asked.

Suddenly the conversation had turned serious without the wives knowing it. How could he explain where the Chief came up with that phase without upsetting Jo. If he told her where the Chief first had the thought, that would bring back the memories of rushing up to the hospital in Newark not knowing how badly he was injured. If he brought it forward and used Mark as an explanation, that would resurrect the memories of supporting Jill. They were five minutes into getting to know their daughter's future in-laws. He didn't want to dump that on them.

"It just means, Jake is someone I can trust," Kevin said.

The answer would not have been accepted if Jake had given it, but it came

31

from Kevin and Jo was too polite to push the issue. That would come later when they were off the phone. Jake anticipated a snide remark about inappropriate levity, but not much more.

"So, did Kevin float his idea past the two of you?" Kate asked.

"How could I?" Kevin protested. "There hasn't been time."

"Then I will," Kate pushed on. "We were wondering if the two of you would be interested in seeing Chicago from the point of view of natives?"

"Natives?" Kevin laughed. "I might be a native, but you my dear are a suburban girl."

Jake sat and listened to the banter of the Moores. It reminded him of the give and take of the firehouse which somehow also became the give and take of a fire department family. The job drew in every member of a firefighter's family.

"Suburban girl? Why because I lived a couple of towns away. It's Midwestern hospitality we're offering. We thought since the girls are out here it would be easier if you could come out and kind of get to know . . ." Kate said before trailing off at the end.

Jo jumped in enthusiastically, leaving Jake to listen to his fate.

"That's so kind of you," she said. "We would love to. When did you have in mind? I can rearrange our schedule to fit in any time you like."

Jo and Kate both began laughing, leaving Jake trying to figure out how they would pull off this sudden trip to the Midwest. Jo would clear the family schedule, but he had clients to consider.

"We have plenty of room," Kevin assured them. "No need to worry about hotels or motels. We can drive into the city or hop the train in."

"Oh, you don't want to take the train," Kate protested.

"The train sounds interesting," Jake said. He always thought if you want to get a feel for a city, ride mass transit at least once while there. Then you got to see the locals. Jo never agreed with this concept.

32

"Jake," Jo said. "We're not in college going to Chinatown or Little Italy anymore. I think I've earned a little comfort after forty years. No train."

Kevin and Kate laughed.

"Yes, dear," Jake said in a sarcastic voice. "We're old and gray and gimpy. Only door to door service will do."

"Honestly," Jo replied. "Accept the fact that you're no longer twenty-five, Jake."

"You know you're getting old when your wife reminds you, you're no longer twenty-five. Used to be I'm no longer eighteen."

This caused another round of laughter before the conversation turned to practical matters.

"We were hoping you could come out next month when the weather gets a little warmer," Kate suggested.

That would be April, Jake thought. Not a good time for an accountant to be away from the office. Before he could say anything, Jo jumped in.

"April is a really busy time for an accountant. How about May? Things should have calmed down by then."

"Oh, you're right," Kate said. "I should have thought of that. Elizabeth wants to be a CPA also. I'm going to have to get used to the hours."

"Then May it is?" Kevin interjected.

"May it is," Jake answered. "How about the week before Memorial Day? We'll get there ahead of the crowds."

"And you can stay until after the crowds go home," Kate said.

They chatted for a few more minutes just introducing themselves to each other. Then it was back to the kitchen and dinner.

Jake stepped up to the stove, turned on the gas, and continued where he left off. Thank God the call came before the beef was cooking. Peppers didn't dry out the way beef did.

33

"We'll have to call Pauli later," Jo said.

"You think so?" Jake asked. "Why don't we just show up at her door? The look on her face would be worth the secrecy." He added the beef and began stirring it vigorously. The smell of the ingredients mixing made him realize he was now really hungry. He looked at his wife, surprised by her silence. She was at the rice cooker scooping out its contents. It appeared she was actually seriously considering his suggestion.

"No, I don't think that would go well with Liz," Jo pointed out. "We have to give her time to be presentable."

"That was not a serious suggestion, Jo," he laughed. "Pauli would disown us."

She slapped him on the arm as he shut the flame. Two bowls with steaming rice were waiting on the table. Jake carried the wok over and poured his creation on top of the rice. The best part of cooking was the instant gratification of enjoying the fruits of your labor.

Chapter Six

Jake sat at the kitchen table finishing up the last bites of his creation. He always changed things a little when he cooked. Have to keep the wife on her toes with a little variation was his philosophy.

"I'll start the dishes," Jo said as she stood up with plate in hand. Over the years they had adopted the firehouse rules for dinner. If you cooked, you didn't clean up. Of course, he knew not to take that too far and helped out, but tonight looked to be a little different. They had to get in touch with Pauli.

"Should we call, text, or email?" he asked

"You mean to Pauli? Maybe you should text first," Jo said after a moment's hesitation. "That's the most private. I don't want to spook Liz. Best to do it gradually."

"How do you do it gradually?" Jake laughed.

"You know what I mean," Jo snapped impatiently. "If you text first, Pauli can get Liz up to speed gradually instead of just dumping it on her. Remember, Liz is the only one who hasn't spoken to us."

"What? Am I that bad?" Jake asked. "I try not to be an ogre."

"Yes, I know dear, but to Liz you're probably very intimidating."

"Me? Laidback, easygoing Jake, intimidating?"

"Laidback and easygoing? Well, at times that's true," Jo chuckled. "But you're also the father of the love of her life and you're a CPA. An old hand at something she aspires to be."

"Old hand? Ouch, that hurt."

"Do something for thirty or forty years and you eventually become an old hand."

"Okay. So, the old hand is going to take out the newfangled device and text his daughter," Jake announced. With that he reached into his hip pocket, retrieved his smart phone, and began to input a text message to Pauli.

"How about we come to Chicago?"

He put the phone on the table so they could both hear and see it. Then he stood up to help out with the cleanup. A few minutes passed before the phone chirped announcing a text message.

"What? You want to come here? Let me run it past Liz. Maybe you can meet her folks."

After reading the message, Jake sent a response. "Already 'met' her parents. Had long talk. They invited. Will stay with them."

"Liz is thrilled!!! But I've been worried. She's spending so much time prepping for the CPA exam. Think you'd be able to help her prep? (My ? not hers.)"

Jake chuckled when he read the tutoring request. How to bond with your daughter-in-law, help with the CPA exam. The modern world was getting stranger by the day. The phone rang as this thought passed through his mind. Jo dried her hands and picked it up.

"Hello Pauli," Jo said. "No, I don't know any details about what your father sent to you. Yes, we were invited by Liz's folks. Hold on dear, let me put the phone on speaker phone." With that Jo pushed a button on the phone and placed it on the counter between herself and her husband.

"Go ahead, dear. He can hear you now."

"We'd be thrilled if both of you could come here," an unfamiliar voice announced before Pauli spoke.

"Mom, Dad, this is Elizabeth Moore, soon to be CPA and my partner," Pauli said.

"Nice to meet you, Liz," Jo replied.

"When is the exam?" Jake asked.

This drew a glare from his wife. "You could at least welcome her into the

36

family, Jake."

"I'm sorry," Jake chuckled. "That's the insensitive male coming out of me." He instantly regretted it. Would Pauli or Liz take offense to that comment?

"No, I wouldn't say that," Liz countered. "I think it's more the practical accountant coming out."

He laughed. Jo shook her head. It looked like he was going to get along just fine with his future daughter-in-law.

"The exam is in May," Liz said

"Beginning, middle, or end?" Jake asked.

"End," Liz said.

"Good. We are planning on going in May, right after tax season ends," Jake informed them. "Just have to line up flights, etcetera. We can cram for the exam when I get there. All that's required is a table, lights, and a lot of coffee."

"Okay, we can do that," Pauli said.

"Any suggestions for preparing for the cram sessions?" Liz asked.

"You know what you can read," Jake said after a moment's thought. "This may sound a bit off the wall, but I do know one book full of studying techniques. If you went through it, you might find one method that helps you focus better."

"And what book is that?" Pauli asked sounding suspicious.

"The Study Techniques of Fire Officers by Deputy Chief Robert Brendler," Jake replied. "It's part of an oral history of the NFD. You might remember Chief Brendler, Pauli. He was in charge of the Training Academy when you were a girl. Tall guy, white hair, thin, always stayed in shape."

"Isn't he married to someone famous?" Pauli asked.

"Famous?" Jake said. "Well, she's a reporter on the national news, Kathy Stanley."

"Kathy Stanley? I've seen her. Doesn't she report from Asia?" Liz asked.

"Yeah, that's her. She's half Chinese. Her mother's from Taiwan. Father

37

was a fire captain up in New England somewhere. Anyway, the Chief wrote a series of books based on an oral history of the department. One of the questions he asked was about studying for promotion, So, Liz, read this book and you'll have a couple of hundred ways of studying for high pressure exams."

"I have to talk to my dad," Liz said. "He might have a copy."

"If not, search on line. The Chief used one of those on-line self-publishers. Told me no commercial house was interested because the subject was too specialized, so the audience was too small. Personally, I think he did a bang-up job. More than a few guys used the stories to set up a studying routine."

"Thank you, I'll do that," Liz said.

"Now you're selling books for a Deputy Chief?" Pauli teased.

"I am not selling anything," Jake countered. "Besides, her old man might already have it."

"Okay, now let's get practical," Jo interrupted. "Which airport is the most convenient for Liz's parents?"

They spoke for a few more minutes, nailing down the preliminaries of traveling in May. When they got off the phone, Jo turned to her husband and asked, "So, you're going to help Liz pass this exam are you?"

Jake smiled and shook his head yes.

"I guess you're not a useless piece of shit after all."

They both laughed, then walked over to the sink to complete the cleanup.

Chapter Seven

"Yo!" Paul Nereto shouted over the sound of Route Three traffic outside the Tick Tock Diner. "Where's Mark?"

"He's waiting inside, still can't stand for too long. The body heals slower than it used to," Jake said

"I was worried he'd have to bail out on us," Paul said after throwing a bear hug around Jake.

"No way," Jake replied. "We're here for John's birthday. If he had to crawl, he'd be here. John was one of his guys. You don't bail out on a brother firefighter. It still bothers him that he couldn't save John."

"How could he?" Paul asked sadly. "It wasn't a fire that got John. It was his demons."

"Mark still thinks if he had gotten John help, he could have saved him."

"Help? From where? The fire department didn't have an employee assistance program, remember?" Paul reminded his friend. "Mark caught a lot of flak that time he went through the cops' program."

"Thought he conquered the demons with that one," Jake sighed. "Mark did take a lot of heat for that."

"Honestly, how's he doing?" Paul said changing the focus.

"Mark's adjusting," Jake answered his childhood friend. "He's trying to figure out a way to stay relevant."

Seeing the diner again brought back memories of Paul working as a roadie for a local band and studying pre-med while Jake fought fires and studied accounting. They were rooming together in an apartment in Nutley. There was a steady stream of girls looking for Paul's attention. Jake had Jo in his senior year. He had no social life to speak of at the time. It was hard dating when you worked fulltime and attended school fulltime.

"Are you still stuck on that whole relevant thing?" Paul asked. "My boy, you have to realize most of the world isn't relevant. At least not outside of family and friends."

"You sir, have a jaded attitude," Jake replied. "But let's get inside before starting a philosophical debate." He agreed with the comment about family. That had been one of his preoccupations since Pauli told him she was a lesbian. How to stay relevant in his own family. It was a thought for another day.

As they moved toward the diner entrance Paul got more serious. "I thought Mark was setting up that training company. Using all those years and certifications to teach the next generation not to do what he did."

"Oh, he tried, but it got to him. According to Mark, training firefighters when he can no longer fight fires is like being a priest in a brothel. If you can't partake in the activities, you shouldn't be there."

Paul laughed, then broke into a dry cough.

"That doesn't sound good," Jake commented. "Thank God Jo isn't here. She'd have you in bed with a thermometer in your mouth. Once a nurse, always a nurse."

"And you wonder why I didn't get married?" Paul asked. "It's just a tickle that developed after I took a lady to a Devil's game. Strained my voice from shouting and can't seem to shake it."

"You took a lady to a hockey game?" Jake laughed. "How romantic."

"Her choice. I would have preferred Broadway," Paul replied.

"Have you tried being quiet and letting it rest?" Jake asked facetiously. Paul was known for his reassuring chatter when dealing with patients.

"A good doctor has to talk with his patients. You know that. Otherwise, they go somewhere else."

"Come on, let's get inside. No need to irritate your throat with the cold air," Jake said as he moved toward the diner entrance.

"You remember the first time we came here?" Paul asked.

"Yeah, like it was yesterday. You were doing the roadie gig. I was off that night. The band played at . . . what was it? Dodd's?"

"Dodd's," Paul confirmed as they climbed the stairs to the door. "It was one of my last times with them."

"You didn't improve your hours," Jake reminded him. "Roadie of a club band to bartender, same hours, same crowd, different function."

Paul laughed then protested. "Not the same crowd. I went to work at a respectable restaurant, remember?"

"You went to work at a casual dining restaurant catering to the twenty somethings, same crowd, different venue."

"You have always thought too much," Paul laughed as they reached the door. He coughed once more before grabbing the handle and pulling. Mark was sitting at the counter.

"Here he is," Paul said. Mark stood up stiffly, grabbed Paul's hand, and gave him a hug. "Sit down. No need to get up for me."

"We have to move to a table anyway," Mark pointed out. "It looks worse than it is. Just a little stiff when I get up too quickly."

"Careful, you don't want to loosen the bolts the surgeon used to put you back together," Jake laughed.

"I don't think he has to worry about that," Paul countered. "Doctor Gupta says she did some of her best work on him."

"Doctor Gupta says?" Mark asked. "You spoke with my surgeon?"

"Yes, Doctor Sandra Gupta, orthopedic surgeon UMDNJ," Paul answered. "Did you know she's a big Devil's fan?"

Jake had quietly let his friends exchange banter, but the mention of hockey brought him out. "Woah, are you telling me the lady you took to a hockey game is his surgeon?"

"Devil's fan?" Mark asked. "You took her to a Devil's game?"

41

"She insisted."

"This is the cute little doctor from Ivy Hill?" Mark continued.

"That's where she told me she grew up," Paul said. "We spent a lot of time talking about Vailsburg."

"My boy, she's too young for your old ass," Mark laughed. "Your heart is going to give out trying to keep up."

"Maybe, but I'll go out with a smile," Paul replied.

"Okay," Jake interrupted. "Let's get a table and the two of you can fill me in on Sandra Gupta."

They moved from the lunch counter to the receptionist who picked up three menus and led them to a table in the middle of the dining room. There were booths open around the busy, well-lit room, but the receptions didn't ask for their preference.

"So, you spoke with the young lady before we arrived and requested a table instead if a booth?" Jake asked, guessing Mark's back was not doing well today.

"Yeah, got here early so you wouldn't see that," Mark chuckled. "Hard to get out of one of those right now, but I'm improving."

Paul placed his hand on Mark's shoulder and gave it a squeeze. "It's going to take a while, but it'll get better. Just keep up with the exercises and stretches the therapist gave you."

"Yes, doctor, but we're supposed to be here to commemorate John's birthday, remember?"

"Okay, no more medical advice," Paul laughed and then began to cough.

"That doesn't sound good," Mark said. "Make sure you order a nice hot cup of tea with lemon. Cures all that might ail you."

"Now who's giving medical advice?" Paul asked.

They sat down, ordered, with Paul getting the hot tea to soothe his throat, then leaned back to talk. That's why they had come.

"So, how do you know Doctor Gupta?" Mark asked. Jake was all ears. Paul could tell as good a story as any firefighter. It looked like it would be an entertaining night.

"Sandra and I have had a working relationship for years," Paul started. "When she first started her practice, she came to my office to ask for referrals of patients who needed more than a chiropractic adjustment. I thought that was brave for a newly minted orthopedic surgeon."

"And it didn't hurt that she was good looking," Mark pointed out.

"Well, yeah." They all laughed. "But she was so young and I didn't need any youthful melodrama. Over time we became friends, but don't read anything further into it."

"Oh, come on Paul, she's attractive and available," Mark said. "You're not interested?"

Their appetizers came as Mark finished, so Paul waited to answer. "No, I'm not the marrying type," he said after the waitress left.

Jake knew they were now on shaky ground. He and Paul had had this conversation numerous times over the years. They never turned out well, so Jake had given up.

"Why not?" Mark asked.

Paul took a deep breath and plunged into his reasoning one more time. "In the modern world, people marry to start families. I have too many flaws to pass on to the next generation."

"Flaws?" Mark asked. "You're a standup guy with a big heart. Would have made a great firefighter just like your brother. What's not to pass on?"

"I have my demons the same as John had his," Paul admitted. "I just chose to deal with them differently."

"His sons are great," Mark pointed out.

"Luck of the DNA draw," Paul sighed. "I don't want to risk it."

Mark accepted that and moved the conversation to the reason they came to the Tick Tock Diner on John's birthday. "How are John's sons doing?" he asked.

"Oh, they're great," Paul laughed, lightening the mood. "They drive their mother crazy, of course. She doesn't always understand why boys do what they do, so I go over and give her a break. You know, take them out and let them blow off a little steam. Soccer and fishing seem to do the trick."

Jake found it ironic that Paul spent so much time with his nephews. He had always told Paul he would have made a great father, but Paul had resisted. Now he was doing just that, but as an uncle. John's widow Beth appreciated his efforts and his example. She came from a family of three girls. Little boys were a mystery to her. Jake remembered a conversation he had with John. Beth had insisted on taking their first son to the pediatrician a month after he was born. She thought he was hyper-active, always in motion. The doctor had reassured her. That's the way boys are. Paul was now the surrogate father. Jake wondered how that would play out when the boys hit puberty. As this was passing through his mind, Mark moved the conversation back to John.

"Did Beth ever apply to the 9/11 fund?" he asked.

Paul leaned back in his chair and shook his head no. "Beth doesn't think it's worth the effort," he told them. "John had his demons before 9/11."

"Yeah, but he had them under control," Mark insisted. "He was clean until we went over there. Then he developed that cough."

"Mark, the cough isn't what got him," Jake said sadly. "He had too big a heart to take in the mess at Ground Zero. It ate at him."

"Yeah, but he still had it under control until some doctor prescribed medication without asking about his history," Mark reminded them. "But we're not here to remember his demons. We're here to remember his heart."

"He loved his job," Paul said. "Sometimes he would tell me about things he had heard or seen. Like - - -What did he call it? The naked jogger.

44

Mark laughed when he heard this, but not Jake.

"You never heard that story?" Mark asked after noticing Jake's reaction.

"That must be a Ten Engine tale," Jake laughed. "Never heard it."

"Actually, it's a Five Truck tale that Ten Engine witnessed," Mark said. "I wish John was here. He could tell the story so much better than I can."

"I'm sure you'll do fine," Jake said. "Feel free to embellish."

"You doubt the accuracy of firefighters' tales?" Mark asked indignantly.

"Didn't say that, just invited you to add color."

"Well, as John told the story, Five Truck pulled up to a job and a naked woman jumped out of a car nearby, ran to Five's cab, and climbed in. John was pumping, so he saw it. The captain gets out and goes over to the deputy's driver. The driver gets a blanket out of the back of the gig, goes over to the truck's cab, and wraps it around the woman. Turns out she was a hooker who was serving the guy in the car she fled. He made some noises that frightened her and she ran. The captain wrote it up in the company journal as the case of the naked jogger. That was a tough neighborhood for a hooker."

"Where was the job?" Jake asked.

"South Broad Street."

"South Broad Street?" Paul asked. "From what John said, it was a hopping place back in the '80s."

Mark chuckled. "Yeah, it was. But that's when I was at Six Engine with your roommate at the time. It really hadn't calmed down when I got promoted. A lot of blood and gore, with the occasional fire."

"I wouldn't call fires every day 'occasional'", Jake interjected.

"We had our fair share," Mark admitted. "And John loved it."

"But Beth, not so much," Paul pointed out.

"It's hard being a firefighter's wife, at least a city firefighter," Mark said.

"Jill found that out early on," Jake said as their meals arrived.

"Quick service," Paul said. "That's one reason John loved this place."

As the three friends began addressing their meals, Jake thought of the trials and tribulations of Jill. "You know, Mark, when Jo and I were driving up to University after you fell through that roof, we talked about firefighters' wives or I guess spouses now," Jake said making a concession to the small but growing number of women on the job. "I couldn't help but remember the first time you injured your back. John was there."

"Yes, he was," Mark laughed.

"Okay, you can't keep me hanging like this. What happened?" Paul asked.

Jake gestured to Mark, who sighed and began the story. "We had a fire on the second floor of one those new townhouses, the ones with the metal gusset truss construction." Paul had a puzzled look when Mark described the construction type. "Trust me," he said to Paul. "Firemen don't like metal gusset truss construction. You get fire up in those trusses, you got a couple of minutes, then the gussets start to pop and the trusses fail.

"Anyway, there was a report of someone trapped on the second floor, so John and Tom North stretch a line in. John had the tip. Tom was lightening up. I was between them. John and I got to the second floor. The fire was in the back. Anyone back there was gone. So, John holds the fire and I start to go into the front to search. Then the back trusses fail and the roof comes down on the stairs, almost gets Tom. Luckily, he had gone down to get more line.

"So, now John and I are trapped on the fire floor and the hose is buried under the debris. I tell John to go out the front window while I hold the fire. He gives me an argument that lasted a second. Then sees I'm not going to let him stay behind while I bail out. He goes to the window and shimmies across a ledge to a balcony on the townhouse next door. The fire eats up the hose and I lose water. So, I have a choice to make before the whole place flashes over. High tail it out that window and maybe break something or burn inside until they get

46

another line in. Break or burn, I chose break."

"And he did," Jake added. "That was the first time he broke some bones. It was a leg and an ankle at that one. And his back was all screwed up, but no breaks. They sent me to tell Jill. She's one hell of a strong woman. But that's what you would expect. She's married to him."

"See, Jake, you were relevant," Paul pointed out.

This caught Jake off guard. As far as he was concerned, having been relevant wasn't the issue. Firefighters knew they were relevant. It was part of the job.

"I know I was relevant back then," Jake said. "Staying relevant after I retired is the problem."

"You were relevant when I was in therapy," Mark chuckled. "A real task master is what you were. Got me through. Then dealt with my pigheadedness and talked me into going out on disability which was even harder. I owe you for that."

The three laughed.

"You don't owe me a thing," Jake said quietly. "That's what friends are for."

"Like I said," Paul reminded Jake. "The only time relevance really counts is for friends and family."

Then there was a quiet break, before Mark changed the subject. "Speaking of family, what's the news from Pauli?"

Chapter Eight

Jake did a mental stutter-step before he attempted an answer. He had anticipated Pauli would come up in the conversation. Paul was her godfather and Mark had watched her grow up. They would naturally want to know about Pauli and Tim also. But Mark switched subjects quickly, giving Jake no time to adjust. He took a deep breath and shifted gears, then plunged in.

"Complicated subject," he began. Trying to think of a concise way to tell the tale. "She called last week to tell us she had found the love of her life. Funny, the way she told us, it sounded like a business transaction, but she now has a partner."

Listening to himself, Jake thought the impression he was giving was unapproving. Both Paul and Mark knew about Pauli's choice two years before, so there was no need to dance around the issue. He decided to simply dive in.

"Now that they allow same sex marriages, she has decided to get married," Jake said. "We were introduced to Elizabeth Moore, the daughter of a Chicago Fire Department Battalion Chief, believe it or not."

"Woah!" his friends shouted in unison. After a minute of congratulations, Mark asked, "Doesn't Chief Gardiner know someone on the job in Chicago?"

"Went to talk with him yesterday," Jake answered. "Had to do his quarterly taxes anyway, but when I walked in, he said he was expecting to talk with me."

"You mean for something other than his taxes?" Paul asked.

"Yeah, it seems a certain Chicago BC wanted to know if he knew a firefighter by the name of Covey."

"No, really?" Mark laughed.

"Really. Firemen are firemen," Jake chuckled. "There always seems to be someone with a connection to a guy on the job a thousand miles away." He took a sip of water as he waited for the inevitable questions.

"Are they planning to marry in Illinois?" Paul asked before coughing. He picked up his tea cup and drained it of its now cold contents.

"No, they're looking to come to that bastion of liberalism, New Jersey, to tie the knot. Seem to think it would be better here. When I talked with Kevin Moore, it sounded like he agreed."

Mark jumped in after hearing that. "Wait a minute, you talked to her old man?"

"And her mother," Jake responded. "If they had any doubts, they must have gotten over them because they were gung-ho. Kevin invited us out to Chicago and Jo leaped at the opportunity."

Their waitress came over as he finished. "Do you gents want dessert?" she asked.

"He needs a cup of hot tea," Mark said pointing to Paul.

"Thanks for your vote of confidence," Paul replied. "But a cup of coffee would go well with that chocolate mousse cake I've been eyeing since we arrived."

"Coffee and chocolate mousse cake," the waitress smiled. "A man after my own heart."

"Then I'm going to disappoint you," Jake said. "I'll have a cup of tea with lemon and a slice of cheese cake."

"Make that two," Mark said, then followed up on his question. "So, the Chief gave you this guy's number?"

"No, no, the Moores called the Coveys," Jake answered. "They thought it would be best if Jo and I went out there to meet them since the girls are there."

"Let me get this straight," Paul said. "They're coming to Jersey to marry because they felt it would be easier, but it doesn't sound like they want to move into the liberal bastion, even if it's not quite that liberal."

"Well, the label is relative," Jake admitted. "But compared to the Midwest, it might be easier here."

"That's not the point," Paul said. "If they're hesitant to marry out there, how are they going to live out there?"

49

"The impression I got is there wouldn't be as many people attending the ceremony in Illinois as there would be in Jersey."

"So, it's more a family thing than a regional thing," Paul observed.

"If you can separate the two, then yes," Jake agreed.

The waitress returned with their drinks and dessert. Paul coughed a little before reaching for his mug. Each took a second to stir their beverage and take a bite out of dessert.

"You going to go to see someone about that cough?" Mark asked. "You don't want to turn into a Chief Brendler."

Paul cleared his throat and asked, "The name's familiar, but refresh my memory. Who is Chief Brendler?"

"Deputy Chief Bob Brendler," Jake told him. "He was the Training Chief when John went through the Academy."

"He has MS," Mark explained. "Suffered with it for I don't know how long, always making excuses as to why he didn't feel right. As I heard the story, he said it was stress that caused a lot of different problems. Got banged up at a few fires because of it, then eventually relented to seeing a doctor."

"So, you think I'm in denial?" Paul asked. "Don't worry, mama. I got an appointment to see a doctor. One recommended by Doctor Gupta."

"Touché," Mark laughed.

"So, how did they meet?" Paul asked, changing the subject to one he liked.

"They met at a club," Jake said. "Pauli was wearing a Six Engine t-shirt believe it or not, and Liz came over to ask about it."

"Was Liz wearing a Chicago Fire shirt?" Mark asked.

"No, Pauli said she was wearing a Harry Potter shirt," Jake laughed. "I remember reading those books to her when she was in grammar school."

"Time flies when you're having fun," Mark laughed.

"Is that supposed to make me feel younger?" Jake shot back.

50

"Eat your cake and stop bitching," Paul said. "Be thankful you can. That's what John would want."

"To John," Mark said, holding up his mug of tea.

"To John," Jake and Paul repeated, lifting their mugs up

Chapter Nine

Jake pushed a shopping cart up to the entrance of Costco. After flashing his card, he strolled in with a feeling of déjà vu. It reminded him of the way Newark firefighters flashed their badges to the Port Authority Police when they drove through the tunnels in the days after 9/11. He had gone over with John several times, always riding in John's white SUV. If the rest of the people in Costco knew his thoughts, they would say he was crazy. Only Jersey firefighters would understand. So many of them responded the same way until the FDNY closed Ground Zero down.

Remembering John last night had been fun, although he realized each of them remembered a different John. Paul remembered a brother he lived with and emulated. Mark remembered an aggressive, yet quiet, firefighter and good friend. Jake's memories of John were a mix of both. John was like an older brother, even though he didn't live with him. Jake knew an outgoing, boisterous boy who was a role model. He was not introduced to the quiet, shy John until he met him on the fire department. Then the demons appeared and he had watched in frustration as John descended into hell.

With these thoughts in mind, Jake began the slow trek through the cavernous warehouse, list in hand. If he blew it and didn't pick up something on his wife's list, she would begin her disparaging comments about sending a man to do a woman's job. His phone rang when he was halfway through the list. Looking at the number, he saw it was Paul and immediately answered it. His friend had gone to see a doctor today. Jake wanted to hear the results.

"Yo, snorkel breath," Jake said using one of their childhood expressions.

"Hey Jake," Paul said quietly. "Got some news about that cough."

The tone of his friend's voice put Jake on high alert. There was news and it was not good.

"Talk to me," Jake requested.

"Well, the doctor did the usual exam of my throat, then listened to my lungs and he wasn't happy. So, he sent me for a chest x-ray and that showed I have multiple tumors in both lungs."

Jake stopped pushing the cart, trying to absorb what his lifelong friend had just said. Multiple tumors, both lungs. Before he could really digest or at least accept that he heard, Paul continued.

"So, they set me up for a procedure to get a biopsy of one of the tumors. But he is almost certain it will be malignant," Paul recited with a monotone cadence. "From there we'll discuss my options for treatment. The only positive news is Hackensack University Medical is the closest hospital for treatment and my insurance covers it."

Jake's brain was processing the information slowly, as if resisting each word, screaming it's not true, waiting for Paul's familiar laugh as he announced it's only a joke.

"I'm not scared," Paul finished.

You're not scared, Jake thought. I'm petrified. But saying that would only make things harder for Paul.

"I understand," Jake replied. "How can I help?"

"Right now, it's up to modern medicine," Paul said. "Don't worry, if I need anything, I'll let you know. Oh, and one other thing, I really don't want my patients to know right now. No one's going to catch it from me, but I don't want the office to turn into a circus. Some of my patients can be very emotional. So, could you keep it under your hat for now?"

"Whatever you want, brother," Jake assured. "Okay to tell Jo and the kids?"

"Yeah, and I'll tell Mark and Jill."

"Okay, you'll tell Mark."

"Got to go, now," Paul said. " They've had a cancellation which opened up a

53

spot for this procedure. I'll let you know the results."

"Okay," Jake answered. "And Paul, I love you."

"Love you like the brother you are, Jake," Paul replied.

Jake loaded the car after checking out, feeling numb. He had always told Paul and Mark that it was against his rules for them to check out before him. All had taken it as a joke, but now Jake knew he meant it. How would he get through the hard times and celebrate the good times without Paul being there? Who would Tim and Pauli turn to for a second opinion and some advice on how to deal with their sometime unreasonable dad? Then there was Johanna. She has known Paul for over forty years. The three of them had shared life, friendship, and heartaches. Paul was special because he was a friend, not a lover. She could go to him for advice when the emotions inherent in any intimate relationship boiled over. He was one of her pillars of support. Now Jake had to inform her that Paul might soon be gone.

Lung cancer? He didn't even smoke! No, but he spent days in Trinity Church next to Ground Zero adjusting the backs of first responders who were injured working the pile. The car pulled into the driveway after a mindless, autopilot drive. The numbness had seeped into Jake's soul. As he began to unload the items from Jo's list, a debate raged inside him. How to tell the news to his wife? Picking up a cardboard box filled with groceries, Jake moved toward the front door resigned to winging it. When he stepped into the house, Jo was sitting at the kitchen table crying. He should have known. Costco took too much time. Jill had already phoned with the news.

He put the box on the floor as she stood up and walked over to him. Then she buried her head into his shoulder and wept.

Chapter Ten

"Got everything, Dad?" Tim asked Jake.

"Just need your mother," Jake said while standing on the front porch. Joanna dashed out of the house passed her husband, handed her carryon to her son, and climbed into the king cab of his pickup truck. Jake closed and locked the door, then made his way to the front passenger seat. Why his son had a pickup truck eluded him. Yes, he was an architect, but that rarely put him on the grounds of the projects he designed. It seemed to be a lot of steel to drag around for an infrequent need. Leaving the thought in the unanswerable bin in his mind, Jake climbed up, buckled his seatbelt, and settled in for the ride to Newark Liberty. He had long ago accepted the ways of his millennial offspring. Tim got into the driver's seat, put the truck in reverse, and started his parents on their way to Chicago.

"So, how's your social life?" Jo asked her son.

"Nothing unusual, Mom," Tim replied. "I get out on the weekends, but it's all work during the week. Growing a business takes all I have to give."

Tim's answer told Jake there had been no movement toward Tim settling down. The girls loved him. He loved the girls. As far as Jake was concerned, the problem was the "s" attached to girls. He needed it to be dropped. When it was one girl, he had a shot at a grandchild. There was no expectation that what they were going to see in Chicago would be a harbinger of grandparenthood.

"How's Uncle Paul making out?" Tim asked as he navigated his way to Route Eighteen.

"The oncologist seems pleased with his progress," Jake answered. "The tumors in his lungs have all but disappeared. From what Paul tells me, the only concern is a small tumor that formed on his adrenal gland. That one isn't shrinking with the therapy being used. So, they're going to try a different one based on DNA."

"Sounds cutting edge," Tim pointed out as he pulled onto Eighteen.

"I've been reading a lot about the new therapies," Jo said, "If his body can tolerate them, there's real hope he can beat this."

"That's good to hear," Tim said. "He's too good a man to lose so soon."

Tim guided his truck through the mid-day traffic, easing over into the far-left lane. Jo made some impatient sounds then expressed her discomfort with the way the men in her life drove.

"Why can't you just stay in the center lane?" she asked. "You and your father just can't drive reasonably. Always in the fast lane. Just be careful. You're not a fireman. They'll give you a ticket."

Jake sat quietly, not daring to respond. How he got drawn into his wife's tirade was beyond him. They were going to be traveling together in close quarters for hours. A disagreement was to be avoided at all costs.

"I'm not speeding, Mom," Tim reassured her. "Just getting into the lane with the least traffic. Besides, they can only hit me from one side over here."

"Men!" she snapped.

After they passed through the Turnpike toll booth and moved to the north bound side of the road, the sign directing traffic sent them to the car/truck roadway. The car only entrance was closed. Jake glanced back at his wife to check on her. It was obvious Jo was unhappy. Since she had gone through "the changes", Jo rarely drove and preferred to ride in the backseat. Jake knew to never get onto the truck side of the Turnpike. He reached back and patted her knee which produced a weak smile.

Why had changing hormonal levels caused such a shift in perceived risk taking? Jake wondered. He had thought of the question before, but had never raised it with Jo, having always anticipated a decidedly negative response. His thoughts were that biology no longer required risk taking to find a mate and

56

reproduce. The two of them were now biologically irrelevant. The change had been gradual over the past forty years. Passion drove them when they were in their twenties. By the time forty came around, Jake found there were times he needed sleep more than he needed intimacy. Paul had laughed when they discussed it. As a bachelor, he chose when to be intimate and when to just say goodnight. Providing, of course, his date came on to him.

Jo was still in excellent shape, but she now did it for health reasons, not to be attractive for him. At some point after fifty or so, they lost their passion. He had asked her once if she missed it. She had told him to grow up. So, now intimacy was rarer and less physical, more a tender reaffirmation that they were a couple than a hunger to satisfy a need.

The exits slipped by quickly until the Garden State Parkway crossed the Turnpike. Traffic began to build after that and slowed down considerably. At least with Tim's habit of getting into the far-left lane, they kept a little distance between his pickup and the tractor-trailer traffic. Jo slid across the back seat to the driver's side to increase the space. Tim turned on the radio to the news station for a check on the traffic. After hearing a car fire in the car lane was the cause, he chuckled.

"Want me to pull over when we get to the fire so you can get out and give them a hand? You know, once a fireman, always a fireman," Tim repeated something Jake had said after retiring.

"That's okay," Jake replied. "I'm sure they'll have it under control by the time we get there."

"Don't encourage him," Jo said.

Jake knew it keep his mouth shut after that.

Traffic slowed and then came to a halt, becoming stop and go for a few minutes.

Freed from concentrating on the cars around him, Tim asked, "Dad, did you really tell Liz to buy a fire oral history book to study for the CPA exam?"

Jake chuckled. "Pauli's giving a false narrative again," he said. "I only told her that she can read about a lot of study techniques in that book. So, it was advice on how to study, not advice on how to prepare for the CPA exam."

"Okay. And it wasn't Pauli," Tim said. "Liz mentioned it."

"Liz?" Jo asked. "You've met Liz?"

"Yeah, I had to go to South Bend for that last project," Tim explained. "Being that close, going to Chicago was required or Pauli would have crucified me."

"What's she like?" Jake asked.

"Smart, attractive. I guess you would call her a dark celt, jet black hair with bright green eyes. Pauli says guys hit on her all the time,"

"Really?" Jo asked. "How does she react?"

"Pauli says she laughs, thinks it's a fun game to lead them on for a second and then crush their dreams."

"I hope you're joking," Jake said. "You're making her sound like a viper."

"Yes, yes, I'm joking. She's a sweetheart, Dad. Don't worry."

It was only a twenty-minute delay, so they arrived at the terminal with time to spare. Tim pulled into a space by the curb that had just been vacated. There was a Port Authority cop keeping everyone moving, so the two men hopped out and dropped the luggage on the sidewalk while Jo waited beside the truck.

"That's it," Jake said. "Thanks for the ride. We'll text you when we land."

"Okay, Dad," Tim replied. Then he walked over to his mother, gave her a peck on the cheek, and climbed back into his truck.

"Say hello to Pauli for me!" he shouted before pulling away.

They were at the curbside only a minute or so. No complaints from the officer watching. Jake had a Newark Firefighters' Union jacket on which produced a nod of the head from the cop. Jo extended the handles of the carry-ons while Jake did the same for their luggage. Then they hustled into the terminal to check in.

Chapter Eleven

"Dad!"

Jake looked around. It sounded like Pauli's shout.

"Jake!"

The last shout helped him hone in on her voice. Pauli was waving her hand above her head by the terminal exit. A tall, slender woman with dark hair and a shy smile was standing next to her. That must be Liz, Jake thought. Beside her were a man about the same age as Jo and him and a younger man, maybe around Tim's age. Jake assumed this was his first glimpse of the Kevin and Carl Moore.

He turned to Jo and said, "Pauli's by the entrance with Liz, Kevin, and Carl."

"I'll take your word for it," Jo said. "I can't see above the crowd."

"Well, she called my name as usual," Jake said. "Why does she always call my name?"

"I guess for the same reason I married you," Jo observed. "You're taller than me."

The crowd from their flight began to scatter, allowing Jo to see her daughter. As they changed their trajectory, Jake latched onto his wife's last comment.

"Is that why you married me?"

"It's a little more complicated than that," Jo laughed "You looked so needy shivering under the air conditioning vent in the ER with no shirt on. And you were cute, too. But if you weren't taller than me, I don't know."

"That was a hot day and my clothes were soaked with sweat," Jake reminded her. "But didn't I strike you as a heroic fireman saving the city from disaster?"

"Dream on tall boy."

They reached Pauli before Jake could respond. Of course, his responses were a little subdued after a flight, even if their time in the air was limited compared to their usual flights. It had been planes to Europe for the past decade. Jo had fallen in love with the escorted tours available at Costco Travel. Chicago was a short hop compared to London. Now that they were running out of European destinations, his wife had set her heart on Asia. From what he had heard, flights to Asia topped seventeen hours in the air. He wasn't looking forward to it.

"Jake!" Kevin hollered. "Great to meet you." He grabbed Jake's hand and shook it while throwing him a bear hug. This went smoothly since both men were about the same height. "This is my son Carl," Kevin continued after they separated. "You've spoken to my daughter Liz and do you remember Liz's significant other, Pauli?"

Liz looked up at the ceiling and muttered, "Dad." While Pauli laughed and muttered "firemen."

Jake couldn't pass up the opportunity to tease his not so little girl. "Yes, I seem to remember her in some very embarrassing situations."

"Don't even go there, Dad," Pauli warned.

Jo stepped past here exuberant husband and shook the hands of Kevin and Carl, then turned to Liz. "I've been looking forward to meeting you in person," she said before giving a gentle hug.

The airport continued to flow around the small group, not paying attention to what was an all-too-common occurrence. Liz appeared to be tense, but cheerful. Pauli was relaxed, appearing confident that her parents would accept her choice of mate.

Carl stepped forward after Jo released Liz. "Let me help you with your bags," he said, reaching for the bags Jake had been pulling.

"Thank you," Jo said while quickly pushing the bags next to Jake in the

61

young man's direction before her husband could protest. Pauli and Liz grabbed the carryon bags and followed Carl out the terminal exit.

"Kate isn't here because she stayed home to cook," Kevin said. "Wanted to make a good impression."

"She did that over the phone," Jake replied as they followed their offspring into the parking lot where Carl was lifting the luggage into a stretch limousine.

"Woah," Jake exclaimed. "Moving on up! Got to Newark Liberty in my son's pickup."

"Not my idea," Kevin said. "The girls wanted to make it a special day."

Pauli had turned around when she heard her father's reaction. She had a devilish grin on her face as she made a welcoming gesture toward the limo. Liz seemed to be standing a little taller. "Welcome to Chicago," she said.

Jo laughed and climbed in the back where she preferred to be anyway. They all settled in before the chatter started.

"How was your flight?" Pauli asked.

"Our flight?" Jake said. "In a word, short. It seemed we got up to cruising altitude and then quickly began descending. I've spent more time stuck in shore traffic on the Parkway."

"Traffic is no better around here," Kevin said. "It's just Lake Michigan instead of the Atlantic Ocean. I'll take you out to see it. From the shoreline, it looks about the same. Water as far as the eye can see."

"Dad," Liz interrupted. "They've seen the lake. No need to try and impress."

"I'm not trying to impress, Liz," Kevin replied. "Just trying to be hospitable."

"You don't have to try, Kevin," Jo said. "You're already being the consummate host." She extended her hand and moved it across her body as if presenting prizes on a game show.

Liz laughed. "See, I told you," she said to Kevin, then turned to Jake and Jo. "He was afraid the limo would put you off."

"How could a Battalion Chief put off a firefighter?" Jake asked.

Pauli jumped right in. "No shoptalk, Dad!"

Everyone laughed. That exchange seemed to break the ice.

"It wasn't shoptalk," Jake said. "Just wanted to show I'm not overly sensitive. Thirty plus years in the firehouse gives you a thick skin."

Kevin laughed and shook his head in agreement.

"So, I can't talk shop," Jake said to Pauli. "What plans do you have for us? Do we get to taste Chicago pie?"

Liz had a confused look on her face. "Which kind of Chicago pie?"

Pauli stepped in to translate New Jersey English. "In Jersey pizza is often called pie," she said.

"Really, I didn't know that." Liz exclaimed. "How do you know someone's not talking about apple pie or cherry pie?"

"Well, if you're talking about an apple pie, you would say apple pie, but if you want pizza, then you might say 'Let's get a pie.' Which means get pizza. It's kind of the context."

"Lots of Italians in Jersey," Jake said, "Pizza means pie in Italian and all those Italian kids taught their friends what good Italian food is. So, am I going to get a taste of Chicago deep dish pizza while I'm here??

"Without a doubt," Kevin said. "Maybe we can try some deep dish tonight. I know a great place in the city. Maybe we'll get a fireman's discount."

This produced a shocked look from Liz. She immediately shot down the idea. "Dad!" she said. "Don't you remember Mom's cooking a big meal tonight? There'll be plenty of time for the two of you to go out and talk shop. Don't rush things."

"Oh, yeah," Kevin said. "What was I thinking?"

"There are so many really great pizza places," Carl added quickly. "We can try a different slice every day."

63

"I'm going to like it here," Jake replied.

"Your waistline isn't going to," Jo teased, setting off another round of laughter.

Jake thought the exchange was a little strange, so when Liz and Pauli began talking with Jo, he caught Kevin's eye. Kevin glanced at the women, then mouthed "later". Jake shook his head yes and let it drop. There was something up and Kevin had almost blown it. Best to let whatever it was go to avoid stupid mistakes.

He could see the Moores were trying hard to make them feel welcomed. How to assure them they didn't have to work so hard? He tried to keep things simple with his question about pizza. Where the need to explain the use of the word pie came from, he wasn't sure. What Kevin was hiding from the ladies would have to be explained later. No talking shop made it more difficult since that's what firefighters do when they meet.

"So, Liz when is the exam?" he asked.

"No shop, Dad," Pauli scolded.

With that, Jake turned away from his daughter and asked Carl, "How do you pass your time, Carl?"

The young man chuckled as Pauli seemed to debate whether talking about his job constituted talking shop. Apparently, it didn't because there was no protest registered.

"I'm a data scientist," he answered. "I crunch really large data for clients to help them better understand how to allocate resources."

"Seriously?" Jake asked. "That's a brand-new field. Do they even have college programs for it?"

"No, not really," Carl said. "I attended what they called a bootcamp."

"How did you prepare for that?" Jo asked.

"I was a computer science major, so it wasn't that much of a stretch. My professors gave me a recommendation, then I just reviewed all my computer languages and studied like crazy for three months."

"And that's why they call it bootcamp," Jake said.

"That's why they call it bootcamp," Carl agreed.

The limo was smoothly navigating through the evening traffic in a stop and go manner. Jake had hit on Kevin and Carl. His attempt at Liz had fallen flat or at least had been ruled out of bounds. Pauli was the only target left and he was up to date on her career. Where to now? A motorcycle sped past them as they waited in traffic, providing a stepping off point for a change of subject and avoiding an awkward silence. Jo started it off.

"Honestly, why can't they wait like everyone else? If someone decides to open their door to see what's going on, they're going to end up in the ER," she said. "You never rode like that, did you?"

The last question was aimed at Jake.

"You rode a motorcycle?" Pauli asked in surprise.

"Quiet," Jake said. "That's top-secret stuff, not to be told to our children in case they get the idea to ride one of those beasts."

Pauli laughed incredulously. "Mom, you made him keep that a secret?"

Jo smiled before confessing, "I guess it's okay for you to know now. Why he wanted to ride one of those is beyond me. He's seen what happens when metal and people collide. He sold his bike and used the money to buy me an engagement ring. I made him grow up."

"Is that talking shop?" Jake asked Pauli. She shook her head no, obviously enjoying the revelation. "Actually, the first time I was in Chicago or really the first time I passed through Chicago, was on that bike during rush hour. Your Uncle Paul was riding behind me and got very upset because the cars were tailgating."

"Uncle Paul had a motorcycle, too?" Pauli asked.

"Uncle Paul has a motorcycle now," Jo told her.

"He's a doctor."

"What makes you think doctors don't ride motorcycles?" Jake asked. Then turned to Kevin and Carl. "Paul is a lifelong friend and Pauli's godfather. She was partially name after him. Her great-grandmother was named Pauline also, so Paul has to share credit."

"This is the friend who has cancer?" Liz asked, turning the conversation serious.

"Yes," Jake said. "He's fighting. Looks like he has a chance to beat it."

"That's tough," Kevin said quietly.

"Guess it comes with growing older," Jake said. "Seen a lot of guys slip away over the past few years."

This brought a prolonged silence. Jake cursed himself. Idiot! How could you say something like that in a situation like this? They were here to celebrate their daughters moving into the next stage of life, not talk about the end. Thankfully, shortly after this the limo pulled into a dead-end street. Jake was looking forward to a special dinner, but something told him Kevin's slip of the tongue meant dinner would be late.

Chapter Twelve

"Why are there so many cars parked on the street?" Liz asked.

"Your mother said something about one of the neighbors having a baby shower," Kevin answered.

The limo had to pull into the driveway of a large two-story frame house in the middle of the block. Jake hopped out with Kevin and Carl following. They quickly pulled the bags out of the trunk. Jake and Carl pulled them toward the house while Kevin went to tip the driver. Carl seemed to hang back to let the women go ahead which struck Jake as odd. Maybe that had something to do with Kevin's behavior. When Liz opened the door, all could hear a shout.

"Surprise!"

The men stepped into a house full of women there for a bridal shower. Jo didn't seem to be surprised, but Liz and Pauli were floored. The room was dominated by young women. Jake recognized some of them. Jo's aunt Marge made it. So did some of Pauli's school mates, but the Jersey contingent was sparse. Not everyone worked remotely and it was the middle of the week, so nothing that wasn't expected. The guys wrestled the baggage up the stairs to a spare bedroom on the second floor and were then promptly shown the door. Jake hadn't even met Kate.

"I'm heading back to my place, Dad," Carl announced. "Got to meet a certain young lady for dinner."

"Okay," Kevin answered. "Thanks for the help. Have a good time."

Carl hopped into a Ford Mustang and headed down the street.

"So, you still want that deep dish pizza?" Kevin asked as he walked toward a Chevy Malibu.

"Yeah, sounds great," Jake said. "Came close to spilling the beans, didn't you?"

"Oh, yeah!" Kevin laughed. "Kate would have been fit to be tied. Start BSing and you drop your guard. Women and their secrets."

"Jo didn't look shocked. Was she in on it?" Jake wondered.

"It was the two of them," Kevin said as they reached the Malibu. "Kate ran it past Jo because she wanted people from Jersey to come."

Unlocking the doors of the car with the remote, Kevin slid in behind the wheel while Jake made his way around to the passenger's side. After starting the car and backing out of the driveway, he asked Jake, "You said you wanted to ride mass transit. You serious?"

"I'm serious," Jake answered. "Quickest way to get a feel for a city is riding the bus or train."

"Never thought of it, but you're probably right," Kevin said as he turned onto the main drag in this part of town. "We can get on the train at a station a couple of miles from here."

"Great," Jake agreed. "Then we don't have to worry about what the wives think and we can talk shop and discuss how Kate got my wife to keep a secret so well guarded I knew nothing of her plans."

"That's for you to tell me," Kevin laughed.

They drove to the station discussing the cars on the road, the difference in weather between Illinois and New Jersey, and the sports rivalries that were inevitable. Kevin parked the car in a lot by the station and they walked the short distance between. As they approached the platform, Jake made an observation that set off another subject. One that made him feel old.

"Have you ever paid attention to the cell phone use on mass transit?"

Kevin laughed and admitted, " Jake, I can't tell you the last time I rode the train into the city. Couldn't do it before I retired. Needed a car in case they sent me to another part of the city. After I retired, I knew Kate wouldn't go for it, so I didn't even ask."

Jake looked at all the people waiting on the platform. There were dozens of them and if they were under forty a cell phone was in their hands. It seemed every person on the platform other than the two of them and a gentleman about their age standing in the middle of the station was looking down at a screen.

"Well, look now," Jake suggested.

Kevin looked down the platform. "Wow," he said. "I don't think any of them are aware of what's around them."

"If the house across the street caught fire, they probably wouldn't notice until it showed up on their phone," Jake laughed. "When I was a kid, I had a work study job in high school. I used to ride the same bus every work day. The same people rode that bus each morning. These folks were family. They'd talk about their kids, their jobs, knew the bus driver by first name. Asked about his family all the time. Now? Let's be serious."

Kevin shook his head in agreement. "Conversation is a lost art form," he observed. "At least the spoken type. Why talk when you can text?"

As they watched the Millennials and younger staring at their phones, the older man standing in the middle by the railing suddenly grabbed hold of the railing, then lowered himself to the ground. After he sat down, it appeared he simply passed out.

"Woah," Jake said. "I think we've got a problem." He then ran down the platform to the man. Kevin was right behind him. The crowd on the platform took a minute to notice. When Jake reached the man, he did a quick visual assessment, then checked for a carotid pulse.

"You got a pulse?" Kevin asked as he poked 911 into his phone.

Jake waited for Kevin to give the operator the location before he answered. "Yeah, got a pulse, shallow breathing, unconscious."

"Elderly man, collapsed on the train platform. He has a pulse and is breathing," Kevin said into the phone. "Let's get him on his back and feet up," he suggested after putting the phone back in his pocket.

The two of them gently moved the man onto his back, loosened his tie, and unbuttoned his collar. By now the people on the platform had begun to react to the little drama unfolding in front of them. As they began to gather around, Kevin stood up.

"Please, please give him some breathing space," he said with an authoritative tone.

The gentleman appeared to be coming around, so Jake leaned closer and started talking. "Sir," he said "Sir, can you hear me?" The man shook his head yes.

"You seem to have passed out, are you in any pain?"

He moved his head to indicate no.

"Okay, do you think you can sit up?"

With that the man began to push himself up. Jake gave him a hand, slowly getting him into a sitting position.

"What's your name?" Kevin asked leaning down.

"Alfred," the man replied.

"Al, do you have any conditions that would have caused you to blackout like that?" Jake asked.

"I have low blood pressure," Al said. "I'm on my way to see my cardiologist to set up an appointment for a pace maker." He chuckled wryly after that. "I guess I should have gone yesterday."

"So, Al," Kevin said. "How old are you?

"Sixty-six."

This answer hit Jake hard. "Double sixes," he said as jovially as he could. "Same as me. Tough admitting your limits, isn't it?"

Al chuckled, "My wife keeps reminding me I'm not eighteen anymore."

"Ha!" Jake laughed. "That's better than mine. She raised the age. I'm not twenty-five."

The sound of sirens got Kevin up to walk over to the railing and look down the block. Satisfied with what he saw, he came back.

"An engine company is almost here. EMS should be right behind."

A train moving into the station drew the spectators back to the platform edge.

Al tried to get up. "I'm okay," he said. "I'll just hop on the train and go to my doctor."

Kevin put his hand on Al's shoulder. "Al," he said. "You've got like seventy years of first responder experience here. Our advice would be to go to the ER and get checked out. We'd all feel better if you do."

"You think so?" Al asked. "I mean I've bothered you two enough."

"No bother at all, Al," Jake assured him. "You don't want to have to explain to your wife how it was you cracked your head open falling down the station stairs if you pass out again."

"Yeah, I guess you're right," Al sighed.

Kevin got up to see where the engine company and EMS were. When he got to the railing, he shouted down, "Jeff, we have a sixty-six-year-old male who passed out. He has low blood pressure and is in the market for a pacemaker. No trauma. He's conscious."

"Chief!" Jake heard someone yell. "Can't stay away, can you?"

"Trouble seems to find me," Kevin shouted back.

A minute later, two firefighters came up to the platform with a first aid kit and a bottle of oxygen. They had large grins on their faces as they approached Kevin, Jake, and Al.

"Chief, how've you been?" the lead firefighter asked grabbing Kevin's hand. After a hug and a pat on the back from each firefighter, Kevin turned to Al.

"Al, you got some of the best to take care of you," he said with a smile. "I

71

broke them in a while back."

The firefighters went to Al and began to check him out. Blood pressure was taken and a cervical collar was placed around his neck just in case. EMS arrived. Al climbed onto their gurney and was strapped in. Before they started to roll, Kevin introduced Jake.

"Guys this is Firefighter Jake Covey, retired from Newark."

"From Newark, Ohio?" Jeff asked.

Jake smiled. People often assumed he was from the Newark in their region. "No, I'm from the original Newark, at least the original American Newark," he told them. "Newark, New Jersey."

"Really?" Jeff asked. "Then you've seen a hell of a lot of fire in your time."

"Ouch!" Jake replied. "In my time?"

They all laughed, including Al who was listening to a ritual of sorts few outside the fire service really saw.

"I've seen my fair share," Jake continued. "It was a good run. Now we have to get Al to the ER to get checked out."

"Yes, we do," One of the EMTs said.

"Nice meeting you, Jake," Jeff said. "Chief, why don't you stop by the firehouse for dinner sometime?"

"Have to clear it with the old lady," Kevin answered. "She's afraid if I go to the firehouse, I might not come back for days."

The EMTs started Al on his way to the ER and the firefighters went back to their rig. As Al was rolled away, Kevin turned to Jake and raised his hand. Jake gave him a high five.

"Felt good to be helping again," Kevin said.

"Damn straight," Jake agreed. "It's not a working fire, but I'll take it."

They both laughed, then turned and walked to wait for the train.

Chapter Thirteen

They stepped off the red line elevated train at the Chicago Station. Kevin led the way, keeping up a continuous narrative of the city. Everything from why it was called the windy city to how the "L" was organized. It seemed Kevin had fallen back on trying too hard to be a good host. Jake wondered how he could disabuse his host of that notion. All he needed was good conversation, a cold beer, and warm food. He was not a difficult guest.

As they reached street level, Jake brought up something he had noticed on the train and then in the station. There were a lot of young adults in jeans carrying backpacks. He would have expected them to be wearing suits or at least business casual while carrying briefcases.

"Seems to be a lot of kids with backpacks," he said. "Like they're on a college campus or something."

"Well, Loyola University is a couple of blocks north of here," Kevin told him. "So, it is like you're on a college campus."

They weaved their way through the foot and auto traffic until Kevin stopped in front of an Italian restaurant.

"Giordano's?" Jake chuckled. "I worked with a guy named Giordano."

"Really?" Kevin asked. "Think they're related?"

"I don't remember him talking about having rich relatives in the Midwest."

"Oh, I don't think these Giordanos are rich," Kevin said as he opened the restaurant door. "They're certainly not the fashion world Giordanos."

"Fashion world?" Jake scoffed. "I live in Levi jeans not Armani suits. No fashion world here."

The two men chuckled as they moved into the restaurant. Their little tryst with Al had put them behind schedule, but they were still ahead of the dinner rush. Quickly getting seated and receiving menus, Jake turned to Kevin, "Okay, give me your best representation of Chicago pie," he challenged.

"Pie meaning pizza," Kevin shot back.

"Not just pizza, Chicago deep dish pizza," Jake said.

"Let's do the classic tonight, so you can get a feel for starters," Kevin suggested. "You can be more adventurous later."

"Deal."

While they waited for the someone to approach them, Jake raised a topic that had been bothering him since they boarded the train. "Think we should tell the wives about Al?" he asked while glancing around the restaurant. So many young couples just starting out. Which ones will stay together? Which ones will fall apart? Would any of them understand the reason he was asking this question?

"Tell the wives?" Kevin repeated slowly. "You know, thinking about it, I don't see why they need to know."

The waiter walked up before Jake could respond. They ordered a couple of beers and requested time to look at the menu. After the waiter went to get their drinks, Jake responded to Kevin's opaque answer.

"So, you'd catch an earful too."

Kevin smiled. "Probably. Would go something like, 'You're retired. Can't you let younger people do the job?'"

"And once you explained that there were no other options, she would relent, but not before questioning the lack of other options."

"I'm only guessing," Kevin said. "She hasn't had to deal with it since I retired. The 'let the young people deal with it' comment was used when I was on the job."

"Once a fireman, always a fireman, is how Jo puts it."

"Smart woman."

"She also says 'Once a fireman's wife, always a fireman's wife' and that's not a positive thing."

"Tell me about it."

The waiter came up with their beers, causing a natural break in the flow of the conversation. Jake changed subjects after a swig.

"Do you come here often?"

"If I came here often, I'd be as big as a house," Kevin laughed. "People don't eat deep dish pizza that often. It's a bit of a project. You'll see. People love it or hate it. I just say it has its place in the panoply of culinary art. I'd suggest the individual pizza because deep dish leftovers aren't very good. It's one of those dishes you have to eat right away to appreciate."

"I was hoping to bring some back for Jo to taste," Jake said.

"No, best not to, she might not try it again."

"Then the individual six-inch pie it is." Jake said while waving to the waiter. After placing their order, Jake leaned back, took a breath, and dove into the forbidden topic of shop talk.

"So, why a fireman, Kev?" he asked.

"Well, fresh out of high school I got started in the restaurant business. Worked my way up to manager pretty quickly, but just couldn't take the 'great indoors'. From there I moved to real estate. Did okay there. That's what I was doing before I got on the job. Then a buddy suggested I try the fire department. Never looked back."

After another swig of beer, Kevin shot a question to Jake.

"So, let me ask you. You're a CPA, why did you take the job?"

"That's a legitimate question and one that Jo asked frequently," Jake began. "I was appointed when I was twenty. Went to college while I was on the job. Graduated during a recession. By then I was vested in the pension, but really, I just loved the job. Jo reluctantly accepted that. How about you? Why stop at BC?"

"The way it's set up here, anything above BC is appointed by the mayor. I wasn't into politics. Besides I was busy with my parttime job instructing small town and volunteer firefighters. Then there were family obligations that got in the way of politics. And I didn't want to stand outside while others went in."

"So, same as me?" Jake laughed.

"How so?"

"I wanted to be in the fire building."

"Yeah, guess you're right. Gets in your blood."

"Adrenal addiction. One of the guys I worked with got injured, had to go out on a disability pension. When he went for physical therapy, the therapist asked how long he was on the job. Then she told him he had been on thirty-year adrenal high, now had to come down."

They both laughed. Then they each sipped their beer and caught their breath. Kevin broke the quiet interlude.

"So, you have a CPA," he pointed out. "Obviously, you have the smarts to get promoted. Why didn't you go for promotion?"

Jake took a moment, debating how in depth an answer he should give. After reminding himself that his daughter was going to become part of this man's family, he opted for a detailed answer.

"I never took the test. Got to want it to get it and I just didn't want the responsibility," he began.

"Responsibility?" Kevin asked.

"I knew a Battalion Chief when I first got on job. He had a fire in an abandoned building. A building that he had told his battalion not to enter because there had been several previous fires. Some companies from outside his battalion responded and entered the building looking for a quick knock down. There was a collapse and three guys died. This Chief never got over it. Felt it was his responsibility. I just didn't want to have to worry about anyone else but me. Besides I made enough as a CPA. If I got promoted, all the other duties that go with rank would have interfered with the accounting. As a firefighter, I could work on clients' accounts in firehouse."

76

Kevin shook his head quietly. Jake knew he would be well aware of what goes through a Chief's mind at a fire. There was no need for any further explanation with him.

As if to prove Jake's assumptions to be correct, Kevin changed the subject to a more practical one.

"So, you've been out a while. What did you find was the biggest challenge when you retired?"

Jake laughed. "You mean besides living with my wife 24/7?"

"Yeah, besides that," Kevin confirmed with his own laugh.

"Staying relevant in the work a day world," Jake answered without the usual hesitation.

If Kevin's reaction to helping Al had been genuine, here was a man who might just understand how he felt. "If I go back to the firehouse now, I'm out of step. The department moved on, but in my head, it was frozen the day I walked out the door. I kind of stay relevant by do accounting for guys with side businesses, taxes for some others. The accounting business keeps me busy, but it's not the same as the firehouse. On the personal side, I thought I would stay relevant by being a grandfather which would surprise my younger self. Didn't even think about that until I became a father."

"Yeah, that kind of changes things, doesn't it?" Kevin agreed

"I'll say," Jake answered as the waiter delivered their pizzas.

Jake looked at the small deep-dish pie with wonder. The sauce was on top of everything. Where was the cheese? Kevin saw his puzzled look and offered up an explanation.

"With Deep Dish pizza, you have the crust turned up at the edges. That's why you need a deep dish. Then they put the cheese down. Next comes any toppings, and finally the sauce is poured over the whole deal."

"Really?" Jake said. "It sounds like an upside-down pizza."

"I guess you could look at it that way," Kevin chuckled. "You'll probably want to eat it with a knife and fork. It really doesn't lend itself to eating by hand."

"Viva la difference!" Jake said as he reached for his cutlery. He continued on with his thoughts while cutting the pizza.

"No one ever warned me about being a father. I guess my folks' generation just accepted it, but when I thought about, my life priorities changed. I mean, if I died before the kids were born, my wife is a young widow. She eventually moves on, gets remarried, has a family. I would just hope that she would think kindly of the time we shared before I checked out. When you become a father, you become very relevant to your children. I mean, no matter how good a stepfather might be, he's not the biological father. There's no hereditary connection, no DNA, you know what I mean? So, I lived for my kids until they became adults. After that I felt I became less relevant, but as a grandfather I'll be relevant again in a set position of family life. I get to spoil them rotten and then hand them back to their parents. But my son thinks he's Pygmalion and he's looking for a Galateas."

The last sentence seemed to go right over Kevin's head. "Pygmalion? What are you talking about?" he asked Jake with a puzzled look.

Jake kicked himself. How could he expect Kevin to understand what he just said. Until Pauli had explained it, he had never heard of it. He owed an explanation quick or it might put a squash on conversations for the rest of the night.

"Pauli saw My Fair Lady on campus and then went through the trouble of pointing out to me what the play was based on," he started. "Believe it or not, Eliza Doolittle is based on a Greek myth about some guy name Pygmalion who carves a statue of the perfect woman and gets some goddess to change it into a real person. Then she tells me that the original myth didn't name the woman, but the French philosopher Rousseau wrote about the myth and did name her. Which is probably why I remember. Had to take a philosophy class in freshman year, so I had heard of Rosseau."

"You do hear some strange conversations among firemen," Kevin commented.

"Firehouse culture is unique."

"Yes, it is," Kevin agreed.

They finished their pizzas in silence. After Jake washed down the last bite with the last drop of beer, he moved the conversation into new, uncharted territory.

"How'd you hear about Elizabeth's new identity?" he asked.

"New identity?" Kevin marveled. "I thought you were a numbers guy. That's an imaginative way to put it."

He hesitated for a moment as if having the same type of debate that Jake had just had with himself. If he did, he came down on the same side that Jake had earlier and dove right in.

"First she told her mother, who freaked out," Kevin said. "Then I came in to see what they were fighting about and was handed the news. It was hard. All the hopes and dreams you had are shot. No grandkids, no son-in-law to bond with. I mean, my father-in-law and I are the best of friends. We go on a flyfishing trip together every year. You're convinced that she'll never be happy because society won't let her. Of course, that was based on my experiences years ago. Now people seem to be more accepting".

"You think so?"

"Society has changed," Kevin answered as if trying to convince himself.

"What's society got to do with it? It's you who have to accept it," Jake pointed out.

"You think I'm happy my daughter is a lesbian?" Kevin asked quietly but in an angry tone. "You know what that does to her chance for happiness? Look, I only want her to be happy and have grandkids of course. If society accepts her choice, she has a better shot at happiness."

"Do you think society has changed or are you hoping society will change?" Jake asked.

"That's a hard question," Kevin said. "What are your feelings about it?"

Jake looked Kevin directly in the eye and said, "If she's happy, I'm happy. And God help the person who attacks her cause I'll be down their throat before they realize I'm after them."

Kevin burst out laughing while Jake had a satisfied smile on his face. Kevin picked up his beer bottle and raised it to Jake. "To firemen the world over, craziest bunch of bastards in and out of the firehouse."

"To all the wackos," Jake said in return. "So, you've met my daughter, got to know her a little. What do you think?"

"That's as direct a question as you can get," Kevin said. "Okay, here goes, I think she is an attractive - - -why did I say that first? I don't know, but she's smart, caring, and my daughter loves her. How about you? What's your opinion?"

"My opinion of Elizabeth?" Jake asked. "She seems like a wonderful woman, but I don't have your advantage of knowing her for a period of time. Her father's a firefighter and she's an accountant, so I'm guessing we have a lot in common. As far as the situation is concerned, I have to accept it or Pauli might just walk out of our life."

"That would be a nightmare," Kevin agreed. Then he waved to the waiter for the check. When he turned back to Jake, he pointed out, "It was fortunate that we were on that platform when Al lost it. You may not have felt it, but we were both relevant today."

Jake shook his head in agreement.

Chapter Fourteen

Jake slipped out of the guest bedroom quietly. Jo was still sleeping soundly and he wasn't about to wake her, not after the big bridal shower. When he and Kevin had returned from the city, they were given a blow-by-blow account. After their husbands called it a day, Kate and Jo sat up and talked for hours like two long lost sisters. He crept past the master bedroom and went downstairs to wait for Kevin. When he reached the kitchen, his host was already there.

"You made it down early," Kevin said. "The ladies aren't getting down anytime soon."

"Yeah, that's what I figured," Jake replied. "Jo crawled into bed way too late to be up now."

"You know what we can do?" Kevin said, "We can make the little ladies a firehouse breakfast."

"You think they want something that big?"

"Well, it'll be brunch by the time they get down."

"What ingredients do you have?" Jake asked gaining enthusiasm.

"Let's have a look," Kevin answered as he opened the refrigerator door. "We have bacon, sausage, eggs. Well, look at that. We've got diced potatoes. Add some coffee and the guys would be content until lunch."

Kevin began to hand the makings of breakfast to Jake who lined them up on the counter.

"You give me the tools and I'll fry up a meal fit for the firehouse," Jake said.

Kevin produced a frying pan, spatula, knife, and fork. Jake organized the ingredients and reached for an apron. No need to ruin the gesture by getting his clothes full of grease. As the production got under way Jake asked, "Think we should bring it upstairs and give them breakfast in bed?"

Kevin shook his head no. "Kate wouldn't appreciate food on the second floor. Says it's an open invitation for unwanted critters."

They both laughed, then Kevin turned serious and said, "Liz tells me you've been having a tough couple of years with your friends."

"Pauli must have needed to share," Jake answered quietly. "Yeah, one of the guys I worked with back in the 'war years' fell through a skylight, one of those level ones. He went down twenty feet, landed on his back. Thank God he was wearing a mask. Still, he broke lots of bones. Was a BC like you, up checking that the roof guys were safe. He would be 'Uncle Mark' to Pauli. Then there's Paul, who is her godfather. You heard about his battle with cancer. Yeah, the last few years have been tough."

He started cooking the potatoes while Kevin absorbed the information.

"You've known Paul since you were kids?" Kevin asked.

"Since second grade," Jake replied. "Grammar school, high school. We attended different colleges, but even then, we were roommates."

"Liz said something about Ground Zero."

"Paul's a chiropractor and his brother was a firefighter, so he has a big heart for firefighters," Jake told him. "He went into the city with some of the guys and then adjusted the sore backs of firefighters. He'd qualify for that fund Congress passed, but he doesn't have a wife or kids and it'd be hard to document him being there. So, he just accepted it. Insurance is covering the expenses."

"That's good," Kevin said. "Mark still on the job?"

"No way in hell would his wife put up with that," Jake laughed. "Go out on disability or meet me in divorce court."

By now Kevin had produced a second pan and was starting the sausage.

"How about you?" Jake asked. "Has time caught up with the guys you worked with?"

"Of course," Kevin admitted. "One of the guys from my old company made

82

it to ninety-five, but a lot more didn't make it out of their sixties. It's the same old story. Guys are working to provide for their families, so don't have time to stay in shape. It takes work to stay in shape and the older you get the harder you have to work. Where do you find the time? Plenty of heart disease and cancer on the Chicago Fire Department."

"Do you ever get the feeling you're running out of time?" Jake asked.

"God, yes," Kevin sighed. "It started to get to me, so I tried to prove to myself it was all in my head. I sat down and made a list of people who had passed away before they got to my age. I stopped when the names on the list passed sixty."

"I know the feeling," Jake said as he poured the potatoes into a metal bowl. "Yesterday didn't help any."

"How so?"

"Al and I are about the same age," Jake replied. "My man's going to see a doctor about a pacemaker."

Kevin chuckled, "We're not Spring chickens anymore."

"That's supposed to make me feel better?" Jake asked. "Do you ever talk to Kate about it.?"

"You mean my mortality?"

"Yeah."

"Not a good subject," Kevin confessed. "Her attitude is Liz will be able to wade through the financial portion of it and Carl can do the heavy lifting, so she'll get by."

"Oh," Jake moaned. "That kind of makes you expendable, doesn't it? Jo avoids the subject, says there's insurance and savings. Of course, the pension gets cut in half, but that's what the insurance and savings are for. All the practical daily stuff, that's what kids are for. So, that puts me in the same boat as you."

"Ha!" Kevin reacted as he finished the sausage and reached for the bacon.

"What do we leave behind? A house, a savings account, a pension, some memories that will vanish when she passes away. The only thing that really matters is your kids. A part of you lives in them, right?"

"I'd like to think so," Jake sighed. "But if they don't have children, then it's as if we never existed, isn't it?"

"Jesus, this is a depressing conversation," Kevin admitted.

"You started it," Jake laughed. "Had a few like this in the firehouse before I retired. You?"

"Only in companies with older guys," Kevin admitted. "The young bucks are oblivious to the end of life. At least until the memories of fire victims start to build up. Then some begin to appreciate how precious life really is."

"True," Jake agreed. "Young companies don't usually have these conversations. They just solve the rest of the world's problems while they sit around the kitchen table."

They both laughed. Jake shut off the stove and said, "I'll hold off on the eggs until the ladies come down."

"Okay, I'm going to check on today's weather, so we know what we're facing." Kevin headed for the den while Jake waited for the ladies.

"Jake," Kevin called. "We might have a problem."

Doesn't that sound familiar, Jake thought as he walked from the kitchen to the den.

"The mayor is asking the public's help in identifying two men who participated in a rescue yesterday," the news reporter started. "Alfred Korn, special assistant to the mayor, suffered a cardiac event on the train platform behind me. The heroes of the day were the usual suspects, a couple of firefighters. What makes this so unusual is we don't know who they are. One was apparently a Chicago Fire Department chief officer. The other a retired Newark, New Jersey firefighter."

84

Kevin quickly turned off the television.

"Did you say anything to Jo?" he asked.

"Not a word," Jake said. "How do you want to play this?"

"The mayor wants to know," Kevin muttered. "The mayor? This isn't going away. The department is going to try to use this for PR. Right now, the news apparently thinks I'm still on the job."

"What did we say in front of Al?" Jake asked himself. "You said we had all these years of experience and he should take advantage of our advice."

Kevin shook his head in agreement then reminded Jake, "It's not what we said to Al. It's what I said to Jeff. That's the only way they know you're from Newark. They even know which Newark you're from."

Kevin's cell rang as he finished.

"Hey, Carl," he answered. "Yes, I saw. It's on the radio also? No, she's sleeping in after the big day. And how was I supposed to know this guy works for the mayor? They dispatched an engine first, the ambulance came a few minutes later. Yes, I knew one of the guys on the engine. I broke him in. Surveillance video? Great. Yeah, thanks. Talk to you."

He hung up the phone and looked at Jake. "That was Carl, he said it's all over the radio news. The mayor's office is asking businesses in the area to check their surveillance video to see if they have a picture of us," he said with a chuckle. "We're wanted men. You didn't say a word to Jo?"

"Not a word."

"There's no way we can dodge this bullet," Kevin said. "All they have to do is ask dispatch who they sent there. Then they ask the guys. The guys will think it's hilarious and sell me out."

Jake thought about the circuses he had seen over the years when the news got hold of an entertaining or sensational story. They could be relentless. But this was a public relations play, not a screwed-up response to a fire. Still, however innocent their inquiries would be, one slip of the tongue and too much private information goes out to the world.

"You think they'll send a television crew?" he asked.

"I think department headquarters is going to jump on it and try to milk it for all it's worth," Kevin replied as he began to pace. "Can't have that mess come here. Kate will flip."

"You could try to head it off and call them," Jake suggested.

"Call who? The network? Which network? Hell, we didn't do much of anything other than call it in."

"You talked to him," Jake said. "Seventy years of experience and all that."

"Don't give me all the credit," Kevin warned. "You saw him go down; you checked him out. I never touched him. And you're from Jersey. That's what makes it newsworthy. Chicago/Newark cooperation saves mayoral assistant's life."

"Whoa," Jake protested. "The man fainted. Saved his life?"

"Tell me I'm wrong," Kevin challenged.

Jake was silent for a minute. "The girls are going to get up soon. What are we going to do?"

Kevin thought for a second. "They haven't heard it yet and the news doesn't know who we are yet."

"Slow it down, Kev" Jake cautioned. "Remember what you said to Jeff with Al lying there, 'This is retired firefighter Jake Covey from Newark.' Al knows who I am. The mayor's office probably called the firehouse and knows who you are. Like you said, they're playing this up for some good publicity."

"Do you think Jo's up for some good publicity?"

Jake walked over to a chair and sat down. Jo wouldn't really get angry over him helping. She would get furious if the press brought in the girls. That would be a threat.

86

"We have to get control of this story before the press digs and brings in the girls," Jake said. "There are too many wackos in the world looking to hurt people who are different. If Pauli and Liz somehow become part of the story, we'll both end up in divorce court."

The sound of movement upstairs told the men their wives were up.

"Does Kate watch the morning news as soon as she gets up?" Jake asked.

"She might if she wants to know the weather or she's following a story."

"Jo watches religiously while she does her morning workout."

"No workout this morning," Kevin said.

"If they don't watch anything, then we can tell them nonchalantly. You know, kind of build up to the whole mayor's office thing."

Sounds coming from the stairs told them the time for planning was over.

"That's what we'll do," Kevin agreed.

They moved back to the kitchen and continued to prepare the firehouse breakfast. Kate and Jo walked in silently, looking neutral, not a good sign after yesterday's success.

"What are the chefs preparing?" Kate asked.

"Sausage, bacon, eggs, potatoes, and coffee," Jake answered from in front of the stove.

"Coffee will be up in a minute," Kevin informed them standing at the counter next to Jake.

"So, we told you about our night," Jo said. "What did you guys do?"

"Kevin took me to try deep dish pizza," Jake told her as he turned off the stove.

Kevin stepped over to the opposite side of the kitchen to retrieve plates.

"Where'd you take him?" Kate asked

"Giordano's."

"Which one?"

87

"On North Rush Street, over by the college," Kevin replied.

"How'd you get into the city?" Kate pressed.

"Jake wanted to experience the L, mingle with the people of Chicago. So, we took the red line in," Kevin explained. "He pointed out how everyone was staring at their phones, never noticed before."

"Of course not, you haven't ridden the L in years," Kate countered. "Is that where you ran into Mr. Korn?"

Jake looked up at the ceiling while Kevin stutter-stepped before responding.

"Yes, he was on the platform waiting."

"Who did the chest compressions and who did the mouth to mouth?" Jo asked. "Or did you switch on and off?"

"Chest compressions?" Jake asked. "He had low blood pressure, passed out after lowering himself to the ground. Said he was on his way to the cardiologist to see about a pacemaker."

"Really?" Kate asked. "The news said it was a cardiac event."

"I guess cardiac event plays better than fainting from low blood pressure," Kevin pointed out.

"The two of you are on the most wanted list right now," Jo said. "How do you intend to handle this one?"

"Well, we want to fess up ASAP to keep it under control," Jake said.

"We figure they probably already know who I am because they dispatched an engine company to the scene and Jeff Orteze was on the rig," Kevin told them. "And I introduced Jake to Jeff, so Mr. Korn heard that part."

"Then why make like it's a mystery?" Jo asked.

"Publicity," both men replied.

"Kevin, no, no, no," Kate insisted. "Not on my lawn, not in front of my neighbors. What about the girls? If these - - -these vultures start poking around who knows what they'll start up."

"We are of the same mind, dear," Kevin agreed. "Jake and I have been working on a plan."

Jake tried to look convincing as he shook his head in agreement, praying Kevin had a plan. The nonchalant informing one was dead.

"I'm going to call headquarters and ask a few questions.," Kevin began. "Then we can negotiate a way for them to get their positive publicity while we maintain our privacy."

Kate took the cordless phone off the wall and handed it to Kevin.

Chapter Fifteen

"I can't thank you enough," Jo said to Kate before giving her a hug. "You two have been fantastic hosts."

"Oh, it was just a little bit of Midwestern hospitality," Kate replied. "With some Chicago drama thrown in."

The two women and their husbands laughed. They were standing beside the Moore's car at the departure drop-off of Midland airport. Jake thought the week had flown by. After the "rescue" of Mr. Korn, Chicago Fire Headquarters had tracked them down. They were summoned to headquarters where the Chief of the department presented a commendation signed by the mayor for the aid they had given Al. The day turned into a media circus with the encouragement of the powers that be. Jake considered the whole affair embarrassing, but Kevin took it in stride. Of course, all Kevin's firefighter friends couldn't stop with the sly comments. These remarks were given for the most part in the three firehouses they were invited to for a meal. The ladies had declined to accompany them, both continuing their low opinions of firehouses.

"Thanks for all the help you gave Liz studying," Kevin said to Jake. "It's given her a real boost in confidence."

"She's a smart woman, Kev," Jake said. "She picked up on fire promotional exam study techniques quickly. Then used them to create her own. If she were on the job, I would think she'd make Battalion Chief easily."

"If she were on the job, Kate would have a nervous breakdown," Kevin laughed. "A CPA is much preferred."

Jake looked up to see if there were any police in the area chasing people out. He spied one about ten cars away making its way toward them.

"The cops are doing a slow roll toward us," he told Kevin. "Let's get the last of the luggage onto the sidewalk."

They reached into the back of the car and lifted the carryon luggage out, dropping it next to the check-in baggage.

"Doesn't look like I have time to help you get them into the terminal," Kevin said while looking toward the police cruiser.

"Not a problem, they have wheels."

With that the two men shook hands and gave a hug with a quick pat on the back. Then the ladies said their goodbyes and the Moores climbed into their car. Jake and Jo waved as the car pulled away.

"I'll take the carry-ons, you get the baggage like the big strong man that you are," Jo told her husband. The couple headed into the terminal as the police cruiser rolled slowly passed the space just vacated by Kevin.

Checking in and boarding went smoothly. The plane took off on time, but it wasn't until they reached cruising altitude that they had a chance to lean back and relax.

Jake turned to Jo and asked a question about something that had piqued his curiosity for the better part of a week.

"You know, we were so busy all week, I never go to ask you," he began. "What did you and Kate talk about all those hours that first night? You were like two long lost sisters trying to catch up after not seeing each other for years."

Jo leaned back into her seat, the sound of the plane filling the silence for a moment. "What did we talk about?" she asked. "How did that reporter put it? The usual suspects, two firefighters. We definitely felt like two sisters. Both our husbands were big city firefighters. Then we talked about our children and about what the girls might face."

"What the girls might face because of their relationship or face from life in general?" Jake asked.

"Both," Jo answered before falling quiet.

"She couldn't have asked for better in-laws," Jake admitted.

91

"Kate and Kevin are a wonderful couple," Jo agreed. "A perfect match really. How many professional firefighters are there in the country? It's like one in a thousand Americans are professional firefighters and it's an exclusive brother/sisterhood isn't it?"

"So, you saying the chances of Pauli finding a soulmate whose father is a professional firefighter were one in a thousand?"

"Once she left Jersey and her father's orbit, yes," Jo said. "Obviously, you know a lot of firefighters in Jersey, so she knows their children. Once she was out from under your influence, she could have fallen for anyone."

"Well, the NFD t-shirt got Liz's attention," Jake pointed out.

"True," Jo sighed. "I guess she couldn't wander too far from your influence. Not as long as she wore identifying clothing."

The stewardesses began coming down the aisle offering drinks and snacks. That pause let Jake think about it. If what Jo said was true, then the money spent on that t-shirt was well spent. They both opted for the orange juice to go with their peanuts and sat quietly for a while.

Jake spent the time reviewing the past week. He remembered the conversation with Kevin about mortality. It wasn't a good subject, but it was a necessary one and his wife was trapped. Her usual response was to say something trite and walk away. How to raise the subject now and get her to agree on reviewing their finances and their will? Using that conversation as a jump off point he began, "Kevin and I had a mortality conversation after helping Al."

"Oh, give it a rest," Jo sighed. "Let's enjoy the afterglow of Pauli's triumph."

Jake wasn't surprised by her wish to avoid the subject, but Pauli's triumph? It seemed a bit much.

"Triumph," he asked. "Sounds like Liz was conquered."

"No, not what I meant," she laughed. "No conquest involved. She just used all the lessons we had taught her to choose the perfect soulmate. Remember, she only has ten percent of the people to choose from."

"Ten percent?" Jake asked. "Why ten percent?"

"That's what science says is the number of people who are not straight."

"Is it?" Jake said. Obviously, his wife had researched the subject, so he wasn't going to argue.

"We really have to talk about the will and insurance and the pension in case I have my own cardiac event," Jake persisted.

"Here? On a plane?" Jo asked incredulously. "How about we wait until we get home. I promise not to dodge you."

"Okay, but let's not put it off too long," Jake answered. "After dealing with Al, that feeling of running out of time came back big time."

"What did you guys talk about?" Jo asked.

"Like I said, mortality," Jake answered. "Kevin tried to convince himself he was unrealistic. He went through the trouble of writing down the names of everyone he knew who had died at a younger age than he is now. He stopped when it went past sixty names."

"Sixty? Seriously?" Jo said in astonishment. "Now I understand why you're bringing up the subject."

They sat in silence for a minute, then Jo asked, "Do you want to slow down and do things?"

"Right now, we have to worry about Pauli's wedding," Jake replied. "But yeah, maybe we should. What's the sense of making money if we can't enjoy it?"

"It'll just be the two of us," Jo sighed. "Like when we started out."

Jake felt there was a shift in his wife's mentality. Afterall, it had been just the two of them for a few years already. The escorted tours of Europe had mostly been taken when the kids were out of the house. Deciding the shift had been brought on more by a wedding than fear of a funeral, Jake didn't push the issue

93

any further. She had said they would review everything. That was good enough for now.

"Kate and I talked about another bridal shower in Jersey," Jo said. "It wouldn't be a surprise, but Liz should get a feel for Pauli's family don't you think?"

Jake just grunted an affirmative response, knowing it was beyond his control anyway. The rest of the flight was uneventful. Jake used the time to rest and think of what Jo said about Pauli not being under his influence. A thought crossed his mind. The hardest part of parenting was accepting that you are no longer the coach on the field calling the plays. Somewhere along the line he had become a spectator in the stands cheering Pauli on. He just wasn't sure where the change had occurred.

After landing they made their way through baggage claims and went toward the arrival door. Tim had called, but Jake thought he sounded strange. As soon as they could see out into the pickup area he saw why. The Deputy Chief's gig was parked there with its lights flashing. Directly behind it sat Engine Twenty-seven's rig. Either an alarm had been transmitted for the airport or he was walking into an embarrassing trap. It was only then that he remembered Chief Gardiner's buddy in Chicago.

"Why are the Chief and Twenty-seven here?" Jo asked innocently.

"To bust my balls," Jake replied.

Jo began laughing as soon as she heard it. "You think they heard about Al," she asked. "How do you think they found out?"

"Could be our son told Mark," Jake answered as he slowed his pace. "Or could be the Chief's buddy in Chicago told him. Hopefully, it's just them and nobody tried to get New Jersey News or worse involved."

Then he spotted the Chief of Department gig. This didn't look good. He had known Chief Monroe for decades and knew he had a good sense of humor, so it

94

might still be contained to the fire department only. He stepped out of the terminal with trepidation. Tom North was in the captain's seat of the rig. When he saw Jake, he turned on the siren and gave the airhorn a tug. The guys on the rig began to cheer and Chief Gardiner stepped out of his gig, Chief Monroe had been chatting with a few Port Authority cops. He instantly broke into a smile, went to his gig, reached in, and pulled out a plaque.

"Jake!" Chief Gardiner shouted. "Our hero has returned."

Jake felt his face redden in spite of himself. At least the mayor wasn't here, he thought. Then the union president and the mayor came from around the other side of Twenty-seven accompanied by the Star Ledger reporter who covered the police and fire departments.

Half an hour later, Tim was pulling onto the New Jersey Turnpike with Jake sitting next to him and Jo in the back seat. Jake had a small plaque on his lap which read:

"For the longest response ever made by a Newark firefighter. From Brick City to the Windy City. Always ready to serve. Jake Covey."

"How did they find out?" Tim repeated Jake's question. "Well, from what Uncle Mark told me, the Chief in Chicago called Chief Monroe. Then Chief Monroe called Uncle Mark. How did he know to call Uncle Mark?"

Jake was shaking his head in disbelief. "He was the captain on the fourth tour when Uncle Mark and I were on Six Engine."

"Okay, I get it," Tim said. "So, anyway the Chicago Chief explains that you helped out someone from the mayor's office and the mayor wants to play it up for publicity. Officially, a letter arrived from Chicago thanking the NFD for the assistance given by you. Oh, and Chief Gardiner's buddy also told him, so there was no way you were getting away with this."

"I loosened a guy's tie," Jake said.

"As Uncle Mark told me," Tim countered. "It's tough being a hero, but someone has to do it."

"Funny," Jake said. "Really funny."

"Hey, you said you want to stay relevant right?" Tim asked.

Jake ignored him entirely.

"What did you ask the mayor?" Jo said

"Well, Pauli had mentioned that it would be great to get married under the rotunda in City Hall," Jake answered. "So, I ran it past the mayor. He said he'd ask the city clerk and then tell Chief Monroe."

"You didn't," Jo gasped.

"I did," Jake laughed.

"Did you tell him the girls' situation?" she asked. "Will it be a private ceremony or packed with the press?"

"We don't even know if it's possible," Jake reminded her. "It will all work out one way or the other."

"I hope so," Jo said.

The rest of the ride was spent getting Tim up to date on Pauli's plans.

Chapter Sixteen

"He's resting right now," Jo said quietly over the phone.

Jake was in their bedroom. He had called his wife as soon as he woke up. She had spent the night just as she had spent every third night for the past two weeks, caring for Paul. Jo, Jill, and Sandra Gupta had spent those weeks doing their best to keep Paul comfortable.

The months after they had returned from Chicago had been a nightmarish, rollercoaster ride. They started out with such hope. The oncologist had given such a positive assessment of the new treatment, but he had also been honest. If this didn't get the tumor on Paul's adrenal gland under control, they had no other tools to bring into play. The disease had metastasized from the lungs to brain lesions to the adrenal gland. All the lung tumors and brain lesions had reacted well to treatment, the adrenal gland tumor had not. That's when the treatment based on Paul's DNA had started. Paul's body had rebelled. He developed atrial fibrillation which led to a massive stroke. Now he was home. The only medication being administered was morphine. Jake could do nothing but watch. He understood now more than ever the helpless feelings of fire victims waiting to see if the firefighters reached their loved ones in time. Like them, he could now only be a spectator and he didn't like it.

"I think you should come up here quickly," Jo said. "Jill is going to bring Mark. Sandra is on duty. She'll be up after she completes her rounds. Jake he's fading fast."

Jake hung up the phone and was instantly assaulted by a lifetime of memories. How to say a final farewell to someone who shared every part of life with you? He and Paul had been through it all. They had been patrol-boys together, altar boys together. Paul had gotten Jake his first job. Jake had gotten Paul his second job. Grammar and high school alma maters were the same. It wasn't until college that the diplomas varied and even then, they were roommates. They had shared dreams as boys, shouting and laughing their way through childhood. Now they were just two old men, quiet, reflective, and forced to be accepting.

Jake knew he would have to be strong for Jo, but how could he be? A part of him was dying. He remembered a comment Jo had made after seeing how he and Paul interacted.

"So, I have to accept Paul as part of the deal, don't I?"

"Yeah, I guess you do," he had responded.

She had grown to love him like a brother. Now they would both grieve the loss. With that thought, Jake bowed his head and wept knowing the void would never be filled. The phone rang, pulling him back from the abyss.

"Jake," Mark said. "We're on our way up to Paul's. Do you need a lift or can you handle it?"

"No, I got it, Mark," Jake said. "And Mark, thanks for asking."

He got himself together and headed out. When he arrived at Paul's, Jo was there to meet him at the door.

"He's gone, Jake," she whispered and then broke down. They stood in the doorway weeping. Mark and Jill were in Paul's living-room doing the same. How did they arrive at this day, Jake thought. They were just two little boys who somehow grew old.

Chapter Seventeen

"Yo! Kevin, Kate," Jake shouted. He was standing next to the family car. Kevin and Kate had insisted no limo for them. The couple heard his shout and strolled over with smiles on their faces.

"Jake!" Kevin shouted then grabbed his hand and threw an arm around him. Kate then gave him a peck on the cheek. The men tossed the luggage into the trunk. Kevin opened the rear door for Kate before hopping in the front passenger's seat. Jake slid in behind the wheel and drove off before the Port Authority cop even noticed them. He headed for the Turnpike, passed through the toll booth, and turned toward the car lanes.

"I'll come back with you tomorrow to pick the girls up," Kevin said.

Jake eased through the entrance ramp and accelerated onto the main roadway.

"If you want," he chuckled. "But the driving doesn't bother me. Spent twenty some odd years going up and down this road. It got to the point where I couldn't tell you where I was, other than between Exit Nine and Exit Fourteen."

All three laughed knowingly.

"There is an advantage to a residency requirement," Kate pointed out.

"I sat in traffic instead of doing sixty-five on a highway," Kevin replied. "Probably spent the same amount of time in the car."

Jake suppressed an urge to tell his friend about the daily battle with traffic congestion heading into Newark or continuing on into New York.

"Have the girls finalized their plans?" he asked moving away from a bad subject as he moved over to the fast lane. Traffic was light. They might be home in forty-five minutes.

"Well, they finalized their honeymoon," Kate said. "Pauli announced that they had bifurcated it."

"Bifurcated? She was an English major," Jake laughed. "Tell me how they did that."

Both Kevin and Kate tried to answer at the same time. Kate motioned for Kevin to continue. Jake was sure if Kevin missed anything, Kate would jump in.

"It happened like this," Kevin began. "Pauli wanted to go south, to Disney World, for a little warmer weather. It's only December, but she's already tired of the cold. Liz? She has never been to New York. She wants to see the city, go to Broadway, see the Statue of Liberty, Christmas in the Big Apple."

"That's why they decided on December twenty-eighth," Kate interjected. "Liz thinks she's giving folks from the Midwest a double vacation. Come for the wedding, see New York at Christmas time."

"Tell me when you're done, dear," Kevin sighed. This earned him a light slap on the shoulder.

"Is she always this violent?" Jake asked.

"Yeah," Kevin laughed. "And I love it."

"Firemen," was all Kate said.

"So," Kevin continued. "They decided instead of spending two weeks in one location, they would spend a week in each."

"Kind of late to be changing plans, isn't it?" Jake asked.

"I said the same thing," Kevin replied. "Liz said they're only doing this once, so they're going to do it right. Pauli said with a little extra money, you can do anything, as long as it's legal."

"And she's not even an accountant," Jake laughed, continuing to cruise smoothly in the fast lane.

"She's going to marry one," Kate said. "So, you know they can afford it."

Things went silent for a few minutes after that. Jake didn't want to push the conversation, best to leave the initiative with the guests. They were the ones fresh off a plane.

100

"How are you doing after Paul passed?" Kevin asked quietly.

Jake had anticipated some sort of question like this. The conversations he and Kevin had over the past few months had covered this territory lightly at best. Even though he had only known Kevin for a short period of time, the two men had made a connection. His new friend was already able to see through false bravado.

"It's tough," Jake confessed. "Sometimes I just want to call him and say, come on over for some good homemade food, always eating out is not good for your health."

"You're telling a holistic doctor what is bad for him?" Kevin asked.

"Yeah. He never listened, but he used to drop by. Occasionally, he even brought a date. Jo would give him an assessment the next day, so the dates stopped coming."

Everyone laughed.

"That happened less and less. He got busy with his practice. I got busy with the firehouse, my business, and family. After his brother died, he took on some of the father duties with his two nephews when John's wife needed it."

"I can imagine the need," Kate said. "Boys are different. Sometimes they need a man's involvement."

"Especially since Beth comes from a family of three sisters."

"Oh, that's hard," Kate agreed.

The miles had been rolling by quickly. Jake began to maneuver to the exit lane which caused a pause in the conversation. They eased off the main roadway into the lane for Exit Nine, then began the gradual slow down to the toll booth. It wasn't until after he merged on to Route Eighteen that Jake continued.

"What makes it so much harder for me is we should have pushed to hang out more together. I had responsibilities. He had responsibilities, but there was always time. We knew there was always time. Until there wasn't."

He heard Kate choke up in the back seat when he finished the last sentence. Not good form to make a guest choke up. This was supposed to be a celebratory week, so he did a one-eighty and took a page out of Kevin's playbook.

"So, welcome to the suburbs of New Jersey," he announced. "You'll notice the highway cutting through town with stores lining both sides of the road. We have two Burger Kings, two McDonalds, a Louisiana Chicken, a KFC, an IHOP, several pizzerias, three supermarkets, two multi-plex theaters, a couple of car dealerships, a shopping mall with Macy's and JC Penny, just about any other type of retail store you can imagine, and no main street."

Kate and Kevin laughed, lifting the dark cloud that had descended on them. Jake pulled off the highway and began the familiar meander through tree-lined streets to the two-story frame house that they had called home for the past thirty years. He pulled into the driveway and parked. There were no excess cars on the street today. The Jersey bridal party was not a surprise. That would happen in two days. He and Kevin would be expelled from the house again. Hopefully, without the drama this time.

Jo opened the door and came out armed with a smile and exuding energy.

"Welcome to New Jersey!" she shouted. "I hope you brought your appetite."

The men lifted the bags out of the trunk while Jo escorted Kate into the house.

Chapter Eighteen

The house was quickly filling with women young and old there to celebrate with Pauli. Jake didn't see anyone from Illinois among them, but that was to be expected. Any who wished to attend Liz's bridal shower would have done so in Chicago. He and Kevin were standing by the front door waiting for Jill to arrive. Mark would be with her, no more welcome than the two of them. It would be another guys' night out, hopefully with a little less excitement than the one in Chicago.

"Did Mark have a preference for what we would do tonight?" Kevin asked.

"No, he's up for whatever you want to do," Jake said. "It's the Jersey guys turn to show you a good time."

The ladies were crowding into the back room of the house, the volume of their voices rising steadily. Jake glanced back at the doorway leading to the room. The thought crossed his mind that he would rather stretch a line into a burning building than walk into that room. So many women in such a small space was frightening. They'd beat him into submission with their tongues, no need for physical violence. Feeling playful, he turned to Kevin with a challenge.

"I dare you to go into that room and tell those women they're too loud."

Kevin looked back and said, "I'd rather lead a line into a working fire."

They both laughed and then returned to watching for Mark's rescue. Mark's car turned on the block shortly after. The two waiting men breathed a sigh of relief and stepped out of the house. Neither Jake nor Kevin had the nerve to walk to the back room and announce they were leaving. Mark pulled into the drive and Jill hopped out of the car.

"You boys play nice," she said while walking past them. "We don't want to bail you out tonight."

The two men chuckled and headed for Mark's car. Jake let Kevin ride shot gun, sliding into the back seat.

"So, Kev," Jake said. "What are we doing with the rest of our day?"

"We have to stay out of jail, so I thought the two of you could show me one of those famous Jersey diners."

"Got just the place," Mark said before putting the car in reverse. "This diner has a special meaning for us."

"The Tick-Tock?" Jake asked.

"The Tick-Tock," Mark confirmed.

"So, I asked Kevin if he would be willing to go into the back room and tell those ladies that they were talking too loudly," Jake started. "And he said he'd rather lead a line into a working fire."

"Lead a line," Mark asked.

"Lead a line," Kevin laughed. "I know you say stretch a line here, but in Chicago it's lead a line."

The three men spent the rest of the drive discussing the different terminology used by their departments. Mark pulled into the Tick-Tock parking lot, parked, and shut the engine. Jake suddenly felt a reluctance to get out of the car. He put it off and pushed himself out. When he turned to face the diner, his stomach flipped. Before they could move toward the front door, he stopped them with a suggestion.

"How about we eat somewhere else and maybe come back for coffee and dessert?"

Mark looked at him with concern, then turned toward Kevin. "I said it had a special meaning for us," he reminded Kevin. "After Paul's brother John died, the three of us would come here on John's birthday to celebrate his memory."

"It was John's favorite diner," Jake said. "Paul and I also made a lot of teenage and early twenties memories here. We roomed together in an apartment the next town over, so we'd stop here for a bite at three in the morning when we were out partying."

Kevin shook his head. "I understand. No need to push it on account of me."

"No, no," Jake protested. "We'll come back later, after I get my head in the right place. There are a lot of great memories here."

He began searching for a way to spend their night. Looking at the rush hour traffic on Route Three, he noted the congestion coming out of New York. But traffic was light going towards the city. That gave him an idea.

"You know, when we were doing college, we'd go into Chinatown and sometimes come back here instead of going to Little Italy for dessert. You guys think you're up for Chinese food?"

Kevin laughed, but Mark looked skeptical. "How are we going in?" he asked first.

"We can drive into the city or just go to a PATH station in Jersey City. Either way is cool."

"I don't think I want to do the train," Kevin said. "Don't think the ladies are up for another drama on a train."

They all laughed, then Jake took out his phone and checked the parking app to reserve a space. Before he touched the screen to finalize it, Mark stopped him.

"Hold on," he said. "Kevin may not know the lay of the land. Chinatown is right next to Ground Zero. I did the Tunnel to Towers run a few times, but you haven't been back there yet. You really up for that?"

Jake looked up from his phone and said, "If Kevin is, I am. We're bound to go to the memorial with the girls while they're here. Better to get over the initial shock, if any, now."

"Then let's do it," Kevin and Mark said.

Jake touched the screen and turned back to the car.

"I reserved a space in a lot between the memorial and Chinatown. Where do you want to go first?"

Mark looked at Kevin and motioned for him to choose.

"I think the memorial first is better," he said. "Then we can debrief one another at dinner."

Chapter Nineteen

As they approached the memorial, each was lost in his memories. Jake was trying to get a "lay of the land" as Mark put it. Where were he and Mark when Tower Seven came down? Where had they helped stretch the line up from the fireboat on the river? Where was the Deutsche Bank Building they had operated in? The memories came back fresh and raw. The smell of those days. The drive to help the FDNY find their brothers and other victims in the rubble. The frustration when they realized there would be no survivors. When the condition of the debris told them the collapsing towers had become grinders tearing everything and everyone to shreds.

It was good they came now. The experience would dampen the shock when they came back with the girls. Their daughters would not experience it the way he was. Lower Manhattan had been rebuilt. The Freedom Tower loomed over the district. All was clean, tidy, modern, and respectful of the sacrifices of that day. None sacrificed more than the FDNY. He wanted to see the memorial pools commemorating those sacrifices, having heard so much about them.

When they stepped up to the south pool, the soothing sound of water running filled the air. They stood quietly at the edge, reviewing the names of the firefighters who were lost. There were three hundred and forty-three names of people who chose to go into those buildings while they were burning.

"Hey," Mark whispered, pulling Jake out of a trance. "Isn't that Chief Brendler?"

Jake looked in the direction Mark was pointing. "Yeah, that's him or his twin. It's got to be him. That's Pat Parker next to him."

Kevin was looking in the same direction. "The guys standing on the right looks awfully familiar," he said. "Who is he?"

"That's Pat Parker," Mark said. "He was a Rescue Squad captain. Came over with his crew the first day and then every day until they closed it down. The squad knew all the rescue tools and had the specialized training, but what counted most was Pat knew a lot of FDNY rescue guys. It's all in a book that Chief Brendler put together. He wrote an oral history of the NFD years ago. Pat and his guys found a rig under the debris early on."

"Wait, wait," Kevin said. "That's it. We helped some Jersey guys and New York guys dig out a rig."

"You know Pat?" Jake asked.

"Know him?" Kevin laughed. "I wouldn't say that. I worked with him and his crew. They called me Chicago."

"He was one hell of a firefighter," Mark said. "Let's go over. It's time you met him. He made Battalion Chief before he retired just like you."

The three of them started weaving through the people gathered around the pool. Jake could see Pat was talking to the Chief, pointing to where they had been. The three of them came around from behind Pat and the Chief. Pat turned back and spotted them. He started laughing, said something to the Chief, and waved.

"Pat was on Rescue for years as a firefighter and captain. He rode with one of the New York Rescue companies for years, so he knew a lot of guys who died on 9/11," Jake informed Kevin. "The Chief is an old Six Engine guy who retired as the Commandant of Training."

"Is this the guy who married the news reporter?" Kevin asked.

"One and the same," Jake replied.

By now Chief Brendler and Pat had turned to face them, each wearing a big smile.

"What's this, a Six Engine reunion?" the Chief laughed.

"Deputy Chief Bob Brendler, Battalion Chief Pat Parker, may I introduce Battalion Chief Kevin Moore of Chicago.?

"Chicago," Pat said appearing to be trying to place Kevin. "Chicago! You were here when we found that truck!"

"Yeah, I was one of the Chicago guys that day," Kevin admitted.

"So, is this your first time back in all these years?" the Chief asked.

"Yes, it is," Kevin said. "It's a bit of a hike from Chicago."

"It's my first time back, too," Jake said.

"Not easy, is it?" Pat said.

"Not as hard after seeing the two of you," Jake said

"I know Mark did the Tunnel to Tower run until his little mishap," Pat recalled.

"Right alongside you, Pat," Mark said. "How are the guys' families doing?"

"Most have come to terms with it," Pat answered quietly. "Some have remarried, others concentrated on raising their kids. And some of those kids are now on the job. They're a strong brunch of ladies."

All in the group shook their heads in agreement.

"Actually, I'm here to commemorate one of my friends from Rescue Two," Pat said. "Today's his birthday. Talked with his wife earlier. She said his youngest son starts the academy next month,"

"I always wondered how the New York guys and their families got through it," Jake said. "I mean, it's hard when one guy dies on the job. Three hundred and forty-three? There's no place to hide; no one on the job is unaffected. Even with 13,000 members, everyone has to know someone or someone who knows someone that was killed in those towers."

This observation was followed by silence among them as each grappled with the thought. The enormity of it came back to Jake. He could picture the acres of debris, hear the PASS alarms sounding, smell the acrid fumes emanating from the pile. So many lives gone, so much talent wasted, and so much courage and compassion displayed. It was the seminal event of his generation and he was content to have done his part. He was relevant those few days right after the collapse, even if they didn't find anyone alive. At least they gave closure to the families of the people they recovered.

"You guys in the city just for the memorial?" Chief Brendler asked.

"The ladies are attending a bridal shower," Kevin laughed. "And we were asked to vacate the premises. Jake thought that maybe a trip to Chinatown was in order. Kind of like when he was in college."

"Chinatown?" the Chief laughed. "Really? We were just about to go there. How about you join us? I know the best place. Lots of good food, reasonably priced, and they don't mind loud firemen."

All agreed to follow the Chief's lead. As far as Jake was concerned, it took the pressure off. He had been the one who suggested Chinatown, but so many of the restaurants he knew in college had not survived 9/11. The entire area had been covered in dust from the collapse. It was a tourist location without tourists. No one wanted to go below Canal Street. Chinatown businesses withered on the vine. The old businesses had been replaced, but between work and family, he and Jo had no time to come into the city to test the new ones. Picking a restaurant by himself would have been a gamble.

The Chief led them to a Sichuan restaurant on East Broadway. It was still early for the dinner crowd, so they settled in quickly. Jake felt a little guilty since they had spent so little time at the memorial. Maybe that was best. The sheer volume of memories that had flash through his mind made him doubt his ability to take it all in at once. Was it a mistake to have put off visiting until now? Age seemed to have worn away some of the armor he had built up over the course of his career. The lock box of challenging memories in the back of his mind would now pop open with certain triggers and leave him awash in emotions. Emotions that were getting harder to control with each passing year. Deciding that it was better to get acclimated than to just dive in, he let go of the guilt and focused on his companions.

The Chief took up the position of Incident Commander as soon as they stepped in. The four other men acquiesced out of respect for his rank, even if they were all retired. Jake chuckled to himself as he looked around the table. All the guys he was with had attained the rank of chief. He had remained a firefighter and yet he did the taxes of three of them. So, when Chief Brendler announced it was his treat, Jake didn't protest. He knew the Chief could afford it. After ordering the meals and filling their tea cups, the firehouse chatter began. At first it followed the path of least resistance and settled on the World Trade Center.

"So, Kevin, tell us Jersey guys how a bunch of Chicago firefighters ended up on the pile," Chief Brendler said, reverting to his oral history role.

"The Chief of Department organized a task force," Kevin began. "There was, of course, some jockeying for position to go, but they got this task force together. There were no flights, so they had to drive. The Chief actually gave them his personal credit card to pay for the gas. On top of that official response, a lot of guys just hopped into their cars and came. I was one of them."

"Newark's the only one that threatened the guys with charges if they went," the Chief pointed out. "But being firefighters, they went anyway."

By now the tea had been replaced with beers, so they toasted the brotherhood.

"Chief, did you respond?" Kevin asked.

"First, you don't have to call me chief. Bob will do," he began. "But no, I didn't. I have MS. If I had come in that heat, I would have been a liability. New York had enough to worry about. They didn't need a pigheaded Newark Battalion Chief collapsing on them. I had to wait until the smoke cleared to contribute."

The three Newark guys raised their bottles in salute. Kevin appeared unsure of what to do.

111

"Remember, Kev," Jake reminded him. "The Chief is the one who wrote all those books including a volume on the experiences of the NFD on 9/11."

"Right, right," Kevin remembered. "My daughter used your study practices book to help prepared for her CPA exam."

Everyone looked at Jake when they heard this.

"Studying is studying," is all he said in defense.

"So, who's getting married?" Pat asked.

There was a slight pause before Jake stepped up to answer. "It's complicated," he began. "It's a non-traditional wedding."

"Non-traditional?" the Chief asked. "Sounds like you're still adjusting to the reality that your kids choose their mates."

"You have that right," Jake exclaimed. "But it's more complicated than that. Actually, I really do love my daughter's choice of a mate."

"Then what's complicated?" Pat asked.

"His daughter's choice of a mate is my daughter," Kevin replied.

"My daughter just went to a wedding like that last month," the Chief laughed. "All that counts is they're happy, no? So, what about grandkids?"

The last question hit Jake hard. There was a reason this guy made deputy chief.

"Well, yeah, their happiness is what counts," Jake agreed. "Just makes having grandkids more difficult."

Kevin shook his head in agreement, but the Chief wouldn't be put off.

"Nonsense," he laughed. "Now you get to hand pick the gene pool you want. No more crapshoot of the heart."

"Crapshoot of the heart?" Kevin laughed.

"Chief, you have no sense of romance!" Mark said with mock indignation.

"Romance? That's for forming a couple," the Chief pointed out. "They've already done that." He paused for a moment, then added. "Oh, and when I say

'You get to choose', I mean you. They can't shout, 'But Daddy, I love him.' like in the Little Mermaid and then run off to see the sea witch."

They all laughed at the analogy, knowing the girls were of the generation that would best understand it.

"Now it's a rational decision and you can have input," the Chief continued. "Of course, they have to want to have kids."

"Pauli says she wants to be a mother," Jake said.

"Then you have your work cut out for you."

The group groaned in unison.

"So, when's the wedding?" the Chief asked.

"They're just going to do a civil ceremony," Jake informed him. "They haven't decided if it will be in the reception hall, in a municipal building, or what."

"Would you mind if some of my old crew attended? Make it a Six Engine family thing. Just for the ceremony, we don't need to stay for the banquet. Couldn't even tell you if they could, really, but just to show some support and appreciation of romance."

"We'd be honored, Chief," Kevin said.

"Who from your crew are you thinking of?" Jake asked. He had worked with many of the guys included in that group. He hadn't seen them in a few years.

"Just a few guys, really. Maybe Frank and Chingli Helms. Have to see if they're home. They've been talking about a business trip to Taiwan. Then there's Ray and Stacey Friedrick, depends on the time and day for Stacey. She'd have to finish her rounds at the hospital and see whatever patients she has that day. Ray's now a freelance investigator, so he'll probably be able to make it. Jack Romanov is the Deputy OEM coordinator for Newark these days. Unless he has some meeting, he should be able to shake loss an hour. You say they might just do a municipal civil ceremony. Have they chosen a municipality yet?"

"Not yet, Chief," Kevin answered. "They just have to give a few days' notice, but not everybody is enthusiastic about same sex marriage."

"Pauli said she prefers Newark City Hall under the rotunda," Jake informed him. "When they came to the airport to bust my balls after my little escapade in Chicago, I mentioned that to the mayor. He said he'd ask the city clerk."

"Sounds promising, give me a contact number and I'll ask around if you want," the Chief offered.

"You got it, Chief," Jake said, then he pulled out his phone. "What's your number? I'll call you now, so my number will be on your phone."

Chapter Twenty

"No, Jake!" Jo protested. "No public ceremony under the City Hall rotunda. It's a wedding, not a spectacle. You don't know what crazy is going to hone in on it to make a point for some perverted cause!"

Jake looked toward Pauli and saw there was no support there. Both families were sitting in their living room discussing the options for the location of the marriage ceremony. Chief Brendler had just gotten back to him that morning. If they wanted, Newark's mayor would be happy to perform the ceremony under the rotunda in City Hall. Jake had gathered everyone together and submitted his proposal. Jo's reaction had been instantaneous and visceral. Glancing at Kate, he saw hesitancy. Kevin looked willing. Liz was in shock, probably from the strength and speed of Jo's reaction. Tim and Carl looked neutral. Pauli? She looked like she just wanted to avoid upsetting her mother.

"Easy Jo," Jake began his negotiation. "It wouldn't be a spectacle. First things first, the mayor would be happy to perform the ceremony."

"He's going to want some publicity to do it," Jo insisted. "Why else would he agree?"

"Well, there's the Six Engine connection," Jake pointed out.

"The what?" Jo asked genuinely puzzled.

"You see, Chief Brendler reached out to the guys he worked with at Six. So, Jack Romanov is the Deputy OEM coordinator. The OEM coordinator is officially the mayor. But the Chief didn't stop there. He then called Frank Helms. You remember Frank and Chingli, don't you?"

"How could I forget them after that whole stalker thing?" Jo replied.

"Frank has been a great help for the mayor in dealing with that whole sister city thing with Xuzhou and getting business between Newark and China," Jake said.

"Why is the Chief going through all this trouble?" Pauli asked.

"To show some support and appreciation for romance," Kevin interjected.

"What?" Liz asked.

"It's a long story," Jake said. "Let's just say that among his talents the Chief writes poetry, so he has a soft spot for romance."

"So, you're saying the Chief put a full court press on the mayor?" Tim laughed.

"No, I didn't," Jake insisted. "I said the Chief knows guys who can talk to the mayor. It's the mayor's choice; they just asked if he would do it. Ironically, another reason he wants to do it is because of Kevin."

"Because of me?" Kevin asked. "How so?"

"The Chief told the mayor that you are the other half of the Chicago rescue team," Jake said.

That made even Jo laugh and seemed to bring the tension down a notch.

"Okay, the mayor wants to do it, but how can he without drawing attention to the girls?"

"Mom," Pauli said. "We're not that worried about people knowing. We are getting married after all. That makes our relationship pretty public."

"You don't understand," Jo snapped, seeming to revert back to her original position. "Splashing it all over the news is going to bring all the crazies out."

"Who said anything about splashing it all over the news?" Jake asked. "It will be a private ceremony. The mayor can give us twenty minutes, half an hour at best. The reception probably won't even be the same day. We're going to end up with the girls, immediate family, and maybe some retired firefighters."

"Under the rotunda in Newark's City Hall?" Jo shot back. "That's private?"

"How about we take a step back and look at our options?" Carl suggested.

Jake motioned with his hands for him to continue. Maybe he analyzed the data and had a solution.

116

"Liz and Pauli are under time pressure since they haven't locked down who will marry them, but have committed to a reception hall and a caterer," he began. "And we don't want too much attention from the outside. Can the mayor wed them in his office and then have like a commemorative photo shoot under the rotunda?"

Jake looked around the room. Jo looked receptive. Liz and Pauli weren't objecting. Kate looked comfortable. Tim looked relieved. Kevin appeared supportive.

"Then I'll call the Chief and ask him if the mayor would be agreeable?" Jake asked.

"Wait," Jo said. "If we take a commemorative picture and people ask why, what do we tell them?"

"We'll tell them about the Chicago rescue," Kevin laughed.

"Okay, we're all in agreement? What else has to be done before the opening night of the Liz and Pauli show?" Jake asked.

"Liz and Pauli show?" Pauli laughed. "Please Dad, not the time for levity."

"You are your mother's daughter," Jake countered.

This earned him a scathing look from his wife.

"We have to finalize the menu," Liz said. "Invites are out, RSVPs are coming back, limo for the ceremony has to be reserved. We have fifteen days until the reception. When will the mayor be available?"

"Good question," Jake said. "Haven't gotten that far yet. I'll call the Chief and tell him your choice."

Jake took out his phone and walked to the kitchen while the rest of both families planned.

Chapter Twenty-one

"I just want to thank you, Chief, for all the help getting this set up," Jake said to Chief Brendler. "It means a lot to me."

They were waiting outside the mayor's office in Newark's City Hall, leaning against the marble railing that lined the rotunda. Frank Helms and Ray Friedrick were talking to a police officer on the mayor's security detail. Frank's wife Chingli and Ray's wife Stacey were with Pauli and Liz, Jo and Kate, and Kathy Stanley. The girls appeared to be overwhelmed by the enthusiasm of the older women. Jake realized that Pauli and Liz didn't know the depth of the bond between Chingli, Kathy, and Stacey. He called them the first tour wives. The three woman and Jack Romanov's ex-wife Gloria had known each other for close to forty years. They each had helped the others through myriad crises and the everyday troubles of modern life. Much like their firefighter husbands, it was the adversities they had faced that welded them together.

"Nonsense Jake," The Chief responded. "I made a couple of phone calls. It seems to have given the old first tour at Six Engine an excused to get together and celebrate."

"At least the ladies are happy to see each other," Jake observed. "Only missing Jack. Do you think Gloria will come?"

"Don't think she'd give up a chance to celebrate with her best friends," the Chief said.

"But if Jack shows, wouldn't that be awkward?"

"Nah, Jack and Gloria are good friends. They just can't live together."

They both chuckled.

"You know you did more than make a couple of phone calls," Jake said. "You helped me stay relevant in my daughter's life. Now she can remember that I had helped fulfill her wish to be married here."

The doors of the elevator down the hall opened and Jack Romanov stepped out with Gloria next to him. Most of the firefighters from Six Engine's first tour circa 1980s were now here. The only one missing was Hector Perez. He had moved to Puerto Rico to live like royalty on a New Jersey pension. That was too great a distance to cover in a few days. Jake thought it ironic. The first tour was here to celebrate Pauli's wedding and he was from the third tour. Mark and Jill should show up at any moment to help represent that tour. Then the wedding party would be complete.

"I think you owe Frank and Jack the credit for arranging this," the Chief said. "They are the ones who spoke with the mayor. Kathy and I played a small part."

"Kathy knows the mayor?"

"You didn't know that? She helps him cut with that Xuzhou sister city thing."

"I thought that was Frank's gig," Jake said in surprise.

"They tag team him," the Chief laughed. "Chingli and I are support personnel, so the mayor has all the help he can handle. As soon as Jake heard this, he understood why the mayor had agreed to get involved.

Frank and Ray broke off their conversation with the police officer and walked over to greet Jack. Gloria went to greet the ladies. Jake noticed Tim and Carl talking with Kevin by the door to the mayor's office. The boys seemed shell shocked by the reunions taking place in front of them. Jake waved for them to join the guys at the atrium railing. Frank, Ray, and Jack came over as the boys and Kevin crossed the hallway.

"Let me introduce everyone," Jake began after they all met up.

"Frank Helms, Ray Friedrick, and Jack Romanov meet Kevin and Carl Moore," Jake said. "You may not recognize the young gentleman accompanying them, but he's the same boy you saw at the union picnics."

"No! That's Tim?" Frank moaned. "God, I'm getting old."

"Yeah, you are," Jack laughed then turned toward Kevin. "So, you're Kevin, the Chicago rescue mate."

"Not my most spectacular grab," Kevin admitted. "But my only claim to fame in Jersey." They all laughed.

Then Ray said, "The kid standing guard at the mayor's door is the son of one of the guys we worked with on the police."

Kevin looked a little confused. Carl couldn't help but ask, "On the police? I thought you were all firemen?"

"Before we saw the light, Frank and I put a few years in chasing bad guys."

"Your pension allows you to switch?" Kevin asked.

"Yeah, most of the switching goes from police to fire," Chief Brendler said. "Word gets out that it's the best job in the world and they can't help themselves."

"I understand why," Tim said. "Carl and I were discussing the obvious connections here. The camaraderie is breathtaking. Even the wives seem to have it."

"Those particular wives have been through a lot together," the Chief told him. "Adversity binds people."

The door to the mayor's office opened as he finished. Everyone stepped in. When they came back out, Pauli and Liz would be legal spouses.

Chapter Twenty-two

After the ceremony in the mayor's office, the wedding moved to the ground floor of the atrium under the rotunda. Jake was amazed that the mayor joined them and had one of his staff tag along. His honor was in an expansive mood and, as always, gregarious and funny. There was a reason this man held the position he did. Surprisingly, Kathy monopolized his time talking about Newark's relationship with Xuzhou and what economic opportunities that might present to both cities. Not a subject Jake would have guessed to be a topic of conversation at Pauli's wedding, but today had surpassed all expectations.

When they reached the ground level of the atrium, the mayor began directing everyone on where to stand. They formed a line with the mayor in the center, Pauli and Liz on either side of him, the parents and brothers next to the girls, and the guys from Six Engine filling in the ends. Before agreeing to the whole affair, Jo had insisted the mayor be brought up to speed on the excuse for a photo shoot under the rotunda if questions should arise. Kathy had been given that task.

"Okay," the mayor shouted, his voice reverberating around the atrium. "Everybody ready? Look at the camera and smile."

At the moment the picture was taken, Pauli and Liz leaned up and kissed the mayor on his cheeks. This produced a huge grin on his face and caused laughter up and down the line.

"Mr. Mayor," Chingli said. "The young girls still find you irresistible."

When the laughter quieted, his honor tried one more time.

"We want a serious picture to remember the day," he said. "Now everyone, smile."

By now people were standing at the atrium railings on all three floors below the rotunda watching. As the wedding party line broke up, a young Asian woman approached Kathy.

"Excuse me," she said. "Aren't you Kathy Stanley?"

"Yes, I am," Kathy answered politely.

"I'm Christine Lin from the Star Ledger. First, can I tell you how much I admire your reporting from Asia? You're one of the reasons I entered journalism."

"Thank you," Kathy said. "You're too kind."

"I cover City Hall; can you tell me why you're taking pictures with the mayor?"

"You don't want to ask me," Kathy told her. "You want to ask the mayor." She turned toward the mayor who was speaking with Jack, and called out to him. "Mr. Mayor, the Star Ledger has a question for you."

When Jake heard this his stomach dropped. What was a reporter from the newspaper doing here? He stole a quick glance at Jo and saw a panicked look on her face. Did Kathy make the cover story clear? If he tried to interfere, the reporter would know something was up. Their fate was in the hands of the mayor. Jake closed his eyes and prayed his honor would honor his word.

"Christine, how are you today?" the mayor said.

"I'm doing well, Mr. Mayor," Christine replied. "Can you tell me why you're having a photo shoot under the City Hall rotunda today?"

"Why under the rotunda?" the mayor began. "Well, City Hall is on the National Registry of Historic places. It was built in 1902 and has one of the prettiest atriums of any building in the country. What better place to take pictures?"

"But why take pictures at all?"

"You may remember a story your paper carried a few months ago about a rescue made by a retired Newark firefighter while he was in Chicago."

Christine appeared to be unaware of the story.

122

"Well, the gentleman to your left, Jake why don't you raise your hand?"

Jake complied, relieved the mayor was sticking to the script.

"Jake was half of that rescue team," the mayor continued. "The other half was a retired Chicago Chief, Kevin. Kevin, could you raise your hand?"

Kevin did so with a grin on his face. The mayor was obviously going to ham it up.

"This is the first time Kevin has been to Newark. He and his family are friendly with Jake and his family. Now Jake, Jake was a firefighter at Six Engine, that's the firehouse on Springfield Avenue, back in the bad old days. Back before you were born. I thought the city was going to burn down, but Jake and Newark's bravest saved the day. But that's a long time ago. Things have improved tremendously since then. And these other men, they were also at Six Engine. They're all old and gray now, but back then they were young and were running into burning buildings to rescue Newark citizens. Now when I heard Kevin was coming to Newark, I said I wanted to honor him. Can't give him a commendation or anything like that. The rescue took place in Chicago. They already got a commendation in Chicago, but I still wanted to thank him for his years of service as a firefighter. I've been in Chicago, so he helped protect me while I was there. Just like Newark firefighters protect everybody who visits our city. And my administration has given our firefighters the best equipment to do their job. We've placed the jaws of life on every ladder company and all fire department trucks have defibrillators on them. We've begun a program to replace aging vehicles so the trucks responding to emergencies will remain reliable. Did you know that every traffic accident in the city receives a fire department response? The modern fire department does a lot more than fight fires. But back in the old days when these guys were in the firehouse, they had too many fires to do all that modern stuff."

"I see," Christine said. "So, we can call this an echo of the Chicago rescue."

"I like that," the mayor said. "That's an interesting way to put it. Yes. It's an echo of that rescue."

"Thank you, Mr. Mayor," Christine said as she put away her notebook.

"Now I have to get back to serving the citizens of Newark," the mayor announced. "Good luck to all of you. Enjoy everything Newark has to offer. There are some great restaurants Down Neck."

They all shouted thanks to the mayor. Just listening to his monologue had left Jake breathless. He couldn't believe a reporter for the Star Ledger was walking past when they were shooting the picture. Thank God the mayor had followed the script. Jake felt like he had just bailed out of a building seconds before it exploded.

Chapter Twenty-three

Carl and Tim went ahead of the group to get the cars from the parking lot and bring them around to the front of City Hall. Jack, Frank, and the Chief followed. Jake and Kevin remained with the ladies just inside the front entrance. Kate, Jo, Jill, and Kathy were with the girls. Chingli, Stacey, and Gloria were chatting off to the side.

"Thanks for running interference, Kath," Jo said. "But how did you know the mayor was up for it?"

"There's a little bit of the devil in him." Kathy laughed. "He thought it would be fun to cover up the real reason for the pictures, so I was sure he would remember."

Chingli walked up to Kathy and said something in Chinese to her. Whatever it was, Kathy agreed instantly and turned back to Jo, Jill, and the girls.

"We don't want to hear any protests," she began. "Bob and I and Frank and Chingli want to host a little lunch at the Spain Restaurant on Market Street."

The girls looked shocked and were about to protest, but their mothers spoke up first.

"Kathy!" Jo said. "We couldn't possibly accept that. After all the Chief did to make this day happen, we should be hosting you."

Chingli smiled then said, "Consider it a wedding present. Frank and Bob are such romantics at heart. They have enjoyed themselves today. So, you see setting everything up was very self-serving. Hosting a wedding lunch would - - - how do you say it? Put a cherry on top."

"You guys are amazing!" Pauli said. Liz shook her head in agreement, unable to voice her thanks.

Kate appeared about to say something, but then thought better of it. Instead, she moved the focus of the conversation to the wedding ceremony.

"I thought the mayor did a wonderful job with the ceremony. It was simple, but dignified."

"Yes," Liz agreed. "He made me feel comfortable. I thought I'd be all nerves. And his staff was so welcoming."

"One of the secretaries thanked me for having it in their office," Pauli said. "She said they never see romance at work, so it made their day."

Kathy laughed when she heard that, then felt a need to explain. "Bob and I were told something similar to that by a nurse in an emergency room."

"I think I heard about this," Jill said. "Mark said something about Bob not having to propose. How'd he put it? 'Me Tarzan, you Jane. You marry me."

They all laughed, then Kathy told the true story. "Not quite like that. From the sound of it, Ray told him the story. It actually went like this. I dragged Bob to the emergency room and they said only family members could accompany him in. He asked if a fiancé counted. They said yes. He said I was his fiancé and that's how he proposed to me."

This produced a new outburst of laughter.

"I'm sure the Chief has a different version," Jake said. Then he looked outside and saw Tim pull up.

"Let's go ladies," Jake ordered. "Your sons are here and we have to move fast. No parking in front of City Hall."

It took twenty minutes to cover the mile from City Hall to the restaurant. There they ran the same drill in reverse with everyone jumping out of the cars before the drivers went off in search of a parking space. Jake and Jo rode with Kevin and Kate in the family car driven by Carl. The girls went in Tim's truck. The others followed in their cars. Hopefully they could find a lot in the area with room for five cars.

When they had all arrived, Chief Brendler took on the role of Incident Commander again. He had a relationship with the staff and was greeted warmly.

Tables were moved together, allowing them to sit as a group. The girls sat at mid-table with their fathers on one side and their mothers on the other. An arrangement insisted on by Jo and Kate so they could talk. Jake had no objection for the same reason. Soon, the appetizers were on the table, the sangria was being passed around, and the firehouse chatter had commenced, with snippets about the wedding and how the girls met.

Jake sat quietly for a while listening to the conversations. The thought crossed his mind that Paul should be here. He quickly put that aside, not wanting to put a damper on the day. The seating arrangements had placed him between Pauli and Kevin and across from Tim.

The girls explained the significance of the Six Engine t-shirt Pauli had worn the day they met. The Chief gave his rendition of how he proposed to Kathy. Ray explained his comment about Tarzan and Jane was referencing how hard a time he had proposing to Stacey as opposed to the Chief's accidental proposal. Then the girls explained their calculated approach which produced moans from the men and approval from the women. Just from that reaction, Jake concluded that women being more romantic than men was bullshit.

Jake was listening to it all, but was having a hard time shaking the mayor's words about the bad old days. The "bad" part of the expression didn't hurt. It was the "old" part that bit. And the old and gray and the before you were born and the long time ago and the back in the old days when these guys were in the firehouse. Now his daughter was married and he felt old and irrelevant. The day had been a huge success. He had helped set it up. How memorable would it have been without his fire department connection? But it was now over. That evening the girls were going to be picked up by a limousine and driven to a hotel in New York to begin their honeymoon. How could he ever be relevant in their lives again?

The meals came and the conversations slowed. Jake heard the Chief explain the nicknames of the guys. Frank tried to defend his nickname of $59.95, the price of a helmet at the time he earned the moniker. Claiming someone had to get water on the fire that was blowing over his head. Chingli then pointed out she had her reasons for pushing him to resign. Their table was loud and overflowing with the camaraderie of the firehouse. Then the Chief asked about Frank and Chingli's children and they said they were expecting their third grandchild. It hit Jake hard.

The only thing keeping his spirits up was remembering the Chief's comment that now he could have input in choosing the father of his grandchildren. As he reached for his glass of sangria, he glanced across the table at Tim and Carl. The two had apparently struck up a friendship that was beyond being brothers-in-law. Pauli's first description of Carl had been accurate. The two young men were very much alike. Science and engineering types who loved the same kind of music, sports, and it seemed even women. He took a sip of his sangria and then realized he was looking at the solution to his family relevance problem. The fathers of his grandchildren might be sitting directly across from him and Kevin.

Chapter Twenty-four

"You girls didn't talk yourselves out yesterday?" Jake asked Jo. They were sitting in the kitchen finishing breakfast. The sun was shining through the windows with the bare trees filling the view. Christmas was a week away, so he thought the ladies would spend their day shopping. When Jo announced they were meeting at a special Chinese restaurant, he was surprised. It was kind of ironic when he remembered the last time he had been in a Chinese restaurant. Kate and Kevin sat around the table nursing cups of coffee and relaxing.

"Talk ourselves out?" Kate asked. "No, of course not. You guys were around. We couldn't share half the subjects we wanted to. Chingli mentioned an excellent Chinese restaurant she'd like us to try, so we're all going to meet there for lunch and a chat."

"Are my ears going to be ringing?" Jake asked

"You mean will we be talking about you?" Jo laughed. "Yes, we are. No subject is off the table. In fact, husbands are a prime target. You two might want to come along."

Both men shook their heads in the negative.

"We wouldn't want to crimp your style," Jake said.

"Didn't think so," Jo said.

"No Christmas shopping in your plans?" Kevin asked.

"Whatever suits our fancy," Kate replied. "We're free now that the girls are on the first half of their honeymoon."

"New York for a week, then the reception, then Disney," Jake said. "They run a tight ship."

Jo looked at him like he was crazy and then just moved on.

"What are you gents up to today?" Jo asked.

"Kevin wanted to experience a Jersey diner," Jake said. "Then we might swing past the firehouse or maybe do Christmas shopping."

"Christmas shopping?" Jo reacted. "Who are you shopping for?"

"The love of my life, obviously," Jake chuckled.

"Well, the love of your life isn't looking for anything that takes up space, so just go on line and get some tickets for Broadway."

"Whatever happened to romance?

"It raised two kids. I'm beyond romance," Jo sighed.

"Ah, that hurt," Jake moaned.

"You'll get over it," Jo assured him. "What diner are you planning on going to?"

"The Tick-Tock," Jake said.

Jo turned serious. "Are you sure?" she asked in a concerned voice.

"Yeah, been preparing for a while," Jake said. "Couldn't do it the day we hit Chinatown, but I think my head is in a good place now."

"You can always come join us for Chinese again," Jo said.

This was followed by a minute of silence as both Jo and Jake wrestled with memories of this particular diner and the friends associated with it. Kevin and Kate seemed to realize their need to process thoughts and emotions, so they quietly sipped their coffee and waited.

"So, besides your better halves, what do you ladies talk about when we're not around?" Jake asked breaking the silence with levity.

"Better halves? Really Jake, you shouldn't pat yourself on the back," Jo said with a smile. "What do we talk about besides you? Our kids, our grandkids if we have any. Talk of our kids and grandkids makes us smile. The men in our lives? Not so much."

The men groaned.

"You know, Jake," Kevin said. "Maybe you should pick another subject. We're getting beaten up with this one."

130

Jake shook his head in agreement as he reached for his coffee, but Kevin's advice brought Kate into the conversation.

"What is it you guys talk about without your wives dragging the conversation to a higher ground."

"Higher ground?" Kevin asked with indignation. "I'll have you know, my dear, that our conversations are of the highest caliber."

"You sound like the mayor; don't dodge the question," Kate insisted.

"We talk about the bad old days," Jake answered. "Just like the mayor said."

"He said you were old and gray," Jo pointed out. "He didn't say you talked about the bad old days, just that you were in the firehouse then."

"Is that supposed to make me feel better?"

"Feel better? Kate's question was about what you talked about not how old you feel."

"We talk about the job, the changes on it, and all the fun we had fighting fires," Jake said, trying to move the discussion away from their aging.

"You, sir, have a strange definition of fun," Jo said.

"That's why you married me," Jake replied.

"Ha!" Jo laughed. "But enough of our morning chat. You guys may not have a deadline, but we gals do."

Jake and Kevin gathered up the dishes since Jo and Kate had prepared breakfast. Firehouse rules kept the peace. Jake was happy this conversation was over. If it had continued in the direction it seemed to be headed, he was sure they would have talked about funeral arrangements.

Chapter Twenty-five

"You okay?" Kevin asked.

They were standing next to Jake's car in the Tick-Tock Diner parking lot. This was as far as they had reached before Jake pulled the plug the last time they were here. Jake felt differently now. He was more at peace with the capriciousness of life. Now he felt a need for closure, a need to embrace his memories instead of being haunted by them. Paul and John would want it that way,

"Yeah, I think so," he answered. "I'm here for closure. There's a lot of personal history here."

"I got that impression the other day," Kevin said.

"I wish you could have met Paul. The two of you would have hit it off, I'm sure."

They started a slow stroll toward the entrance. Traffic on Route Three was light, so the noise level was low, matching the subdued tone of the conversation.

"You said the two of you roomed together in college."

Jake smiled remembering those early days and the first time he had come here with Paul.

"We lived about a mile south of here," he started. "But the first time we came here was about a year before we moved into that apartment. I was on the job a couple of years and Paul was working as a roadie for a local band. Before college and marriage and all that, I was still living at home with my parents and faced a dilemma. All my friends worked normal hours and all the guys at work had part-time jobs. The only exception was Paul who worked nights when the band had a gig. If I wasn't working, I'd hang out with Paul and follow the band. They'd finish at three in the morning and then go for an early breakfast. The only places open were diners. This one was their favorite."

By now they had reached the entrance, so the conversation paused until they were seated. Mid-afternoon on a weekday made seating easy. After they ordered, Kevin continued the conversation.

"Did Paul play with the band or was he only a roadie?"

"Well, we both learned the guitar when we were teenagers," Jake said. "Paul had a knack for it. I just had a love, but no talent to speak of. But to answer your question, they dragged him onto the stage once or twice. It never went anywhere. Paul needed to help people, not serenade them."

They both chuckled as their beers came.

"I did a stint in a local band while I was in high school," Kevin confessed. "We played high school dances and things like that. Mostly standard rock and roll stuff, you know, Stairway to Heaven, Gimme Shelter, that sort of thing. There were five of us. My brother, three friends, and me. Four of us became firefighters. My brother was the contrarian. He became a cop. That's the kind of neighborhood I grew up in. You became a fireman, a cop, or a criminal."

"Here's to teenagers and rock and roll," Jake said lifting his beer. Kevin raised his in response. Then they both rested for a moment, before Kevin completed his tale.

"Remember I told you about the list of people I knew who died before my age?" he asked.

"When the number went above sixty, you stopped counting," Jake said.

"Three of the guys in that band are on the list," Kevin told Jake quietly. "A car accident, a heart attack, and pancreatic cancer. It's just me and my brother left."

"God, that's got to hurt," Jake said. "The pension wins again."

"The accident happened before he retired, so he wasn't out on pension yet. But the other two? Yeah, the pension won."

Kevin tried to move the topic away from death. "So, I have a brother. How

133

about you? Any siblings?"

"Got an older brother," Jake said. "He was on the job. Made captain, then retired and moved out to Arizona. He's flying in for the reception, so you'll meet him in a few days."

"Kate comes from a large, happy family. They're scattered all over the West. We see them occasionally at weddings and funerals. So, we should see some at the reception."

"Jo has a sister, but they haven't spoken since her parents passed away. Pauli talks to her cousins, so they were invited. No one told me if they're coming or not."

"Mind if I ask what caused the break?"

Jake gave a wry chuckle. "This is not to be mentioned, even to Kate," he began. "Although I suspect Jo already told her, but there was finagling with her mother's will that created a lot of bad blood."

"Always comes down to money, doesn't it?"

"Jo's father did quite well and Jane's husband - - Jane being Jo's sister - - - didn't. Jo swears he's the reason, but she still hasn't forgiven her. Says if they needed the money, why not just ask?"

Jake wanted to change the subject to something other than family problems and death. Mentioning the pension gave him the opportunity.

"What's your pension like in Chicago?" he asked before taking another swig of beer.

"Our pension?" Kevin asked. "Well, we have twenty and out at fifty percent, but only guys with a good side job do that. After twenty, you get two and a quarter percent for each year until you top out at seventy-six percent."

"You have to leave at sixty-five?" Jake asked.

"Sixty-three."

"Really? We get thrown out at sixty-five. Have to stay twenty-five years,

134

then you get sixty-five percent. Anything after twenty-five gets you one percent per year, but it stops at seventy percent. Only exception is anything past forty years gets you a percent per year. Only know one guy who did that."

"Sounds livable," Kevin said.

"Depends on how good you are with money," Jake replied. "We had a cost-of-living adjustment, but they took it away from us."

"Oh, so the new guys don't get it," Kevin said.

"New guys? They took it away from everyone."

"What? Even guys who were already retired?"

"Yeah."

"You mean after decades of planning for retirement, they pulled that out from under you. I'm sure that screwed up a lot of retirement plans. How can you recover from that? You have to start saving again to replace the COLA. That must have kept you busy."

"Still does," Jake chuckled. "Most guys do alright. Some guys struggle and won't listen to advice."

"Spoken like a true CPA," Kevin laughed.

Their lunches came, switching their focus more towards food than talk. Between bites, Jake changed subjects again to ask, "How's Kate adjusting to her daughter getting married?"

"In a way, better than me. Liz is still my little girl, but I suspect when we get home there will be more of a reaction."

Jake shook his head in agreement. "I feel the same about Pauli, guess it's being a father. I'm still trying to figure out how I'll fit into her life from now on. Jo hasn't said anything yet. I think that's because she has Kate to talk to."

Kevin laughed. "That just supports my supposition that I'm going to get an earful when I get home."

"You have the advantage of the girls being in Chicago," Jake pointed out.

"I'm dreading the next couple of months. It may be a really rough ride."

Kevin waved down the waitress after the bus boy cleared their dishes. They ordered coffee and dessert, leaned back, and then dove back into the morbid.

"So, you've had that feeling your time is running out," Jake said.

"God yes!" Kevin replied. "I've had that feeling since before my little list of those gone before me. Kate says it's a mid-life crisis. A little late for a mid-life anything, don't you think?"

"Mid-life? I'm playing my end game. Whatever mark on the world I was going to make has been made. Now it's what part of me will be left behind?"

"Jake, we've been through this already," Kevin reminded him. "At least we have offspring to pass our genes on to the next generation."

"Will they?" Jake asked. "Has Liz spoken with you about being a mother?"

"Not to me," Kevin answered. "She's spoken with her mother about it. From what Kate says, yes, she wants to be a mother."

"Adoption or giving birth?"

"Shit! That's a good question. As I understand it, by giving birth."

"Pauli said the same thing," Jake admitted before moving the conversation to the next level. "Remember what the Chief said?"

"You mean the Little Mermaid comment?"

"Yeah, the 'It's a rational decision.' comment. Avoid the crapshoot of the heart."

Dessert came with coffee, slowing the conversation and letting ideas percolate to the surface,

Jake had been sitting on his idea of choosing the father of his grandchildren. Now he was ready to share it.

"Who do you think Liz would choose for a father?" he asked.

Kevin put his fork down and was lost in thought for a minute. "I don't know who," he began. "But I suspect a type of man. She didn't come home with many

136

dates for obvious reasons. Really, the only one I have to go by is Pauli. So, I'd say she'd pick a guy who's intelligent, physically fit, good looking, and maybe a bit artsy. What about Pauli?"

Now it was Jakes turn to think. He really should have been ready with an answer since he was the one who brought up the topic, but Kevin had approached it differently than he expected. The response he expected was someone like Pauli, only male.

"What about Pauli?" he began. "Someone like Liz, only male."

They both laughed.

"So, where does that leave us?" Kevin asked.

Jake hesitated for a minute, then dove in. "Did you notice that Carl and Tim are getting along great?"

Kevin put his fork down and looked directly at Jake. "What are you suggesting?"

"Well, someone like Pauli, only male is Tim. And someone like Liz, only male is Carl."

"Wait, wait, wait," Kevin interrupted. "Are you suggesting that the fathers of our grandchildren should be our sons?"

Jake burst out laughing at the absurdity of the question. Kevin joined as soon as he realized what he said.

"I would hope so," Jake laughed. "But after they find the right woman to marry."

Calming down, Kevin appeared to be mulling it over in his mind.

"At first it sounded ludicrous," he said. "But that's in a regular relationship. We have an extraordinary one to deal with. If it worked out, then Liz's child would Pauli's child's cousin?"

"And Pauli's child would be Liz's child's cousin," Jake calculated. "But they would have the same DNA mix, Moore-Covey and Covey Moore."

"That's wild," Kevin said. "Only trick would be how to persuade them to do it. I mean at first blush it sounds strange, but there's no reason not to do it, is there?"

"And every reason to do it. It takes the unknown risks away. They know exactly what they're buying into."

"Now let's not get ahead of ourselves," Kevin warned. "We have to time it perfectly and present it rationally or all four ladies will shoot it down."

"So, do some basic research. Start conversations about family traits and what a great match the girls are. That's the foundation. It'll be a couple of years, I think. They are both too practical to just jump into motherhood without planning it out. Liz is thirty-four, right?"

"Yeah."

"So, she gets first shot since Pauli is younger and we have to consider their biological clocks," Jake observed. "At least if we're being rational about it. Let's get the foundation laid. Then we'll talk to the boys. Then we'll lobby the ladies."

"Sounds like a plan to me," Kevin said. "A damn good plan."

They raised their cups of coffee to toast it.

Chapter Twenty-six

The front lawn had a dusting of snow on it, but the streets were clear when Jake looked out the window. The perfect white Christmas considering that Tim and Carl were driving into New York to pick the girls up for Christmas dinner. Jo and Kate were bonding in the kitchen preparing a traditional turkey dinner with all the fixings. They had spent yesterday laughing while they baked cookies, cake, and pie. The men had slipped out of the house for some last-minute shopping. After forty years of marriage, Jake was not foolish enough to believe his wife's remark about gifts. He had better have something to present to her when they gathered around the tree. Kevin was upstairs completing the job of wrapping the gifts. Jake's job was to keep an eye out for wives going upstairs or kids arriving.

Everything considered, this would appear to be a Norman Rockwell Christmas. The only thing missing was grandchildren coming to visit for the holiday. Of course, the underlying complication was the four young adults coming. There was only one couple and they were both women. A picture of the two families together would look promising if not for that fact. He felt a tinge of frustration rising to the surface, but quickly suppressed it. Taking solace in the knowledge that Pauli was happy. Tim's truck pulled into the street, ending the time for contemplation. Today would be the first Christmas with the in-laws. Ironically, it didn't feel like it. It felt more like Christmas with friends.

Opening the door, Jake stepped out to welcome the newlyweds and their brothers. Pauli and Tim would think of the visit as a return home. Kevin and Kate had spent the past week and a half here, but Liz and Carl had only passed through. Tim having invited Carl to "crash" at his place so they could stay out late without their mother's complaining. He would have to be particularly attentive to making the Moore children feel at home. The four climbed down

139

from Tim's truck, reached back inside for presents, and then marched to the front door.

"Merry Christmas, Dad!" Pauli shouted.

"Merry Christmas all," Jake said in return. "I hope you brought gifts that can be consumed."

"Yes, Mom already told me her preference," Pauli laughed.

When they stepped into the house, the noise level went up exponentially, drawing Kevin down the stairs with arms full of presents.

"Put all the gifts under the tree," Jake instructed. "When the kitchen ladies take a break, we can open them."

"Kitchen ladies?" Pauli said. "Really, Dad."

"Don't look at me," Jake said in defense. "We're not allowed in there. Maybe you girls can go back and help, but we're not wanted."

The girls shed their coats, put the gifts under the tree, and went to the kitchen. The guys hung out by the tree, hoping the ladies would make quick work of prepping dinner so they could eat. After some kitchen chatter, all four women came out. Everyone moved to the living room to exchange gifts. Jake noticed that Carl and Tim looked expectantly at two large boxes, one for Liz and one for Pauli, so he signaled Kevin to pay attention.

"What did you guys pick up that requires such large boxes?" Liz asked with more than a hint of suspicion.

"If we told you before you opened them, it won't be a surprise," Tim said.

Pauli had a doubtful look on her face, "Is it going to pop or explode?" she asked.

"Glad I talked you out of that one, Tim," Carl laughed.

"You guys didn't do anything silly, did you?" Jo asked.

"Not silly Mom," Tim answered. "I think they'll love the gifts."

Liz and Pauli began to warily unwrap the presents. They opened five boxes,

140

each inside the one before. This produced increasing laughter and wry comments from the girls. They finally pulled out two envelopes containing tickets to the hottest show on Broadway which produced squeals of delight.

"We've been trying to score tickets for this show for months," Pauli said.

"Worth the effort of opening all those boxes?" Kevin asked.

"No, but that's okay," Liz smiled. "I expected nothing less from my kid brother."

"He's done this to me before," Pauli said. "Only that time he gave me a lump of coal."

"And that necklace you're wearing," Tim pointed out.

"I was so angry I started to cry," Pauli remembered.

This gave Jake an idea that might add to how special the day was. He quickly walked over to a cabinet, reached in, and produced a VHS tape.

"Where'd you get that?" Carl asked. "That's an antique. Do you even have a machine to play it?"

Jake felt outdated, but ignored the comment and opened a cabinet under the television. There sat a machine that could play the antique, a VCR.

"Whoa!" Carl shouted. "I haven't seen one of those since I moved out."

"Please Carl," Kate said. "There's one in your father's den."

"Really? I didn't know that. Does it still work?"

"Yes, it works," Kevin answered.

Jake had continued his mission while his guests had exchanged views on VCRs. Pushing the tape in, he fast forwarded it, knowing exactly which year of Christmas video recordings he wanted. He stopped the tape where the index on the cover said he should. Then he pressed the play button and stepped back. If this were a television episode, it would be called Pauli's revenge.

When the image came up on the screen, they could see a five-year-old Tim opening gifts. Everyone watching had a smile of their face until Tim spoke. The

141

high, tiny voice of a five-year-old came through the speakers. This instantly brought laughter from the girls. Jo and Kate looked emotional, as if they were remembering when their sons were just little boys.

Tim looked at Carl then protested, "You ladies don't have to go through this. Your voices don't change."

"Women's voices do change," Jo reminded her son. "But we don't sit around waiting for it to happen as if the change somehow makes us more feminine."

"Okay," Kate jumped in. "There's food to be eaten. No more kids here, only hungry adults. Gifts can wait, let's eat."

All agreed and moved into the dining room. Jake was delayed a second putting the tape safely away and shutting the VCR. Kate's comment about no more children reverberated in his mind. Christmas gift giving was for children. Watching adults open gifts was like watching the grass grow. The true joy of the season would only return when they had grandchildren under the tree.

Chapter Twenty-seven

"These cookies are delicious," Liz commented.

Jake held back on the urge to respond, waiting to see if Pauli could recite the story of great-grandma Covey's hard cookies. He doubted she would remember his tales of sneaking into the attic of his childhood home to steal hidden cookies his mother had baked for the holidays. If she could tell Liz the history of the recipe, he would be content.

They were still seated at the dining room table. Opening presents was forgotten. Although any presents would probably be anticlimactic now that the boys' gift of Broadway tickets was revealed. Following firehouse rules, he and Kevin had begun clearing the table of dishes. They were quickly supplanted by the younger generation. Now was the time for coffee, cake, cookies, pies, and family tales. Pauli didn't disappoint him.

"Those cookies are made from my great-grandma Covey's recipe," Pauli said. "Some are hard, my favorites, and some are soft."

"And when she was a kid," Tim said. "She'd make these really weird faces when she guessed wrong and got a soft cookie."

Jake chuckled at the memory. The first in-laws' dinner was a great success. He had done the traditional turkey carving required of every father, at least when he was growing up. Now, Jo and Kate were cutting the pies and cakes they had baked, asking for preferences, and then passing them out. He leaned back and waited for someone to initiate the after-dinner conversation that bonded families together or drove them apart. He wasn't worried. The Coveys had always laughed at family gatherings. Jo's family, not so much, but Pauli and Tim inherited the Covey trait.

"This pie tastes just like yours, Mom," Carl said.

"That's because it is my pie," Kate answered. "You think I was just an observer yesterday? We taught each other our favorite recipes; great-grandma Covey's cookies are headed for Chicago."

"Fantastic," Carl said.

"So, how'd you get those tickets, Tim?" Pauli asked bringing the food conversation to an end.

Her brother leaned back as if enjoying the focus that question placed on him.

"You want me to reveal my trade secrets and clandestine contacts?" he asked.

"Yes. Impress me Mr. Man-about-town."

Jake took a bite of Kate's apple pie and waited to enjoy the playful clash of wits that was inevitable when his children got together.

"Well, it all started with someone from New York calling about a small job at their New Jersey office," Tim began. "They wanted to see if they could use the office space more efficiently or would they need a new office. I submitted a proposal that showed they didn't need a new office which saved them a ton of money."

"Really? And they gave up their two tickets to the hottest show in town for that?"

"Oh, I'm sorry. I forgot to mention," Tim said with a wry chuckle. "This guy owns the theater. I was going to hold out for backstage passes, but I thought you would want to see the show in the audience."

"Really?"

"Of course, I could just be making that up to impress our guests."

That brought a burst of laughter from around the table.

"Actually, you mentioned the show last year, so I picked up tickets for around Christmas, figuring you'd be back."

"And what would you have done if I hadn't come back?"

"I would have gone to a club or bar that had exceptional women and waved the tickets around to find a date" he bragged.

"Exceptional women?" Pauli asked after the laughter stopped.

"Yeah, you know, like a Pygmalion type of woman," he answered.

"A what?" Carl asked.

"Ah, you see, there are advantages to having a CPA for a sister and there are advantages to having an English PhD for a sister," Tim pointed out, seeming to want to drag the conversation out for as long as possible.

"He's referring to the Greek myth about a sculptor who creates the perfect woman in marble and then talks a god into bringing her to life," Pauli informed them.

"But how does he know what she's like?" Carl asked. "I mean, I'm sure she was a beautiful sculpture, but what about her personality?"

"Agreed," Tim said. "I've dated more than one pretty bitch."

"Timothy!" Jo scolded as everyone else laughed.

"I call it like it is, Mom."

"You know, that begs the question, how did you choose your mate?" Carl said.

This brought Jake out of his spectator corner. The potential for new revelations about old topics was too great. He and Jo had just discussed this topic not too long ago. He remembered his being tall was a factor.

"How did I choose your father?" Kate began. "You mean besides the obvious physique and smile, right?"

"Yeah, the traits that told you he was a keeper," Carl said.

Kevin was beginning to look uncomfortable. Kate looked at him with a smile and said, "The looks helped me decide he was worth the effort. Then we dated and I found he was empathetic, kindhearted, and responsible. I felt he would be a good provider and most importantly, a good father."

"You nailed it, Kev," Jake laughed.

"Don't laugh yet, Jake," Jo warned. "I'm up next. Why Jake? At first it was a Clara Barton thing. I was working the ER and he got knocked down at a fire. Poor thing was sitting under an air-conditioning vent without a shirt, covered in sweat, and shivering. He had the nerve to hit on me and I thought since he was a fireman, he was relatively safe."

This brought another round of laughter.

"After a few dates, I found he was checking all the boxes I had for a husband. He was intelligent, polite, compassionate, a real gentleman who I thought would make a good father."

"Okay, that's the ladies' point of view," Kevin said. "I think Carl and Tim are looking for the man's viewpoint."

"Tim?" Tim asked. "How'd I get pulled into this?"

"Pay attention," Jo advised. "You might learn something so you can avoid pretty bitches."

Tim pulled back and held up his hands as if pushing back his mother's comments.

"Why your mother?" Kevin asked. "First, she was cute. I'm not going to deny the physical attraction. But she was also smart, sensible, easy to be with, and appeared to be a woman who would make a good mother. Your turn, Jake."

Jake knew he couldn't avoid answering. He looked at Jo and imagined it was forty years before. What did he see?

"Why Johanna?" he started. "Since she was a nurse, I knew she had a good head on her shoulders. That also told me she was emotionally stable; no drama queen can work in an ER. Even in her uniform, I could see she was put together well."

The last comment brought hoots and laughter from around the table.

"And she still is," he completed his thought. This produced a nod of appreciation from his wife.

"She seemed to be compassionate. I was shivering and too young and dumb to speak up. She saw my distress and jumped on it. That's of course, what made her a such a good mother."

"So, the common thread after animal attraction," Carl analyzed. "Is they would be a good parent."

"Makes sense. Why else would you get married?" Tim asked.

"That's rather cynical don't you think?" Pauli asked. "What about love and companionship?"

"You can have those without getting married," Tim pointed out. "Don't people form families to provide stability for children? And health benefits of course."

"I know this will sound strange right now," Pauli said. "But I'm working on something about working women and satisfaction or fulfillment in life."

"What wall did that come off of?" Tim laughed.

"Trust me. It will make sense in a second," Pauli reassured. "The answers I'm getting are interesting and unexpected, at least by me. Most of the women say the most satisfying and fulfilling experience of their life is being a mother."

The parents around the table shook their heads in agreement.

"So, how about the older generation here," Carl said. "Could you tell us youngsters how you feel about it?"

"Dad, you've really had two careers," Pauli said. "What's your most fulfilling experience?"

"Hands down being a father," Jake laughed. "The only thing I can imagine that would be better is being a grandfather."

Jake regretted the last sentence immediately, but no one seemed to notice, filling the room with laughter instead of comments. He thought he got away with it, but then Pauli chimed in.

147

"Your complaint is registered, Dad," she laughed. "It's under consideration."

Jake looked at Kevin to see if he screwed up. Kevin nodded discretely, acknowledging that Jake's snafu actually provided reassurance that the girls were considering it. Looking at the boys, they seemed to be absorbing the conversation. Hopefully, after processing it, they would be open to their fathers' proposal.

Chapter Twenty-eight

Looking out at Branch Brook Park, the thought crossed Jake's mind that it was a shame it wasn't April. The Cherry Blossom Festival would have made a great backdrop for any pictures. Instead, the park looked like it was asleep, bare trees, brown grass, and a chilling wind reminded him it was winter. He turned and walked toward Nanina's in the Park, the venue Pauli and Liz had settled on after searching the internet. Pauli was familiar with the restaurant/banquet hall, having attended various functions here over the years. It had a special place in Jake's heart. Paul had hosted his parents fiftieth wedding anniversary here when Pauli was a toddler. That was a good memory.

Jo had gone in ahead of him. Kevin and Kate were already greeting the small number of early arriving guests. Pauli and Liz were speaking with the band. Tim and Carl were talking with a group of twenty-somethings, with Tim paying particular attention to one woman. None of the group looked familiar to Jake, so he assumed they were from Chicago. Jo commandeered Kate as soon as they met up, leaving Kevin to Jake. He walked up to Kevin and asked, "Do you know the woman Tim is talking up?"

Kevin glanced over at the group and answered, "That's Clare Donahue. She's one of Liz's best friends. They grew up together."

Jake nodded his head and looked more closely at Clare. Remembering the conversation around the Christmas dinner table, he did a quick evaluation. She passed the "animal attraction" test he thought.

"What can you tell me about her?"

"She's a nice girl. We watched her grow up. Carl dated her for a little while, but he's too analytical for her. They're friends, but that's all. Why do you ask?"

"Tim seems awfully focused," Jake chuckled. "Too analytical you say. Tim has that touch of artistry in him."

"Are you suggesting he might be interested?" Kevin asked.

"Suggesting he might be interested?" Jake laughed. "I'm not suggesting. It's obvious he's interested, but do you think the young lady would return that interest?"

Kevin went quiet for a minute. Then he smiled slyly and said," "You know, she just might. Architecture does have a hint of the artistic in it, right? It's going to be an interesting evening."

Guests began arriving en masse, so Jake took up a position next to Kevin. With seating chart in hand, they directed guests to their tables, talking in between.

"Did you get any push back from my slip of the tongue?" Jake asked.

"You mean the grandfather comment?"

"Yeah."

"No, nothing on this end," Kevin said. "Pauli's comment is still the last word on the subject."

"Good," Jake sighed. "You think Pauli meant that they're looking to move on this quickly?"

"I'm suspicious," Kevin told him. "Liz has been talking with Kate and Kate has been very closed mouth."

"You think we should expedite our planning?"

Before Kevin could answer, Jake noticed his nephew Pete had entered the hall. Not a surprise; he was close to Pauli and was on the list in his hand. As he was about to turn back, he saw Pete reach out to help Jo's sister Jane. Bells began to sound in his head. Did Pauli invite Jane? The two sisters hadn't spoken in years. Why push tonight, the biggest night of Pauli's life? Jake waited a moment before saying anything to Kevin, Jane here tonight could be very emotional for Jo. If Jane's husband Gary showed up, it could evolve into a physical confrontation. His sister-in-law looked thin, exhausted, and more than a little

150

anxious. Jake had to head this off while it was still manageable.

"Kev, got to do something really quick," Jake said. "Be back in a minute."

"Got it Jake," Kevin acknowledged.

Jake quickly made his way to Pauli. Walking up to her, he shot a quiet question out before she could even turn to face him.

"Did you invite your Aunt Jane?"

Pauli turned around and asked, "What did you say, Dad?"

"Did you invite your Aunt Jane?" he asked again while keeping an eye on Jo.

"Well, yes," Pauli admitted. "She is my aunt and I thought it would be impolite not to invite her after inviting Pete. I don't expect her to come. She didn't return the RSVP."

"She's here with Pete," he said. "They just walked in."

Jake made his way over to Jane, his heart aching for the woman. The closer he got, the frailer she appeared. She was only two years older than Jo, but it looked like there was a decade between them. Life had not been kind to her. What was most worrisome to Jake was the absence of her husband, even though that simplified the situation. He was a domineering man, who brooked no independent thought from his wife. Jake feared there would be a price to pay for her accompanying Pete.

"Jane, how are you?" Jake asked sincerely.

"Not well Jake," she answered. "I need to speak with Jo."

Need to? Jake felt his stomach drop. Between her physical appearance and her domestic situation, any news would not be good. Jake offered his arm to her and led the way to his wife. When Jo noticed them, she showed an instantaneous change in her demeanor. Jake thanked God it did not appear to be anger, instead it was a genuine sadness.

"Jo, could I talk with you for a second?" Jane asked.

151

Kate was standing beside Jo and began to move off so they could speak in private. Jo motioned for her to stay, appearing to need some feminine support.

"Sure Jay," Jo said blandly. "What's up?"

"I moved out and filed for divorce," Jane began. "I accused him of spousal abuse, but I'm going to need to borrow your husband to sort through the finances and insurance. I'm going to have some hefty medical bills soon."

"Medical bills?" Jo asked in shock.

"Yes, and we have to talk," Jane said. "It might be genetic, but right now we have to help Pauli celebrate."

Jo began to cry and gave her sister a hug. Then she turned to Kate.

"Kate this is my big sister Jane," she said. "She was just reborn."

Jane and Jo laughed.

"I'm not supposed to get excited or emotional," Jane worried.

"Okay, we'll be low key." Jo promised. "Let's go see Pauli and her new mate."

With that Jake gave a sigh of relief and made his way back to Kevin knowing all would be made clear before the night was through.

"You looked relieved," Kevin commented.

"It was touch and go for a minute, but after Jane explained her situation, Jo proclaimed her reborn and set off to present her to Pauli."

"Reborn?" Kevin asked.

A couple that Jake didn't recognize stepped in. Kevin gave them a warm welcome and pointed out where they were seated. Jake waited until they were out of earshot before beginning the story of Jane.

"Jo's sister has had it rough," he began. "She got married young to a newly minted lawyer. Everyone thought he was a good catch, but I sensed there was something off the minute I set eyes on him. Of course, they had been married for a few years by then. Turns out he's got a gambling problem, so their finances

152

have always been tenuous at best. When Jo's father died, Gary, that's Jane's husband, drew up a new will for her mother to sign. No one thought anything of it until their mother passed away. Then the terms of the will became public and we found out that Jo was basically left out. By then he had become violent and Jane wouldn't do anything because of Pete. Gary had convinced her that she would lose all rights as a mother if she filed for divorce. All unethical, all too much for Jo to take."

"So, the sisters didn't speak for years," Kevin repeated what Jake had said the other day.

"So, they didn't speak, but - - - Got a question for you. If you helped someone who really needed it even though Kate said you shouldn't, would Kate be ticked off when she found out?"

"Sounds like rescuing Al," Kevinn chuckled.

"It's more complicated. The sisters didn't speak for years, but I gave Jane a hand when she received the money from the will. The money was in her name, not Gary's so I did some accounting magic and hid much of it from him. If she tells Jo, I might be in for a hell of a tongue lashing when we get home."

"Jake, I've only known the two of you for a short time, but I deem myself a pretty good judge of people. It was a necessary skill set for a battalion chief," Kevin began. "I think in the end she'll be grateful that you helped her sister."

"Thanks for the positive vibes," Jake said. "I hope you're right. But now, Jane just told us she filed for divorce and needs my help to square away her finances. Then she said she's anticipating medical bills, so something is going on."

After finishing Jane's sad tale, Jake looked out the door and saw Chief Brendler with Kathy Stanley walking up. A few steps behind were Frank and Chingli Helms. Both couples had been added to the invite list after the marriage ceremony. They would complete the Six Engine table. All the other guys and their wives had already arrived.

"Chief, Kathy, welcome," Jake shouted. "You're sitting at the Six Engine table. That's table number three."

"How'd you guys get hoodwinked into doing the greetings," the Chief asked shaking their hands.

"It's a family affair, Chief," Jake laughed. "Fathers are always given the job of guarding the castle entrance."

"Castle entrance," Kathy laughed. "Thank God it's not a castle. They're very uncomfortable."

"Unless the barbarians are at the gate," Jake replied. Frank and Chingli caught up with the couple and they strolled off together in the direction Jake sent them.

Looking around at the banquet hall, Jake noted a generational divide. Most of the guests from Illinois were young. The ages of the Jersey crowd were more mixed. He also noticed that Tim and Clare were still chatting, obviously enjoying each other's company. Would it complicate matters if they began seeing each other?

He turned to Kevin and shared his observation.

"The Illinois representation is decidedly younger than the Jersey one," he pointed out. "Any thoughts on that?"

"Thoughts?" Kevin asked. "I'll say the girls did a good job planning and recruiting among their friends. From what Liz said, my impression is mostly single or childless couples without holiday obligations came. Seems most intend to stay until after New Year's Eve. The plan is to go into Times Square and watch the ball drop."

"Do it now," Jake chuckled. "May not get another chance."

"That's the mentality," Kevin agreed.

His thought about Tim and Clare's dating complicating their master plan was growing in his mind, so he decided to run it passed his co-conspirator.

"Let me ask you something very hypothetical."

"Shoot," Kevin replied.

"If Tim and Clare were to start dating, a big 'if' considering the distance between their homes, but if they did, do you think it would complicate things?"

Kevin thought for a moment. "You mean would she object to the arrangement?"

"Yeah,"

"First, what business would it be of hers?" Kevin pointed out. "Even if it concerned her in some way, the procedure would be performed in a doctor's office unless they wanted to try at home. But it wouldn't be an intimate arrangement. They would use artificial insemination, I'm sure."

"That's a long analysis," Jake said. "It sounded like you think it won't be an issue."

"Not with a girlfriend," Kevin agreed. "But what do we do if the girls balk at the idea?"

"First, it's our job to present it in a rational manner so they don't balk," Jake said. "What about a backup plan if including brothers somehow didn't sit right?"

By now most of the guests had arrived and dinner was being served. This gave them the privacy they needed for the discussion, but also put pressure on for a quick resolution.

"A backup plan," Kevin said as he looked around the hall. "Well, if brothers wouldn't work, how about cousins?"

Jake laughed at what they were saying. "We sound like the families in Dune," he laughed. "The geneticist breeds for the best genes."

With that they abandoned their greeting post and went to their tables.

Chapter Twenty-nine

Jake stepped into the front door of his home with a bag of freshly baked bagels. Jo and Jane had not had the opportunity to talk yesterday at the reception. Instead, they had spent their time celebrating Pauli's wedding and Jane's liberation. The sisters agreed as they parted last night that Jane would come for breakfast. The bagels were only a part of it. Since Kevin and Kate were flying back to Chicago tomorrow morning, this was their last chance to make a Jersey firehouse breakfast. That's where the bagels came in.

While the ladies talked, the men worked at the stove cranking out breakfast amid feminine laughter. The thought crossed Jake's mind as he and Kevin labored, "What's wrong with this picture?" Knowing the ladies couldn't produce a real firehouse breakfast, he chalked it up to desiring authenticity and pushed on. It wasn't until after cleanup that the ladies paid attention to Jake or Kevin.

"Jake," Jane said. "I never really got to thank you for your help over the past few years."

He froze upon hearing that. She had thanked him numerous times. Why claim she had not? Why say it in front of Jo? With the cat out of the bag, all Jake could do was smile, nod his head, and pray Jo would accept the news lightly.

"Wait," Jo said. "He helped you over the past few years?"

"Yes, his help was indispensable," Jane informed her sister. "Without it I don't think I'd be sitting here today."

"You're giving me too much credit," Jake responded. "Pete did the lion's share of the work."

"He did the legal part," Jane insisted. "You did the financial. That allowed me to keep that money out of Gary's reach so I had resources to strike out on my own."

Jake was keeping an eye on Jo, trying to read her hidden reaction to the news. Kevin was showing signs he was getting nervous with the trajectory of the conversation.

"So, you gave a hand when it was needed?" Jo asked. "Like on that train platform in Chicago."

Kate and Jane laughed at Jo's comment, hinting that the Al rescue had been a part of their earlier conversation. All three of the ladies seemed to find that affair to be funny. Was that a good sign? Jake wondered.

"I just gave some advice to help Jane feel a little more secure," Jake confessed.

"A little advice?" Jane laughed. "You set up accounts so the money could pass through and I could do what you advised and switch it into Pete's name. Then you monitored the account and made sure the taxes were paid without Gary knowing. I wouldn't have known where to start. As far as I'm concerned, you saved my life."

Jake was sweating by now, knowing his wife saw through him. His concerns about her reaction to helping Jane were on display for all to see.

"I don't know, Jake," Jo began. "It sounds like you did a lot of heavy lifting to help my estranged sister."

"Estranged?" Jane reacted. "Come on now Jo, you're being dramatic."

"Well, we weren't speaking remember?" Jo pointed out. "At least the two of us weren't speaking. Apparently, Jake and you were."

Kevin looked at Jake nervously while Jake waited for the other shoe to drop. He had a feeling it would hit the floor with a loud thud. The Moores were only here one more day. Couldn't this have waited. He regretted not swearing Jane to secrecy. Now all he could do was wait for his fate.

"Jake, thank you for your foresight," Jo said before choking up. "I don't know how I would have handled it if something untoward would have happened to her."

She stood up, walked over to him, gave him a smile, a hug, and finally a kiss. "Later you can let me hear my husband's full contribution to your liberation," she said to Jane.

"Oh, you're being so melodramatic again," Jane laughed.

"Not really," Jo replied. "But right now, we have to get to the practical. Where is Gary and what is your legal status."

"Gary? I don't know," Jane began. "When he found out about the bank and investment accounts, he threatened to beat me to a pulp unless I gave him the money."

"What?" Jake asked.

"Did you call the police?" Jo wanted to know.

"I threatened to, then told him to go to hell. He stormed out. I checked the family bank account the next day and found he had cleaned it out," Jane said.

"What's your guess on his whereabouts?" Jake asked.

"My opinion? He's probably in Atlantic City trying to double his money," Jane said bitterly. "It all came to a head because his partners began questioning his handling of escrow accounts and payments to the firm. I suspect there's going to be an audit and he needs to clean up his mess quickly before that starts. When he goes back home, he'll find a restraining order and a request for a divorce on the kitchen table. Pete and his buddies moved my things to an apartment. I'm not going back."

Jake saw that Kevin and Kate had been silent throughout the discussion. It would have been unreasonable to ask their opinion or advice. They were too new to the situation. He felt for them. If he were in their position, he would have felt like an intruder. With the pause in Jane's narrative, Kate reached her limit. She stood up and quickly left the room in tears. Kevin began to stand up, but Jane waved for him to wait and went to Kate. Jo quickly followed, leaving the two men on their own.

"Whoa!" was all Kevin could say.

"You haven't heard half the horror," Jake said. "I did what I did because he is such a bastard, but she refused to leave him until Pete was out of the house. That sits heavy on Pete. I had to do something to give her flexibility."

"You did the right thing," Kevin said. "Sometimes that's the hardest thing."

"Not this time," Jake said. "It was a no brainer."

Kevin looked at Jake and said, "You know, I am jealous of you."

"Jealous? Why?"

"You got to save lives and help people in the firehouse. Like you said, you were relevant there. And now you get to save lives and help people with your accounting knowledge."

Jake laughed at the absurdity of what his friend just said.

"Save lives?" he asked. "To quote Jane, you're being melodramatic, don't you think?"

"From the story I just heard, maybe not," Kevin replied. "Ever been on a domestic violence run?"

Jake stood quietly for a moment considering the question. He had been on domestic violence responses and sometimes one of the couple left in a body bag. The ladies came back into the room as Jake processed this.

"Now we've settled that," Jane said. "Kevin, just to let you know, Kate felt she was intruding on family business. But I told her, after Pauli and Liz, you are family now."

Kevin nodded his head.

When the ladies returned to their seats, Jane moved the conversation to another topic.

"I crashed the reception yesterday because I had to speak with Jo about my health," she began.

Everyone protested her description of attending the reception, but Jane held

159

up her hand to quiet them.

"I was having unusual headaches and other unexplained symptoms," she continued. "So, I went to my internist who sent me to a neurologist who sent me to a radiologist who did what they call an MRA on my brain. The radiologist told the neurologist that I have a large aneurysm in my cerebral cortex just waiting to pop."

Jo sucked in her breath and Kate's hand went up to cover her mouth in shock. Jake and Kevin were speechless.

Jane ignored them all, determined to get her story told.

"Now I have to get my papers in order," she said using her fingers to put quotation marks around 'papers in order'. "I need to draw up a will and change the beneficiary on my accounts from Gary to Pete. I have to make sure everything is in order for the taxman."

Jo reacted to this strongly. "Jane, don't you think you're the one being melodramatic now? Did the doctors say you needed an operation or something?"

"Yes, as a matter of fact they did," Jane answered. "They scheduled me for next week. I should have my affairs in order before then."

Jake watched his wife go over a cliff after hearing that. Her instinctive reaction was denial, pure and simple.

"Come on now, Jane, they do this all the time," she insisted. "It sounds impressive to us, but it's like a car fire to Jake and Kevin. Easily handled by competent professionals."

Jane sat quietly for a moment as if struggling to come up with words to comfort her sister. Then she just quietly said, "Jo, it's brain surgery. They're warning me not to get excited. The note I left Gary told him I moved out because the doctor said any excitement might burst the aneurysm."

Now it was Jo's turn to flee the room. Kate and Jane quickly followed.

"I am so sorry," Kevin said to Jake.

160

Jake sat quietly and thought how unfair life was to Jane. She was a good woman no matter what scale you used to measure her. Good wife and mother who stayed in an abusive relationship, unappreciated, for her son. She was finally breaking free after forty-three years of hell and now this.

"It's like responding to an arson job," Jake said. "One where a couple of innocent kids are killed because of a neighbor's jealous boyfriend. It's so unfair."

Thankfully, Kevin did not counter this with some sort of glib remark about life and fairness. Yesterday had been close to perfect. Today would balance the scale, diametrically opposed to the previous day.

The ladies came back into the room calmer. After sitting, Jane turned to Jake. "Can you meet with Peter and get everything in order?"

"Jane, of course I can," he reassured her.

"Good. I have to get this done before Gary takes me off his medical insurance. One other thing, Jake. I need you to run interference for me. If I could have my phone number forwarded to yours, that would help with the keep calm order. I don't get many calls, just Gary and Pete and I really shouldn't talk with Gary. I'm getting another cell phone, so Pete should call that one. That leaves Gary on the old one. I can't just cancel that because of the insurance issue."

"Okay, not a problem. And I'll reach out to Pete as soon as we're done here."

"Oh, we're done," Jane laughed. "I'm not that complicated an old lady."

They all laughed, some forcing it. Then they stood up to move into the den. They had all afternoon to catch up on what had happened over the past few years.

Chapter Thirty

After loading the car, Jake, Kevin, and Mark were standing next to it waiting. The weather was warm for late December, but they still hoped the ladies wouldn't take too long with their farewells. Jake found it amusing that everyone who had come to see the Moore family off had broken into three distinct groups. The ladies had retreated to the back den to say their goodbyes. Tim, Carl, and Pete were talking in the foyer inside the front storm door. The three old firefighters were conducting business outside away from prying ears

"I was surprised Jane went through the trouble to see us off," Kevin said. "Seems she hit it off with Kate."

Jake shook his head in agreement, looked over his shoulder to confirm the ladies weren't at the door, and then added his observation.

"It's to be expected," he said. "Jane was Jo's role model when they were growing up. They have similar life views and similar temperaments. The only real difference is Jo is a little more ornery. Jane's a little sweeter."

Kevin and Mark laughed at this assessment.

"If Jo could hear you now," Mark said.

"Oh, she knows," Jake said. "And she agrees. That's the reason Jane was trapped in her marriage. Seems it took a health scare to give her the steel she needed in her soul to leave Gary."

The sun broke out from behind a bank of clouds, shining onto where they stood as if to emphasize Jake's statement. Kevin couldn't resist the opportunity for the dramatic to pass. All it took was a simple "ahhhhh", attempting to sound like an angel. They all joined him and then laughed.

"So, you could say Kate got two for one," Mark pointed out.

"Yeah, I guess you could look at it that way," Kevin agreed. "Maybe more than two for one since you didn't include Jill and if you get Jo, you get Jill. I'll have to use that point the next time she's ticked off at me. It'll change the subject and make her laugh."

The sun slipped back behind the clouds and ended the anointed feel of the day. Jake turned again to look for movement from the house, then glanced at his watch. They still had plenty of time. In his gaze back he noted the sons talking. This produced another observation.

"The boys seem to have hit it off as well. A data scientist, an architect, and a lawyer. Their generation is doing okay."

"You think so?" Kevin asked. "None of them have the best job in the world."

"And that would be?" Mark asked

"The only job we ever loved," Kevin said.

"Oh, come on," Jake laughed. "It's a dirty, dangerous, physically and emotionally challenging occupation. They've got it made. That's what we set out to do, give them every opportunity to do better than us."

"You envy them?" Mark asked.

Jake thought for a moment. "Envy them? My twenty something year old self wouldn't. They're stuck in an office trying to be relevant. I never had to question how relevant I was. So, no I don't envy them. But I don't want my son on the job. Not today's job. It's not the same."

"When my son asked if he should take the test," Mark said. "I told him the job isn't the same as when I came on. And he said of course it isn't. Times change, technology changes. The way he put it is, if he got on the job, then the fire department he stepped into would be his fire department. The one I stepped into all those years ago is mine."

"That from a twenty-one-year-old kid?" Jake chuckled. "Impressive. I will say this, one of the benefits of this job is the brotherhood. Do you think we could have connected so quickly if we hadn't all been firefighters? Just knowing that

163

we have the shared experience of the job gives us that connection."

"Yeah, you're right," Kevin said. Mark shook his head in agreement.

"I overheard Tim inviting Carl back over the summer so they can hit the Jersey Shore," Jake said lightening the mood. "There was some sort of comment about bikinis, volley ball, pizza, and beer."

"Sounds like a frat party to me," Kevin said. "What kind of pizza are we talking about?"

"Jersey thin crust, of course," Mark laughed. "It's a shame you visited in December, between the shore, the Big Apple, and some great fishing, July's better."

"We had no control over that," Jake reminded him. "The girls set the date, but Kev, you're welcome to come back when it's warmer."

"How about you come for the Fourth," Mark suggested. "I have a gathering at my place every year. We could see Revolutionary Morris County and maybe catch the fireworks in the city."

Kevin looked interested. "Revolutionary Morris County, really?" he chuckled. "You know, I've never done any surf fishing and we didn't get to Broadway either. It doesn't look like Kate needs any persuasion. You think you could come west again? There's more to Chicago than rescues on the L and Giordano's deep-dish pizza."

Jake smiled and shook his head. "We should get together and finalize our plans," he pointed out. "The campaign began well, but we still have a lot of work to do."

Mark looked puzzled. "And what campaign are you talking about?"

Jake looked over his shoulder one more time and then leaned into Mark for added security. "Remember what the Chief said about being able to have input into the father of the girl's children?" he asked. "You know, the Little Mermaid comment."

Mark reacted to the last sentence, acknowledging he remembered. Then Jake nodded towards the storm door.

"Are you saying the brothers would be the fathers?" Mark asked.

"Well, yes, but not the way you made it sound," Kevin answered. "It would be Carl and Pauli and Tim and Liz. All done in a doctor's office through artificial insemination."

"And everyone is in agreement?"

"Not quite yet," Jake said. "That's why we have to finalize our plans."

"You are one hell of a team," Mark laughed. "Let's see, if you pull this off then any offspring would be cousins, right?"

"Yeah, more like double cousins," Kevin said. "Related on both sides of the family, but we've got a long way to go."

"The girls want to be mothers, but we need to find a way to ensure they don't go off on their own before we present the idea to them."

Mark just shook his head and laughed. Tim, Carl, and Pete stepped outside ending the conversation.

"Your secret's safe with me," Mark assured them quietly.

The young men came over to the older men with a proposal that matched Jake's invite.

"Dad, the three of us were talking," Tim began. "It's a shame Carl didn't come in the summer. We'd have a lot more fun then. You think we could extend an invitation to the Moores to come back in July or August?"

"How about for the Fourth of July?" Jake asked. "We've already got it covered. Why'd you ask? Is Carl going to stay with us?"

"No, no, we were trying to score a week rental down the shore," Tim laughed. "But we were wondering if Carl's folks could make it also."

Kate came to the door looking for the men in her life. After seeing the group outside, she turned and waved toward the back of the house. The sun broke

165

through the clouds one more time as the ladies stepped out.

"We're all set?" Kate asked.

"Loaded up and ready to go," Kevin replied.

The ladies huddled by the door, looking emotional.

"Okay," Kate sighed. "Off we go. Thanks for everything. We have to do this again soon."

"July Fourth," the men said in unison.

"Oh, you guys have it all worked out already?" Jo asked.

"A proposal," Jake said. "Needing the approval of our wives."

"We'll talk after the girls get back," Jo said. "Although I don't see why not. It'll be easier now that Jane can give a hand."

"Jill and Jane haven't been to Chicago yet," Kate reminded everyone.

"Let's get July nailed down," Kevin said. "Then we'll talk about Chicago. We can have a party on Lake Michigan."

Jane and Jill were smiling at the thought, then they gave Kate one last hug.

"Looks like we'll see you in July," Jane said.

Jake walked to the car with Kevin, Kate, and Carl in tow. Carl gave Kate a hug since he was staying until after the New Year. Jake was content with the events of the past two days. Hoping all their plans would come to fruition by the end of the summer, he climbed behind the steering wheel and started the car. Next stop Newark Liberty International.

Chapter Thirty-one

His cell phone went off as Jake was pulling out of the Costco parking lot. The number that appeared on the car entertainment center screen was Jane's. Should he pick it up? Jane had said she only received calls from Pete and Gary on this phone. She neglected to mention the robocalls that came so frequently. What was it about an elderly woman that attracted so many telemarketers? The traffic light right after Costco turned red as he pulled out, so he stopped and pressed the answer button.

"Jane?" Gary's voice came through the car speakers.

"No, Gary," Jake answered, instantly alert.

"Jake?" Gary asked. "Why are you answering Jane's phone?"

The light changed, so Jake began accelerating and moving the car to the exit for Route Eighteen. He now regretted answering the call, assuming the conversation could get heated.

"I'm answering my phone, Gary," he said. "She has all her calls forwarded to me now."

"What? Why?"

They were seconds into this phone call and Jake was already tired of it. He had never really gotten along with Jane's husband, having seen through the man's façade early on. Easing onto the exit ramp for Eighteen, he gave as concise an answer as possible.

"Doctor's orders," Jake said. "She's not to get excited."

"Jake, I have to talk to her," Gary said, beginning to sound a little desperate.

You have to talk to her, Jake thought, or do you have to browbeat her? The sound coming through the speakers spoke volumes. If Gary had gone to Atlantic City, he lost big time. The car responded to the pressure on the gas pedal, allowing Jake to merge onto Eighteen.

"Do you know about her condition?" Jake asked.

"What are you talking about?" Gary countered with distain. "The woman's healthy as an ox."

Jake moved the car into the far-left lane before answering.

"Didn't she tell you about the headaches and double vision?"

"Oh, come on, that's bullshit," Gary proclaimed. "She's had headaches all along. You're not going to fall for that, are you?"

Not fall for that? He couldn't believe what he was hearing. One way that Jo and Jane were different was their health. Jo had been the active, athletic sister. Jane suffered with allergies all her life, making it difficult to be active outdoors in the spring and summer. This had given her a touch of asthma and made her more prone to respiratory infections. Healthy as an ox she was not.

"Gary, she has a large aneurysm in her cerebral cortex. They scheduled her for corrective surgery next week," Jake informed him. "Before then, she's not to get excited."

"I have to talk with her before then," Gary insisted.

"My man, what don't you get?" Jake snapped. "You're toxic to her. Stay away."

"You don't understand," he pleaded. "If I don't come up with some money, they're going to throw me out of the practice. They'll report me to law enforcement. I need to cover a large nut. She's got money that you hid from me. That'll cover everything. Just have to explain it to her."

"Don't go near her," Jake shouted. "If you do, she's as good as dead."

"Bullshit, you just want to keep the money yourself!"

"What?" Jake couldn't believe what the man said. Thank God traffic was light. He wouldn't have been able to handle this crazy conversation otherwise. "Are you nuts? Look, she has a restraining order out against you. The court says don't call her, don't go near her, understand?"

"Court? What do you know about court?" Gary shouted. "I need her to sign that money over to me. Where is she?"

"Gary, do yourself a favor," Jake told him. "Get to Gamblers Anonymous, then negotiate with your partners to come up with a way to repay the money quietly."

Gary cursed and hung up the phone.

Jake made a quick calculation and decided to pull into the next parking lot. Taking out his cell, he hit contacts, then home.

"Did he call you?" Jo asked without even a hello.

"Yes. The man is delusional."

"I just got off the phone with him," Jo said. "I'm really worried."

"He doesn't know where Jane is," Jake said. "Reach out to Pete. Make sure he doesn't tell Gary Jane's address. Then gently talk to Jane, so she isn't startled. We'll call the police if we have to, but right now he hasn't violated the restraining order."

"Okay," Jo said. "I'm going to call Jill. We'll go over there and keep Jane company."

"I'll follow after I drop the groceries. Look around before you go," Jake reminded. "You don't want Gary following you. Maybe we should have Jane pack some clothes and come stay with us until the whole thing blows over."

"I'll see if she'll agree," Jo said. "You know she doesn't want to impose. She can be stubborn."

Jake hung up the phone thinking Jane is not the only stubborn one in her family. If Gary shows up, he's going to be confronted by the ornery, athletic part of the family.

After a quick stop to drop things off, Jake headed to Jane's for a war council. The poor woman was still in the process of moving in and was scheduled for major surgery at the end of the week. They had insisted she use movers just to manage the stress. The heavy lifting should have been completed yesterday afternoon. She had put a few pieces of furniture and all the essentials of modern life into storage. Yesterday was moving storage to the new apartment. Today was supposed to be the house warming, ladies' afternoon tea. Instead, it was now a "prepare for the asshole's harassment" strategy session.

As he pulled into the apartment complex parking lot, he saw Gary shouting at Jane! How did he find her? Jake spied a parking space and quickly pulled in. Jo came out from behind Jane, joining in the shouting match. He threw the car into park and jumped out, walking quickly toward the confrontation. Jane's shout could be heard clearly.

"You don't control me anymore! Leave or I'll call the police."

"You ungrateful bitch!" Gary countered. "I gave you everything you have."

Jane wasn't backing down. "And then you gambled it all away," she shouted.

"Leave or we'll call the police," Jo repeated the treat.

"I already did," Jill shouted from behind Jane.

Then Jake saw Gary push Jo and he began to sprint. Jo did what any red-blooded Jersey girl would do. She slapped Gary across the face. Before Gary could respond, Jake was on him.

"Back off asshole," Jake shouted.

Gary took a step back while Jake inserted himself between his brother-in-law and the sisters. The rage Gary saw in Jake's face forced him back even further. Jo began to lead Jane back into the apartment. They took a few steps in, then Jane raised her hand to her head and collapsed.

Jo stood over her sister in shock. Jake forgot about Gary and leaped through the doorway to Jane. He quickly noted her breathing was shallow and sporadic. After gently shifting her into recovery position, he looked into her eyes. Jake was filled with frustration. This might not have happened if he hadn't stopped home

170

with the groceries.

"Jill, call nine-one-one," Jake ordered, bypassing Jo. The shout awakened Jo, who moved to Jane's head. All they could do now was maintain her airway and wait for EMS.

Gary stood frozen watching his in-laws monitor his wife. Pete came from the back of the apartment. Jake figured that's where his mother sent him to avoid a physical confrontation between father and son. Now the young man stood over his mother knowing that she took the hit for him. If Jane didn't pull through, he would carry that with him for the rest of his life. And still the gambler stood by in silent shock watching the results of his actions.

"Got the police on the phone," Jill said. "Can we provide them with more info?"

"Tell then sixty-eight-year-old female who is scheduled for a brain aneurysm operation has suffered what appears to be a massive stroke. Breathing is shallow and sporadic."

Jill passed the info on to police dispatch.

"There's a squad car on the way," she told Jake. "EMS will be a little later."

In that instant, things went from bad to worse. Jane took one last raspy breath and stopped breathing all together. Jake's stomach dropped. He quickly checked her neck for a pulse. Finding none, he began chest compressions, all the while berating himself. His choices today had been wrong. He could help a stranger in Chicago, but couldn't help his wife's sister. Useless piece of shit was all he could think as he worked on Jane, knowing CPR only helped one in ten victims.

Sounds of a siren came through the frigid air. A squad car stopped in front of the apartment and a cop jumped out. A quick glance on his part told him all he needed to know. He went to the truck of the car and pulled out a cylinder of oxygen. After Jill told him she was an ER nurse, he handed the bottle to her and

171

went to help Jake with the compressions. Jo, Pete, and Gary watched Jake and the cop switch off and on until the ambulance arrived. The EMS crew quickly got Jane into the back of their rig. Jill climbed into the rig after telling the EMS crew she was a nurse. The rig pulled away heading for New Brunswick with Jill and an EMT continuing chest compression on Jane.

It had only been a short time since her collapse, but in his heart, Jake knew Jane was gone. Jo turned to Gary and began screaming at him. The cop stepped in between until Jake could calm her down enough to get her in the car. Pete locked the apartment door, got into the back of the car, and Jake headed for the hospital. All knew there was little hope that Jane would ever talk to them again. If Gary could have stayed away until after the operation, Jake thought, then maybe this could have been avoided. Al was alive and well in Chicago and Jane was gone. Useless piece of shit!

Chapter Thirty-two

Cars lined the street. Clouds blocked the sun. A miserable, gray January day that matched Jake's mood perfectly. Coming home to Jane's repast highlighted the uniqueness of the day. Gary would not be here. Jake had left him at the cemetery after an odd, strained conversation. Part confession, part defense, Gary had acknowledged his problems and had asked Jake's help sorting through his finances. Discovering that Jane had changed the beneficiary of her insurance policy had pushed her husband to the brink. He now faced the prospect of begging his son for money to dig himself out of the hole gambling had put him in.

Pulling the car into the back of his driveway, Jake climbed out wondering what he was stepping into. Would it be an Irish wake or a solemn German gathering of remembrance? Jo's family had the option of both heritages. He climbed the back steps and walked into a divided house. The different sides of Jane and Jo's family had settled in opposite sides of the house. The German branch was in the back den. The Irish branch in the front living room. There was plenty of mixing between the two with the food in the dining room and the fact that they all hailed from the same section of Newark. Many having known each other their entire lives. The fire department had taken up positions in the middle, being neither one nor the other. They were there to support Jake as much as anything else. It had been a rough week for him. The inner questions and guilt haunted him. Why couldn't he have done more to prevent this? Just run interference for a few more days and see if the doctors could perform their magic, repairing the aneurysm. He should have anticipated Gary would follow Pete and given Pete a heads-up days earlier. He should have insisted Jane stay with Jo and him. Then Gary wouldn't have had the nerve to confront her. The questions and alternate choices were endless. He needed to talk with Paul, but that was no longer an option. Now he would have to dump on Mark and Kevin. Thank God Kevin and Kate had insisted on attending the wake and funeral. Mark and Jill would have been overwhelmed if they had not.

As Jake began making the rounds to thank everyone for their support, he came across Pauli and Pete. They were talking away from the crowd. He couldn't help but overhear Pauli's tearful words.

"You were there when I needed you most," she told Pete. "When I decided to come out, you were the first one I told. Then your mom was so understanding. She gave me support, not criticism, told me how to approach my mom. That saved so much grief and so many misunderstandings. When I have a child, if it's a girl she'll be Jane and if it's a boy he'll be Pete."

"You don't have to do that," Pete insisted.

"I want to," Pauli replied. "It's like what my dad says about firemen. They do what they do, not because they should, but because it's the right thing to do. Remembering your mom or thanking you are the right things to do."

Jake felt uncomfortable listening to this very private conversation, so he quietly retreated and went to the front of the house by an alternate route. His purpose today was to support Pete, not intrude on a private conversation with a lifelong confidant. Since Gary wouldn't come to the repast, Pete took on the mantel of male representing the family. Jo was playing the female opposite and Jake was the go between/backup. He made his way around the house, approaching each cohort of relatives and friends to thank them. Jo and Jill were nowhere to be seen. Jake assumed they were in a corner somewhere leaning on each other.

After floating around greeting all who had come, Jake settled down with the fire department guys. Only Kevin and Mark remained. The repast was beginning to wind down. Soon the house would be empty of all the well-meaning friends and families who you saw at weddings and funerals. They had come together for

174

Pauli's wedding last month. None would have guessed that they would come together again so soon for Jane's funeral.

He walked over to Kevin and Mark and dropped down into a chair. His friends waited a moment to see if Jake would say anything, then hit him hard.

"You look like shit," Mark said.

"Is that supposed to make me feel better?"

"No, it's supposed to give you a warning about beating yourself up," Mark replied.

"Who says I'm beating myself up?

"I do. After forty some odd years of watching you do it, I've got it down," Mark said. "You did everything anyone could do to help Jane. And there's no way to tell why that aneurysm popped when it did. So, drop the self-pity party and step up to help Pete."

"Whoa!" Jake said. "That's tough love if I ever heard it."

"Sounds like good advice to me," Kevin chimed in. "You couldn't beat yourself up in the firehouse and you shouldn't do it here. Only knew Jane for a short while, but my impression is she wouldn't want you to."

Jake leaned his head back on the wall behind the chair and sighed.

"I wish it was that easy."

"Jake, you can't bring her back," Mark said. "You can only respect her wishes. Let it go."

Jake took a deep breath and mentally reached for the locked box in the back of his mind. He placed the doubts and recriminations into it next to the 9/11 memories and the pictures of burnt toddlers. After closing the box, he turned to Kevin and said, "I overheard Pauli talking to Pete. But first you have to understand their relationship. They were born a couple of months apart and grew up together. The schism in the family didn't happen until they were in their late twenties. So, they were playmates sounding boards, advisors, more like brother and sister than cousins."

Kevin shook his head showing he understood, but didn't want to interrupt.

"So, I came up from behind them," Jake continued. "They didn't notice I was there and Pauli was crying and talking. She said that she owed Pete, that he was the first one she came out to, and that Jane had given her support and advice when she needed it most. Then she said when, and I'll emphasize that word, when she has a child, if it's a girl she'll be named Jane and if it's a boy she'll name it after Pete. Because that's the right thing to do."

"The right thing to do?" Mark chuckled. "Sounds like something you would say."

"She's his daughter," Kevin reminded.

Jake looked around, but still didn't see Jo, Jill, Kate, or even Liz.

"Where are the ladies?" he asked knowing they were in the house throughout the repast.

"They went upstairs," Kevin said, "Kate was having a hard time of it. Jo was doing no better. So, they retreated to collect themselves. Jill went to comfort Jo and Liz went to comfort Kate. Oh, and they took a bottle of wine with them. That should help them work their way through it."

Chapter Thirty-three

"Don't you think the two of you should leave soon?" Jo asked Jake and Tim.

She was dashing around the kitchen preparing the welcoming meal for the Moores and Liz and Pauli. Jill was at the stove monitoring the spareribs in the oven and stirring the sausage and peppers on the stove top. Jo was putting the finishing touches onto the apple pie before inserting it into the oven with the spareribs. Jake and Tim were debating what to have for lunch before going to the airport to pick up their guests. They had completed their assigned tasks. The backyard patio was cleaned up. The grill was ready to be fired up. Picnic table was covered with a table cloth while a screen tent surrounded it. The mosquito repellant was deployed. Weather forecast was for a warm, partly cloudy, calm day with a bit of humidity, A perfect day for a pre-July Fourth picnic. All they needed were the guests.

When Jo suggested they leave early, Jake knew there was no lunch to be had at home. He motioned to Tim and stood up.

"Yeah, you're right," he said to Jo. "We don't want to leave them waiting."

The two men quietly made their way out to their rides. Before climbing into his car, Jake asked Tim, "How does Burger King sound?"

"The one on the south side of Eighteen?"

"Yeah, that's the most convenient."

"Okay, I'll meet you there."

Jake got into his car and Tim climbed into his truck. Each backed down the driveway and headed for the King.

After collecting their order, father and son deposited themselves in the dining area. Between bites Jake began the process he and Kevin had agreed upon.

"So, I haven't really had a chance to talk with you about your Chicago visit," Jake began. "How are the new couple adjusting to married life?"

"Dad, they lived with each other for a year before they were married," Tim laughed. "There wasn't a lot of adjusting going on."

"You never know," Jake pointed out. "Some people, once they get that legal status, they start making demands they never made before."

Tim took a bite and thought about it. "I didn't see anything like that. They kind of danced around the apartment. No issues."

Jake saw he had to be more specific if he wanted to get a feel for when the girls planned to start a family.

"Did they talk about buying a home or starting a family?" he asked settling on a more direct approach.

"New home? No," Tim said. "Starting a family? Often, but nothing specific. Just general issues. Yes, they want to have a family. When they decide, they'll talk with Clare to set it up. That sort of general thing."

Jake stopped eating as he took in the last sentence so nonchalantly uttered.

"Clare?" he asked. "You mean the friend of Liz's that you were talking to at their reception?"

"One and the same," Tim chuckled. "I've been meaning to talk with you, but don't say anything to Mom right now."

"Mum's the word," Jake assured.

"Clare and I are getting along well, even if we're separated by eight hundred miles," Tim said. "What do you think of her?"

This was a surprising twist to the conversation. He knew next to nothing about Clare other than she was a longtime friend of Liz.

"I don't have enough information to give a realistic answer," he said. "Why would Pauli and Liz want to speak with Clare about starting a family?"

"Well, Clare's a nurse, so I guess Mom and Jill will like her," Tim said. "She works at a fertility clinic, so she's a good source of info about getting pregnant. Liz credits her with inspiring them to get married and become

178

mothers."

Jake sat quietly for a moment to take this bit of information in. Did Kevin know this? How could they use this to their advantage? Maybe they could take Clare out to dinner surreptitiously and recruit her or at least ply her for info. He ate while he thought this through then he jumped on the subject.

"So, Clare would be familiar with the different techniques and interventions used to impregnate women artificially."

"Well, yeah, that's her job," Tim replied.

Jake glanced out at the traffic on Eighteen and thought about how long it would take to get to Newark Liberty. He needed to mine this new vein of precious information before the ladies were around.

"Did the girls talk about how women in their situation choose fathers for their children?"

"They didn't talk with me about that," Tim said. "I overheard more than they told. And Clare tries to use me to encourage them. She seems to think a woman feels most fulfilled when she becomes a mother."

"Yes, but to be a mother you need a father unless you adopt," Jake pointed out the obvious.

"They both want to give birth," Tim said. "That much I know. I can also say they're both very particular about who they would choose. Medical students are good. Guys with no ambition are bad."

"That's reassuring," Jake muttered. "So, would you consider donating to them?"

"What?" Tim asked in astonishment. "How could I donate? I mean, there's a reason all societies have a taboo for marrying your sister."

"Your sister," Jake said. "Not your sister-in-law."

Tim sat quietly assessing what his father had just said. "You mean donate to Liz?"

179

"Think about it," Jake said. "If you donate to Liz and Carl donates to Pauli, then the offspring will be genetically the same. Covey-Moore, Moore-Covey. And we can be reasonably sure they wouldn't have any genetic issues."

Tim sat in shocked silence. "Have you said anything to Pauli?"

"No, not about this. Had to speak with you first," Jake said. "No sense in starting the discussion if you're not willing."

"I'd give it serious consideration," Tim said. "Let me talk with Clare. Is Mr. Moore talking with Carl?"

Listening to what Tim said, the first thing that crossed Jake's mind was why talk to Clare? Granted she was a nurse working at a fertility clinic, but what did that have to do with agreeing to donate sperm for artificial insemination?

"I think we're a little ahead of everyone," Jake confessed. "When you mentioned Clare is working at that clinic, it seemed like an ideal time to raise the subject."

Tim finished his soda while he shook his head in acknowledgement.

His son's mention of Clare piqued Jake's curiosity on another subject besides where she worked. There wasn't a lot of time to discuss it, but he wanted to confirm his impression.

"So, when you visited Chicago to see Pauli," he began. "Did you happen to run into Clare?"

"Dad," Tim chuckled. "The reason I went to visit Pauli was to see Clare."

Jake laughed, stood up, and said, "We better get going. Don't want to be late for your mother's barbequed spareribs."

Chapter Thirty-four

Kevin and Kate walked into the kitchen after dropping their luggage in the guest room. Carl and the girls had stopped with Tim at his place to pick up his luggage. The four of them were staying at the shore rental Tim had reserved back in January. Jake was waiting for Kevin before firing up the grill. The kids would arrive shortly. No one had eaten in four hours, so he anticipated impatient clientele.

"Ready for the obligatory summer father's duty of standing over a hot grill under a blazing sun in humidity so thick you can cut it with a knife?" Jake asked Kevin.

His question earned a sharp response from the ladies.

"Oh, we've been working in a hot kitchen for two days and now you're complaining about flipping hamburgers?" Jo snapped. "Really, Jake."

"Don't worry," Jill chimed in. "Reinforcements are on the way. Mark should be here any minute."

Kevin motioned for Jake to retreat to the outdoors. Jake nodded his head and went for the door.

"Jo left out that they slaved away in central air conditioning," he said after the storm door closed behind them.

"Don't go there, Jake," Kevin warned. "You broke the first rule of marriage. Always validate what your wife says."

Jake chuckled and made his way to the gas grill. After lighting it, he stepped over to a cooler, pulled out two beers, and handed one to Kevin. Realizing that this might be the only time they would be able to converse privately, he decided to bring up his discussion with Tim.

"Have you talked with Carl yet?" he asked.

"You mean about the conspiracy?"

"Conspiracy? Isn't that a bit over the top?"

"What else would you call it?" Kevin asked. "We're conspiring to gain influence over the choice of a father for our grandchildren, right?"

"Okay, maybe you're right, but it's a righteous conspiracy."

Kevin laughed. "You should have been a writer. But back to your question, no, I haven't spoken with Carl yet. Have you spoken with Tim?"

"Just did today," Jake told him. "We kind of stumbled onto the topic. Do you know where Clare works?"

It took Kevin a second to realize to whom Jake was referring.

"You mean Liz's friend Clare?

"Yeah."

"No, I don't," he admitted. "Seem to remember her studying to be a nurse. That's about it."

Jake took a swig of beer and checked how the grill was heating up. Then focused on the conversation again.

"Believe it or not," he said. "Clare is working at a fertility clinic."

"You're kidding me. Wait, wait, I remember now. Her father is an OBGYN. Does he run a fertility clinic? Maybe," Kevin said. "Wow, how can we use that to our advantage?"

"We're already doing that," Jake laughed. "From what Tim said, Clare's the reason the girls got married. Seems she encouraged them to have children and that was the impetus for making their relationship more formal as Pauli put it."

"We have to take that woman out to dinner or something," Kevin laughed.

"Oh, it gets better," Jake assured him. "Keep this under your hat for the moment, but Tim's been seeing her."

Kevin looked shocked. "How? They're a thousand miles apart."

Jake shrugged his shoulders. "Wasn't really explained to me. I'm guessing that Tim's taking advantage of a project he's doing for someone out by you and

182

flying there to check up on it and see her."

Kevin accepted Jake's explanation and moved the conversation back to speaking with Carl.

"Do you think we could have a guys' night out and discuss it with them?" he suggested.

Jake stood quietly considering it. How could we do that? They're going to stay down the shore. It would have to be done down there. But how to persuade the ladies to cut them loose? Then he remembered Kevin's comment about never having gone surf fishing. Could they rent gear and hit the beach to fish early in the morning? Kevin wasn't the only one who had never been surf fishing. It was not like they were going to do anything serious, but he would still have to research it.

"Let me run something passed you," Jake began. "You said you had never been surf fishing. Does Kate go fishing with you?"

Kevin laughed at the thought. "No, it's a guy thing in our family."

"Great! How about we suggest going surf fishing. As long as the girls stick with their previous attitudes, that will give the four of us time away and something to do while we discuss and think it over."

"Sounds like a plan," Kevin responded.

"I just have to do some research," Jake laughed. "I've never been surf fishing either. That's Tim's thing."

They both laughed. The secretive conversation ended just in time. Tim's truck pulled into the drive which caused Jake to reach into a second cooler and bring out the hotdogs and hamburgers. It was time to become a grilling father.

Chapter Thirty-five

"You, okay?" Kevin asked as they hit the deep sand.

"Yeah, why?"

"You're walking funny."

"Oh, that's just my bum knee. Got banged up at a job. Don't mention it to Jo. I'll never hear the end of it. She'll start talking about knee replacement."

"Not a word from me," Kevin pledged. "So, how is Jo really doing?"

They were walking over the fine sand of Long Beach Island toward the ocean. Each was carrying a surf fishing rod borrowed from one of Tim's fishing club buddies. Their other hands were holding one of the handles of a cooler that was suspended between them filled with bait and ice. The sun was just coming up and the sea breeze was cooling, so they wore light jackets. Jake knew by the time they left these would be shed and sunscreen would be applied to their skin. A perfect early summer day to learn how to surf fish. Today Tim would repay for his father teaching him how to ride a bike, swing a bat, shoot hoops, and most importantly, how not to annoy mom.

"Jo?" Jake replied. "She misses her sister tremendously and regrets losing those years after her parents passed. She is finally getting around to seeing a neurologist about possible aneurysms. Next week we go to see the doctor a wife of one of the guys from Six Engine sees. She sees this guy for MS, but a neurologist is a neurologist. They're the ones you see for brain aneurysms."

"Does she have any symptoms?" Kevin asked.

"No, no symptoms, but after seeing what happened to her sister, out of an abundance of caution, she wants to get an MRA done. That's an MRI of the brain's blood vessels. Jane wanted her to do that."

"But Jo was hesitant?"

"She'd never admit that," Jake chuckled. "Let's just say she had to adjust to the idea. It's funny, between what happened to Paul and Jane, Jo now agrees with me. She feels like we're running out of time."

"Well, aren't we?" Kevin asked. "None of us is twenty-five anymore."

"Twenty-five?" Jake chortled. "None of our children are twenty-five anymore."

"You know," Kevin said. "A thought just crossed my mind. Do you think we could use that feeling to help our conspiracy?"

"That's something to think about while we fish," Jake agreed.

Tim and Carl had already staked out an area for them. Their fathers dropped the cooler where Tim had left the tackle box and began preparing their poles for the morning's work. They had agreed that Jake would begin recruiting Carl by acting as a curious father asking about a certain former girlfriend who was now dating his son. That meant Jake had to set up next to Carl.

Tim helped everyone settle in. He had decided yesterday they would use frozen soft bait just off the bottom. That way they could just cast out and leave it. Then Jake could talk to Carl while waiting for the fish to bite. That's what Tim told Jake, anyway. Jake just agreed to whatever his son said. He wasn't really here to fish. That was just a cover for talking with Carl about donating. As planned, Tim set Jake up next to Carl.

Carl cast out and then walked the line back to a beach chair as instructed by Tim. Jake was waiting in a similar chair. Jake let Carl settle in and then said, "From what the ladies told me, you dated Clare for a while."

Carl laughed. "Dated Clare?" he said. "Well, yes and no. We've known each other from childhood. She's one of Liz's oldest friends. I knew it wouldn't work out on the first date. It felt like I was dating my sister. She had the same kind of feeling, so we quickly reverted to friends which Tim seems to appreciate."

"So it appears," Jake laughed. "Have you ever spoken with her about Liz and Pauli?"

185

"What do you mean?" Carl asked. "I mean, whenever I see her, Liz is usually there."

That didn't work, Jake thought, so he switched to a more direct approach. "Clare works at a fertility clinic, doesn't she?"

"Yeah, she does," Carl laughed. "She thinks I'm the perfect candidate for a sperm donor. She says if she could get over the whole brotherly thing, she'd scoop me up in an instant."

Jake laughed, but not so much at the last part of Carl's comment. Clare thinks he's a perfect candidate to be a donor! How sweet is that? He felt giddy, but how to use that to convince him to donate to Pauli? This had to be presented right or it could get complicated.

"Did you ever give it serious consideration?"

"What? Clare's comment about being perfect?"

"Well, not about perfection so much as about donation."

Carl seemed to hesitate, then he turned serious. "I understand her reasoning for saying that. You know, helping infertile couples and all, but I don't know how comfortable I'd feel seeing some stranger's kid who looked like me. You know what I mean? Family resemblances should remain in the family. Clare wouldn't see it that way, but I guess I'm old fashion."

Jake's mind was spinning. Carl didn't feel right donating to strangers because family resemblances should remain in the family. Pauli was now part of the family. A few minutes into this exploratory conversation and he might have a route to Carl becoming the donor they wanted.

"Don't get me wrong," Carl continued. "I think guys who help are heroes, but I wouldn't feel right. I'd feel I should have some sort of relationship with any children I father."

He paused for a second as if thinking about what he just said to be sure it was clear. Then he continued on to a related subject.

"Did Tim tell you that Clare might be coming here tomorrow?"

"No." Jake answered becoming more focused on what Carl said if that were possible.

"Yeah, my girlfriend Marie wants to see the Jersey Shore. She works with Clare and they have a few days off, so Marie is coming and probably Clare too."

Carl's pole began dancing as he finished this announcement.

"Whoa!" he shouted. "I think I've got something."

Tim came over to talk his brother-in-law through the catch. While the younger men were dealing with a fish, Jake moved over to Kevin.

"Did you know that Clare thinks Carl is a perfect candidate for a sperm donor?" he asked.

Kevin looked surprised. "He said that?"

Jake shook his head in the affirmative.

"Did you get to invite him into our conspiracy?" Kevin asked.

"Not yet," Jake said. "The fish hit as I was about to spring it on him."

Tim was coaching Carl so they had a few more minutes if the fish didn't break free.

"Well, what's the plan now?" Kevin asked.

"The two of us request he consider donating," Jake said. "Oh, and if we need a little more help, it seems Clare might be coming tomorrow with Marie."

"Marie?" Kevin asked. "Who's Marie?"

"Carl's girlfriend."

"Really?"

"That's what Carl said," Jake continued. "One other thing, seems Carl rejected Clare's suggestion about donating because he feels he should be involved in the life of any child he fathers."

"Well, that's not an issue now, is it?

"Shouldn't be," Jake agreed. "You'll love his reasoning. He said that family resemblances should remain in the family. That sits perfectly with our Covey-Moore, Moore-Covey justification."

"That's how we should approach it then," Kevin said. "Now you're going to have to get to your pole because some fish is on it."

Jake looked up, saw his pole was bent, and dashed over to handle it.

"I think we should shuffle positions," Kevin suggested. "The two of you got a fish, now Tim and I should get a shot at the hot spots."

Jake jumped at the suggestion, adding a condition of his own to move the conspiracy along.

"Great idea," he said "Why don't you and Tim take over our poles and we'll take care of yours. Just not right away. Since Tim has to set up these two so we can get them back in the water."

"Well, you and Carl just take these two and I'll help Tim set up," Kevin said.

Jake had hoped Kevin would have caught on, but his meaning was too ambiguous. Hit him between the eyes with it, Jake thought.

"Nah, I want to watch how Tim does it in case surf fishing gets under my skin," Jake began. "Setting up surf poles might be a useful skill for me. Why don't you and Carl take over those two right now. You can have a good father son talk while we set up over here."

A light went off in Kevin's head.

"You know, that makes all the sense in the world, I'll speak with Carl about it."

With that the two conspirators split. Jake to help Tim. Kevin to persuade Carl.

Chapter Thirty-six

As they entered the professional building, Jo noticed a poster in the lobby announcing a fund raiser for the North Jersey MS society. The featured speaker was Kathy Stanley. On the bottom of the poster was a small line directing any inquiries to Dr. Ambs office, Suite 203.

Jake was looking at the board listing doctors' offices, too busy to notice the announcement.

"He's in Suite 203," Jo said.

"Now how do you know that?" Jake asked, not bothering to turn around.

"It says so on the poster."

"Poster?" Jake said as he turned around to face her. "Oh, that poster. Kathy's going to be speaking at a fund raiser and the doctor we're going to see is somehow involved. Is that good, bad, or indifferent?"

"Could be good," Jo guessed. "He treats Li Carney and he knows Kathy. Two fire department connections. Maybe he'll give us a fireman's discount."

Jake laughed, happy that Jo was finding some humor in seeing a neurologist. They walked over to the elevator and pressed the up button. The door opened immediately, so they stepped into the car, pushed the button for the second level, and waited quietly as the machine did its job. When they entered Suite 203, Jo went to find seats while Jake went to get the obligatory forms necessary for medical attention in modern America.

After completing the requisite forms, Jake returned them to the receptionist. "Forms completed," he announced.

"I just have to make a copy of your insurance card," she said.

After finishing all the required tasks that go with a visit to a modern doctor's office, he walked back to Jo and dropped into the seat next to her.

"So, Chuck Carney knows this guy?" Jo asked.

"Yes," he answered for the third time that morning. "His wife sees him for her MS."

"Really? Isn't their daughter the basketball phenom?" she asked.

"Yeah," Jake chuckled. "I seem to remember Chief Brendler donating a chunk of cash to the MS society after she won a foul shooting contest."

"You know a lot of connections come out of that little firehouse."

"It's a special place," Jake reminded her.

"Only a fireman could think that," Jo chuckled.

Jake could sense his wife's effort at being calm. Live with a woman for a few decades and you get to know her inside and out. He realized Jo was nervous, but didn't know how to calm her down. One thing he had learned over the years was even if he had no solution, he had to at least acknowledge her feelings.

"How nervous are you?" he began.

"How nervous?" she sighed. "More than a little."

"So am I," Jake admitted.

Jo turned silent again. The waiting dragged on. Patients were called in to see the doctor. By Jake's count there were two people ahead of them. Jo was fidgeting, flipping through magazines, and sighing a lot. She was building up to something. He knew all he had to do was wait.

"What do we leave behind?" Jo finally asked with tears in her eyes. "We strive to raise a family, to teach our children to do what is right, to help others, and all that malarky, but once we're gone, what remains?"

Jake listened quietly, knowing not to contest her interpretation. It all sounded familiar. Didn't he and Kevin have this conversation not too long ago? He decided to repeat their conclusion.

"We leave behind our children. Two intelligent, caring human beings who can contribute positively to society," he began. Then he quickly decided to add the other half of his and Kevin's conclusion. Even if it made him feel a little

190

guilty for bring up the goals of their conspiracy.

"And if we're lucky, our children will have children who will be raised the same way, to make the world a better place."

Jo looked at him with a wry smile and laughed. A tear escaped her right eye. He reached up and brushed it away.

"Chuck says this guy knows what he's doing," he reassured her. "We'll have answers to all of our questions soon. It will all work out."

"What will?" Jo asked. "The grandkids or my health?"

"First things first, my dear," he answered.

The receptionist called Jo's name, so they stood up and walked towards the inner sanction of the office.

When they stepped into Doctor Ambs' office, there were two chairs in front of his desk. The doctor motioned for them to take a seat. As they sat down, Jake shot a question at the doctor to break the tension.

"Doc, do you know Kathy Stanley?"

At first the doctor looked questioning, but then seemed to make the connection. "Oh, you're referring to the announcement in the lobby," he began. "I've met her at assorted affairs for the MS society, but I think I spoke more with her husband than with her. Why do you ask?"

"You spoke with Chief Brendler?" Jake asked. "Then you know he has MS."

"Chief Brendler? Is that her husband's name?" the doctor asked. "But no. I didn't know he has MS. He is doing quite well from his appearance. I have to confess they were very casual conversations. And I'm not known for being a suave conversationalist. Why do you call him chief?"

"He's a retired Newark Fire Department Deputy Chief."

"Is he? It's a small world," the doctor said and then immediately pivoted to the matter at hand. "So, what can I do for you today?"

191

"I have concerns," Jo began. "My sister died suddenly from a brain aneurysm. She had come to see me to talk about it shortly before that happened. She was worried it might be genetic."

"And you hadn't spoken about it before then?" Doctor Ambs asked.

"We were . . .," Jo started to answer, the paused. "We weren't speaking with each other for a few years before that."

"How old was she?"

"Sixty-eight,"

"How about your parents?" he asked. "How did they pass away?"

"My father slowly deteriorated," Jo answered thoughtfully. "The cause of death listed on the death certificate was congenital heart failure."

"And your mother?"

"She suffered a stroke at eighty-two."

Jake could tell the conversation was upsetting her, but realized the questions were necessary. They were on the forms he had just handed the front desk. Apparently, the information had not been entered into the system, so didn't show up on the doctor's tablet.

"Do you know what kind of stroke?"

"What kind of?" Jo asked.

"Was it a blockage?"

Jo paused and got herself centered, then answered. "It was an avulsion not an occlusion."

"You sound like you have a medical background," the doctor chuckled. "I usually ask for a short bio, but you seemed so focused on your concerns. So, how about you tell me about yourself."

Jo smiled at the invitation. "Johanna Covey, doctor. You can call me Jo," she began. "This is my husband, Jake. I'm a retired ER nurse and he's a retire Newark Firefighter."

"Newark firefighter?" the doctor reacted. "Do you know Chuck Carney?"

Jo laughed at the question.

"He recommended you," Jake answered.

Doctor Ambs' smile turned a little more relaxed and natural. "Any kids?"

"Two," Jo replied. "Our daughter is an editor in Chicago and our son is an architect still in Jersey."

"Okay, back to the reason for your visit today. You're concerned because of your sister's death. Do you have any symptoms?"

"No."

"And you came because you want an MRA of your brain's plumbing," he said.

"Yes," Jo smiled. "That was what my sister wanted. It's why she came to talk to me after all those years of estrangement."

Bringing the subject of her relationship with Jane up again seemed to cause a change in the doctor's demeanor.

"Can I ask you something?"

"Ask away," Jo replied.

"Did your sister pass away in January?"

Jo appeared to be taken aback. "Yes."

"Do you know her doctor's name?"

"Doctor DeAngelo."

"He's a colleague of mine. I'm familiar with your sister's case."

This brought Jo up short. Jake had been letting the scene play out, but the doctor's last statement had thrown Jo off.

"You're familiar with the case?" Jake asked. "In what way?"

"Doctor DeAngelo was bothered by the way it played out," he explained. "He had a patient whose MRA showed a very large brain aneurysm that needed immediate attention, but the patient put it off until after her niece's wedding. She

193

planned to speak with her sister there about a possible genetic link since her mother had died from a burst aneurysm in her brain. Days before the operation, this woman had a dispute with her former husband. The stress was too much and the aneurysm burst."

"She was still married to him," Jo said. "But she had a restraining order. Does knowing that change anything?"

"Maybe removes a step or two," Doctor Ambs replied. "Here's what I want you to do, get an MRA. My staff will arrange for one today if you can do it. After we get the results, we'll be able to talk. At the moment, all we have to go on is family history. That's not enough to schedule brain surgery."

Jake sat absolutely still, trying to process what he had heard. Of course, if Jo had an aneurysm brain surgery was the only way to correct it, but the whole process had suddenly accelerated.

The doctor recorded his findings into a handheld device and sent them on their way with words of encouragement. After arranging a mid-afternoon MRA appointment, the two of them went to the car quietly. Jake knew when they got home everything would come out. He prepared himself on the drive for what was sure to be a challenging couple of hours. The conspiracy now seemed trivial.

Chapter Thirty-seven

"What just happened?" Jo asked after they stepped into the kitchen.

"As far as I'm concerned," Jake said slowly, choosing his words carefully. "We got the inside track on finding out if our worries have any basis in fact."

Jo looked at him hard, then turned away. This is not good, Jake thought. Unsure where his wife was going, he waited patiently for her to continue.

"She gave her life for me," Jo said in a whisper. "She delayed her operation so she could warn me." The tears began to flow freely.

Jake gently pulled her to him, now knowing how to comfort her.

"Jo," he started. "Jane made a rational decision to warn you, but had no intention of sacrificing her life. You are not responsible. If anyone is responsible, it's Gary, but even with the restraining order, he hasn't been charged. Jane died a natural death. She would never want you to feel responsible for her decision."

His wife seemed to accept his analysis and calmed down.

"I want to get hold of Pete," Jo said after she recovered. "Just to confirm all our papers are up to date."

Jake didn't like the sound of her request. They had no test results. Why was now any different than last week?

"How about I make lunch," he countered. "We have time before the test. Let's eat and then go through the possibilities that Doctor Ambs didn't bother with."

"You can make lunch, but I still want to talk to Pete," Jo said. "It's been a few years since we last visited our wills. We're not getting any younger. I'll feel better if I need an operation."

It was ironic hearing her say that. They had discussed talking about their will on the plane coming back from Chicago, but had never gotten around to it. Now he didn't want to talk about it.

"No more talk about operations," Jake said while thinking of a way to distract her.

"Have you spoken with Pauli about their plans for the future?"

"You're just trying to distract me," Jo said then gave him a peck on the cheek. "Thank you. And yes, I have talked with Pauli about their plans."

Jake waited for more information, but none appeared to be coming. He went to the refrigerator and took out cold cuts, then got a couple of plates and began building sandwiches with the bread on the counter.

"So, what did you think of my take on what we leave behind?" he asked.

"Ha," Jo responded. "From what you said, we have no control over what that is."

As soon as Jake heard this, he knew it was the perfect opportunity to introduce her to the goals of the conspiracy.

"Maybe we have more to say about it than you think."

Jo looked at him like he was crazy.

"What are you talking about?"

Jake carried the plates with their sandwiches to the kitchen table and went back to the refrigerator for drinks. All the while considering how to present his proposal.

"You said you've spoken with Pauli about their future," Jake started. "What aspect of it did you discuss?"

At first, Jo seemed reluctant to say, but then relented. "Pauli said they want to start a family soon. Unfortunately for us, Liz would get first crack at it since she's older. The whole biological clock thing, you know."

"Did they say how they'd choose the fathers?" Jake asked expectantly. This would be the conspiracy's first insight into the thinking of the future mothers.

"That's one of the particulars they haven't worked out yet," Jo admitted.

"How would you feel about having some input into that choice?"

She paused to consider the question. Obviously, it would be a tempting proposition for any grandparent. Jake saw Jo was struggling with the idea.

"I don't know, Jake," she said slowly. "That's about as personal a decision as any a woman can make."

Feeling relieved the idea wasn't rejected outright, Jake waded in. "We wouldn't be making the decision for them," he pointed out. "Just looking to give input. Lobbying or suggesting a father."

This pushed Jo close to the edge, but not over it. "Lobby for a father?" she asked. "My parents never had a say in who the father of my children would be."

Jake jumped on this idea. If he changed her thought process to remind her that what he was proposing has been done indirectly all along, then he could win her over.

"Whoa, whoa, whoa," Jake shouted. "Run that by me again. You mean if I had been a drunken vagabond, your parents would have been okay with you marrying me?"

"That's choosing a husband not a father."

"Wrong," Jake insisted. "Choosing a husband is choosing a father."

Jo offered no resistance to that idea. Instead, she sat at the table and picked up the sandwich he had made for her. That's a good sign, Jake thought. If she can eat, then she was calming down. His distraction therapy was working. After a bite of her sandwich and a minute to think, his skeptical, sarcastic wife returned.

"Do you have someone in mind?" she laughed. "Are you going to interview every medical student and doctoral candidate? Or maybe take out an ad in the paper or on the internet looking for CPAs. Might as well tour all the firehouses in Newark and Chicago. I'm sure there are some strong, handsome young bucks there. Wanted sperm donor to father exceptional children. Really, Jake. What are you going to say to Kevin and Kate? Don't worry, I've got this?"

Therapy session complete, he thought. Her focus had been shifted from the

MRA so thoroughly that her sarcastic-self had taken over. He didn't respond to her question, just reached into his pocket, took out his phone, pulled up a picture of Tim and Carl with a fish, and showed it to her.

"What?" Jo asked in shock. "That's . . . that's . . ."

"It's not incest if that's your first thought," Jake pointed out.

After a little consideration, Jo slowed down and answered thoughtfully.

"No, you're right," she admitted. "As long as Carl donates to Pauli and Tim to Liz."

With that acceptance, Jake moved onto another level of revelation about the conspiracy.

"Clare says Carl would be the perfect sperm donor."

"Clare? Who's Clare?" Jo asked.

"The girl Tim was talking up at Pauli's wedding."

"And how would she know?"

"She's a nurse," Jake revealed. "Works at a fertility clinic. You might meet her on the Fourth at Mark's."

Jo absorbed the new information without asking any more questions. Instead, she began a practical analysis.

"The boys would have to agree," she said.

Jake suppressed a grin. He never imagined it would go so smoothly.

"Carl had some reservations about keeping family resemblances in the family, but then Kevin pointed out that's what he would be doing."

"Carl, Kevin, Clare?" she asked. "Who's in on this? I haven't heard Pauli or Liz."

MRA worries were now forgotten. Replaced by a negotiation even if Jo didn't realize it yet.

"First we get all our ducks in a row," Jake pointed out. "Then we suggest."

"Lobby," Jo insisted

"Lobby," Jake agreed.

"I have to think about this," Jo said.

Jake knew his chance of prevailing were really good. He relented instead of pushing further.

"Give it some thought," he suggested. "Remember, instead of the biological crap shoot of romance, this can be a rational decision. And any children would be blood relatives. It would be a Covey-Moore, Moore-Covey family. They'll all look alike and think alike."

Jo looked at him, sighed and said, "Thank you. You got me through a tough hour or so."

"Babe, you don't have any symptoms like Jane," he reassured her. "We'll get you tested and, in a day or two they'll give us the all clear."

"You always were the optimist among the two of us," Jo chuckled. "So, does Kate know about your little scheme? She didn't say anything to me."

"I don't know for sure," he answered. "Kevin is in charge of that part. We recruited the guys over the past few days. Don't count Clare in. She doesn't know yet. Just said that to Carl while discussing her job on a date."

"On a date?" Jo asked.

"Yeah, he dated her once, but she's one of Liz's best friends and he's known her for so long he said it was like dating his sister. Oh, and when you meet her, you can thank her for inspiring the girls to marry and start a family."

"Really?" Jo asked. "A nurse, Liz's close friend, and she inspired their marriage. What else can you tell me? Anything about Tim maybe?"

"You should speak with Tim," Jake pleaded. "I'm not authorized to discuss it."

Jo gave a knowing chuckle and stood up. "Shouldn't we be going? We have a test to do and then I have to begin prepping for tomorrow. Today is the Third after all. I have potato salad and coleslaw to make."

199

When Jake stood up, his legs felt wobbly, like he had just bailed out of a building right before it flashed over.

Chapter Thirty-eight

The sky was blue with only a stray cloud floating by. The temperature was warm. The humidity could be felt, but it wasn't suffocating. It was a perfect day to celebrate the founding of the nation. Jake eased the car into the exit lane for the Turnpike. They were headed for revolutionary Morris County and Mark's home for their annual Fourth of July barbeque celebration. How many years has it been since Pauli attended? Graduate school and then the move to Chicago had left her too far away for a one-day holiday. Just another reason why this July Fourth was special, Jake thought.

"Did you remind the kids to get there before the cannon?" Jo asked.

"Yes, I did," Jake replied. "But I don't have a lot of confidence the shore crowd is going to make the trek before it goes off."

"What do you mean by the cannon?" Kate asked.

"When the parade starts, they set off a small brass cannon to let everybody in town know the parade has started," Jo informed her.

Kevin and Kate were sitting in the back seat recovering from a jaunt into New York yesterday. By the time they returned last night they were experiencing what Jake called the "Apple drains". Even though the mass transit system dropped you in the area of whatever it was you wanted to visit, you still had to walk a lot. Tourists striving to get the most out of their visit tended to overdo it. Whether it was Times Square or the Museum Mile, the people, sights, and attractions all took their toll, draining you of all your energy.

It took at least a day to recover and that was when you're young. Kevin and Kate were well beyond that energetic time of their lives. Kate was so exhausted Jo hadn't had a chance to tell her about their medical adventure on the Third before they set out on the Fourth. Neither he nor Jo expected a lot of conversation coming from the back seat.

"Okay, signal cannon," was all Kate could muster.

Looking in the rearview mirror, Jake could see Kevin was sleeping peacefully. It would be a quiet ride up Route 287 to Florham Park.

"Who did Mark say was coming," Jane asked quietly.

Jake passed through the tool gate before replying. "He's expecting Mark junior, Terry, and their little ones, Brian's working today so no Brian, then there will be Chief Brendler, the four of us, and the shore crowd, so that's seventeen there."

"Kathy's not coming with the Chief?"

"I don't know. Mark didn't say," Jack admitted. "It will be overwhelming enough for the Chicago folk."

After that they settled in for the hour-long drive to northwest New Jersey.

Jake turned onto Ridgedale Avenue just ahead of the police closing the road. A few minutes later, he pulled into Mark's drive and was surprised to see Tim's truck. It must have been a tight squeeze with six adults in that club cab, Jake thought. He parked the car and shut down the ignition before waking Kevin and Kate.

"We're here folks," Jake announced.

The sound of a cannon could be heard in the distance as they climbed out of the car. Jake went to the trunk with Kevin and grabbed the folding beach chairs they brought with them. Jake led Kevin to the edge of the lawn and placed the chairs among a forest of others. The parade wouldn't be here for half an hour, but chair space today was as precious as an on-street parking space Down Neck. Their task completed; the two men followed after their wives who had taken bowls of potato salad and coleslaw into the house.

They stepped into controlled chaos. Jill and her daughter-in-law Terry were working at the kitchen stove with Jo and Kate looking to help. Terry's terrors as Mark affectionately called his two grandsons were running around with tri-

202

cornered hats and toy muskets.

"Boys," Terry called. "Why don't you go outside to see if the parade is here?"

The two dashed out the side door to recon the parade. They knew some of the marchers would have real black powder muskets that they would discharge while they marched. It would be the highlight of the little guys' day.

"Jake," Jill called from her position at the stove. "Mark's out back waiting for you to set up."

"Okay, Jill," Jake called. "We're responding."

Jake felt so bad for Kevin. He had been sound asleep when they arrived. Then there was a shout, a dash to the trunk, a quick set up of chairs, and entering a high energy environment. All within a couple of minutes. Kind of like the firehouse. Jake chuckled at the thought.

"It's been a while since you did that instantaneous transition from sleep to work," Jake said as they walked out the side door.

"Yeah, not since I retired," Kevin laughed. "You never lose the ability, do you? It just gets harder as you get older."

"Amen," Jake agreed. "You can still do it, but you just can't bounce back like you used to. Jo noticed it the last few years on the job. That's why she demanded I retire." They climbed down the stairs and headed for the backyard.

"Sounds familiar," Kevin chuckled. "You would think they would be used to it and leave you alone."

"Right," Jake laughed as they rounded the corner of the house. "How did the Chief put it? Women worry about what is possible. Men worry about what is probable."

Kevin laughed. "The Chief is a fountain of wisdom," he said. "That's why they demanded we retire. They figured we're running out of luck, so we shouldn't push it."

"What happened to Mark only convinced Jo more that she was right."

"Yeah, that's a hard way to end a thirty-five-year career," Kevin said.

The subject of the comments was setting up by the backyard grill. The Chief was standing next to him and his son was in a circle of young adults, coffee in hand, being introduced by Tim and Pauli.

When they reached the Chief and Mark, Jake grabbed hands and threw hugs around the two men. Kevin smiled and exchanged handshakes. Mark offered beers all around and the four began the usual firehouse chatter.

"We used to grill in the firehouse all the time," Mark told Kevin. "The grill in Six Engine was in the hose-well."

"In the hose-well?" Kevin laughed.

"It wasn't always there," the Chief assured him. "There was a time before our time when they actually hung hose there."

"Before the Dacron hose we have now," Jake said. "We did hang hose occasionally when a length had to be sent down to the hose shop for repair. We'd dry it out first, then send it down."

"Sometimes it smelled like hamburgers," Mark laughed. "Sometimes like barbequed ribs. Ah, them's was the days."

The four laughed loudly which drew the attention of the young adults drinking coffee.

Tim looked up and then leaned over to Clare. She shook her head yes with a broad smile. At that the two of them left the group and came over to Jake and Kevin.

"Hello, Mr. Moore," Clare said. This produced a chuckle from Jake and a quick request from Kevin.

"Clare, you don't have to call me Mr. Moore," he almost pleaded. "You're an adult now, just call me Kevin."

Clare laughed. "I'll try, but that's going to take some getting used to."

"That's a problem a lot of firemen face," Jake told them. "You come on the job and find you're working with your schoolmates' fathers. Don't call them mister, whatever you do. They won't hear the end of it for a week. The entire crew will call them mister. Firefighters can be brutal."

Clare laughed and turned a bit red.

"Now you went and embarrassed her, Jake," Kevin laughed. "Ignore him Clare, he's harmless."

"I don't know how harmless he could be," she countered. "He looks a lot like that rouge hero you were hanging around with in May."

"Touché," Jake laughed. "I think we're going to get along just fine Clare, but we haven't been properly introduced yet have we?"

Tim jumped right in. "You didn't give me a chance, Dad. Clare Donahue, this is my father, Jake Covey. Dad, meet Clare Donahue an old friend of Liz's."

"Old friend?" Clare shot back. "A lifelong friend maybe, but not that old yet, still young and energetic."

Jake instantly liked her spunk. She'd do well in the firehouse. Maybe Tim was onto something here. Time would tell. Would Jo appreciate spunk? The woman was a nurse, so Jo and Jill might make a connection there. How to get her aside for a friendly conversation and recruitment talk?

"Your mother is in the kitchen," Jake told Tim. "We had that test done yesterday. Results tomorrow hopefully. I'm sure she'd love to hear how the nursing profession is faring since she retired."

Clare reacted with a look of concern to the test statement. Then the nursing statement seemed to animate her.

"What type of test did she have done?" Clare asked.

"An MRA," Jake replied, happy she had asked. It was good information for her to have when meeting her boyfriend's mother.

"An MRA?" the Chief reacted. "She got through it okay?"

"Yeah, Chief, no complaints about being inside the beast," Jake said.

"They can be tough," the Chief said. "I know guys who were in collapses and can't do a closed MRI."

"Guilty as charged," Jake admitted. "Only open MRIs for this old firefighter."

This produced some light laughter before Clare brought the conversation back to center.

"Does she have symptoms or is this because of her sister?" she asked.

Jake was more impressed with each question Clare put to him. Not just a nurse, but a smart nurse. Jo would approve.

"Just a precaution," Jake reassured. "No symptoms. I'm optimistic, but that's a fault in my wife's eyes sometimes."

They all laughed. Then Tim led Clare into the house.

Chapter Thirty-nine

Jake was preparing to perform his share of the grill service. The parade was marching past the house, but he was never one for parades. So, he volunteered to be the lead off griller, allowing Mark to enjoy the parade with his grandsons. He was the only one in the backyard at the moment. The grill was heating up. He had a cold beer next to the tools of a griller's trade. The sun was bright, but the grill was in the shade. Life was alright for the time being.

As he bent down to check the coolers holding the burgers and hotdogs, he saw Clare walking toward him. No Tim, just Clare. His admiration for her rose even more.

"Want a beer?" he asked when she stepped into shouting distance.

"Thanks, that sounds great," she replied.

Jake reached into another cooler and pulled out a bottle of beer. He twisted off the cap and held it out to her.

"Why, thank you Mr. Covey," she said.

"No, no," Jake laughed. "Not Mr. Covey. I'm just Jake. No need for formalities here. Did my wife say how she wanted to be addressed?"

"Oh, Jo and Jill were very welcoming," Clare announced, then moved onto why she had left the parade so early. "Tim thought I should talk with you about my job. Funny thing is Jo said the same thing."

There was a boom from the front as she finished. Jake knew the Revolutionary War re-enactors must be passing the house. Mark's grandsons should be thrilled.

"Perfect timing Clare," he said. "The booms mean the parade is just past the halfway point. We should have time to talk before I turn into a short order cook."

Clare smiled, took a deep breath and said, "First I want you to know how much I admire your reaction to Pauli's relationship. I don't know if my parents would be so accepting."

This caught Jake off guard. How to respond to something like that? All he could do was fall back on the truth.

"I don't know if I deserve your admiration," he said. "The only way to really understand how I could accept Pauli's relationship is to have a child of your own. It's a different kind of love than all the others I've experienced. As far as I'm concerned, there is no other option than acceptance."

"My father would have a hard time," Clare told him.

"Is your father a preacher or something?" Jake asked before remembering Kevin's comment about Clare's father being an OBGYN who might run a fertility clinic.

"No, he's a doctor. Actually, he runs the clinic where I work. He has a tremendous amount of respect for parenthood. Lesbians need help conceiving for obvious reasons. Which is anathema to him. As he sees it, the gift of life is inside them, but it can't be released without a man and they don't find men attractive."

When Jake heard this, his heart sank. He thought Clare would be his ace in the hole. When she confirmed her old man ran a fertility clinic, he wanted to shout halleluiah. Then she inserted a caveat. But when he thought further, it seemed there was a contradiction in what Clare said.

"He runs a fertility clinic, but opposes women without male partners having children?"

"Well, it's more like they don't appreciate the gift and he thinks every child deserves a father, a man in their life."

To Jake, that sounded like there was hope. Since the brothers would be the fathers, they would be involved as uncles in the children's lives.

"So, his problem is more with donor fathers not being involved in the lives of their children when the mother doesn't have a man in her life?"

"Yeah, he does artificial insemination all the time for couples who can't conceive naturally. Refuses to work with single women without a man handy to act as a father figure."

Jake did a quick, but thorough analysis and decided to continue with the recruitment. Liz and Pauli satisfied her father's criteria and so probably satisfied hers also.

"I understand you deserve a thank you for Liz and Pauli marrying."

"You're giving me too much credit."

"Not really, you pushed them off square one. Do you think they will talk with your father about children?"

"They already have. It's hard for him, he has that rule about male involvement. But he's known Liz all her life. He trusts she'll be a good mother. Maybe since she has Carl, who will be an uncle and male role model, he'll be okay with it. They haven't gotten that far yet."

"Is it true you told Carl he'd be a perfect sperm donor?"

Clare giggled and blushed. "I don't believe I'm having this type of conversation with you," she said. "Yes, I said that to him, but it was a comment on his health more than anything."

Jake shook his head in understanding.

"No need to be embarrassed," he told her. "An old man like me understands. I didn't think you said it because he was cute."

"You're not that old," she said.

Jake chuckled at her assertion, knowing she was trying to be polite.

"Firefighters age faster than average and become irrelevant even quicker."

"Irrelevant?"

"You don't want someone like me climbing a ladder to get you out of a burning building. To paraphrase the old saying, "Old firemen never die, they simply fade away."

"I don't think you're going to fade away," Clare protested. "There's something to be said for experience, don't you think?"

Jake had heard that argument before. The State Legislature had allowed for early retirement of firefighters and cops for a reason. That reason was simply safety, the public's safety. Deciding the conversation had drifted too far from the topic he wanted to discuss, he shifted gears.

"That only goes so far," he chuckled. "But back to the subject of Carl's health and him being a perfect donor, would you say he would be perfect for Pauli?"

"If you could talk him into it," Clare said. "Yes, perfect for Pauli, but he won't be interested."

Jake now knew he had this in the bag. "He's not interested in donating to strangers," Jake told her. "We had a discussion on his reasoning and it turns out, since Pauli is his sister-in-law, she's family and so he would be happy to do it."

Clare looked surprised. "You already spoke with Carl about it?" she asked.

"Yes, we have," Jake said. "What would you think of Tim as a donor for Liz?"

She stood speechless for a minute, the sound of the parade filling in the void.

"Carl for Pauli and Tim for Liz?" she said softly. "Then the children would be . . . "

"Cousins, but would have the same DNA mix, Covey-Moore, Moore Covey," Jake said.

"Yes, you're right," Clare agreed. "Cousins but more like siblings."

"Could you keep our little chat on the QT? I guess your generation would say on the down low."

"Yes, on the down low," Clare laughed. "What about it should I keep quiet?"

Jake noticed the sounds of the parade were fading. They were running out of private time.

"Just if the subject comes up between you and Pauli or Liz, don't mention we discussed it," Jake requested. "But please point out the advantages."

"And what do you feel are the advantages?"

"We know the genetic history of the fathers, any offspring will be related, and the father of each will be the uncle of the other, so they'll be father figures."

"Have you spoken with Liz or Pauli yet?"

"Not yet," Jake confessed. "First get all the details worked out so any questions can be answered, then we present our proposal for their consideration."

"You have my word not to mention it," Clare said, "And my prayer they accept. That would form a wonderful and loving family."

Terry's terrors came running from the parade, shouting their orders for hamburgers at Jake. He threw some burgers on the grill, content with the morning's work.

Chapter Forty

The phone ringing startled Jake out of a deep sleep. At first, he ignored it, confident Jo would pick up the handset by her exercise bike. When it rang a second time, he opened his eyes and was shocked to find Jo still next to him. The thought crossed his mind that she was avoiding exercise to prevent a stroke. That would be a major change and not a good one. He reached over and picked up the phone before the third ring.

"Hello," he said in a half-awake tone.

"Good morning," a young female voice greeted him. "This is Dr. Ambs' office. May I speak with Johanna?"

Jake was instantly alert. It was like an alarm over the old bell system in the firehouse. Bells were ignored until you realized you respond on the alarm. Then they commanded your complete focus.

"I'll get her for you," he said, then covered the mouth piece, reached over, and shook his wife. "Jo, it's Ambs' office."

This jolted her out of sleep. She quickly stood up and walked around the bed to take the phone from her husband. Jake put the phone on speaker and handed it to her. This was a conversation he needed to hear.

"Hello," Jo said.

"Good morning, Mrs. Covey," the young voice began. "Dr. Ambs would like to see you in his office today if at all possible."

"But we don't have an appointment until later this week," Jo said still groggy from the sudden awakening.

"Yes, I realize that, but he thinks it would be best to see you today."

Jo was so obviously shaken, that Jake simply reached up and gently took the phone from her.

"What time does the doctor want us there?" he asked.

"I'm sorry Mr. Covey, but I need your wife's permission before I can speak with you."

"We filled out the Hipaa form," Jake insisted. He could see his wife was in a downward spiral and didn't need a twenty-something telling him about the rules.

"It isn't in the system yet."

Before he could continue his argument with a computer, Jo called out, "Yes, yes, you can talk to him."

"Dr. Ambs said any time you can make it would be fine," the twenty-something voice said. "He just wants to see you ASAP."

"Do you have any appointments available?" Jake asked.

"No, there are no appointments available today, so you can just come in whenever you can make it."

"I understand," Jake said. "We'll be there as soon as we can."

"That's in the East Brunswick office," the voice reminded them.

"We'll see you in the East Brunswick office shortly," Jake said.

Jo was crying before he hung up the phone. "This is not good Jake," she said. "Not good at all."

He climbed out of bed and went over to her. "Slow down," he said. "We'll go in and see what he has to say. Then we'll panic together."

She laughed through her tears. "Firemen don't panic," she reminded him. "You always said panic kills."

"Then we'll make calculated decisions together," he said while giving her a hug. "This guy isn't an oncologist. Whatever they found, they can fix."

She looked at him, eyes full of tears and said, "You're optimistic to a fault."

"It's a trait that was valued in my profession."

They arrived at Dr. Ambs office to a full waiting room, but when Jake stepped up to the receptionist, he was told they would be next. Their wait was less than ten minutes.

"Johanna, Jake, please sit down," the doctor greeted. "I have the results of the MRA right here."

Jake sat in amazement as the doctor picked up the results and seemed to peruse them. Common sense said if they were rushed in ahead of a full waiting room, the doctor had read the results and knew they were bad.

"So, the MRA shows some abnormalities in the arteries of the cerebral cortex," he began. "Specifically, there are two aneurysms. Both are operable, but one could be a little tricky. I'd like you to see Dr. Dunn, he's a neurosurgeon up at UMDNJ in Newark."

Jake couldn't believe what he was hearing. This guy had it all figured out. Only problem was Jo hadn't consented to even seeing a neurosurgeon, let alone allowing one into her brain. He looked at his wife. She appeared to be shellshocked. All of her fears had been realized. He knew from her moods and actions over the past few days, that she had been preparing herself for this news. They were about to find out how well prepared she was.

"Dr. Dunn?" she asked. "The elder or the younger?"

"The son is the neurosurgeon," Dr. Ambs replied. "Do you know them?"

"I worked at UMDNJ for over twenty years, doctor," Jo answered. "So, yes, I know of them, but I was in the ER, so I've never met either one. Chief Brendler knows the elder Dr. Dunn. The Chief has MS and that's Dr. Dunn the elder's specialty."

"Yes, I remember you talking about the Chief," Dr. Ambs said, apparently letting Jo direct the conversation as she adjusted.

"I can call and arrange a consultation immediately if you want," the doctor said.

"How urgent is this doctor?" Jo asked.

Jake sat quietly listening, admiring how his wife was handling the news. Would he have been so calm?

214

"I'm not going to lie to you Jo," Dr. Ambs said. "You don't have symptoms, so that's a plus, but if one of those were to rupture, it would be catastrophic. The sooner it's addressed, the better."

"Then please reach out to Dr. Dunn," Jo requested. "I have a life to live, I don't need the anxiety."

Jake was floored. When was Johanna Covey ever so decisive? There were always questions, always worries before making a decision that mattered. His wife could overthink which brand of bottled water she should select at a picnic. Now she was opening her brain to a stranger without so much as a Google search.

By the time they left Dr. Ambs office, they had an appointment for a consultation with Dr, Dunn at three o'clock. That meant they had to leave at one-thirty. It was ten o'clock. He wanted to ask about their options for the day, but didn't dare. She had to set the tone. So, they walked to the car in silence. The dam didn't break until he started the car. He immediately shut the engine down and reached out to his wife. She leaned toward him over the console between the front seats, placed her head on his shoulder, and wept. All he could say was, "I love you, babe. We'll get through this together."

"Are we running out of time, Jake?" she asked through her tears. "I want to have my own little terrors who I can love and watch run around."

"You will, Jo. You will."

Chapter Forty-one

"We'll meet you at the hospital," Jill said. "You're going to need a woman's support. These guys just won't cut it."

"You're on speaker phone, Jill," Jake shouted.

"And?" she snapped back. "I only speak the truth. See you at the hospital in about an hour."

Jake hung up the phone and turned to Jo. What do you say to the woman you love after she's been told she needs brain surgery?

"When we left the doctor's office, you asked me if we're running out of time," he began. "I confess that I've had that feeling for a while now, but not in this context. My concern was always time to be relevant. Now that means nothing. I don't want to face life without you. Whatever I have to do to get you through this I'm going to do."

After his pronouncement, Jake walked over to his wife and wrapped his arms around her. She hugged him tightly and said, "I'm scared, Jake. Scared of dying, scared of being a cripple, scared of losing my mind. It's my brain, Jake. There's so much that can go wrong."

"I'm scared too, babe," Jake whispered. "You make life worth living. I don't know if my body and mind can make it without you. We'll fight the way we have for the last forty years. We'll see our little terrors running around."

They stood quietly for a minute, clinging to each other as their world stood still. No longer young, no longer healthy, but relevant to each other.

"Okay," Jo proclaimed. "Enough of feeling sorry for ourselves. If we're going to fight this, we have to get up to Newark by two-thirty."

"Don't you want to eat something?"

"No, I couldn't stomach anything right now," she said. "I'll pack some protein bars in case my stomach changes its mind. Let's get going."

While Jake guided the car through the late morning traffic, Jo called Dr. Anastasia Friedrick. They hadn't spoken since Pauli's wedding, but Jo knew she could get an honest assessment from Stacey. Sidestepping the receptionist at Stacey's office, Jo called her personal cell. She put her phone on speaker so Jake could hear.

The good doctor picked up on the second ring. "Jo" she answered with her usual exuberance. "How are the girls doing? I heard Kevin and Kate were in Jersey. Did Pauli and Liz come with them?"

Jo looked like she felt exhausted just hearing the energy in her friend's voice. "Stace, I've got some hard news," she began. "I need an opinion about a neurosurgeon."

"She could hear Stacey draw in her breath. There was an instantaneous change from friend to doctor. "The best one I know is Dr. Dunn at UMDNJ," Stacey said. "From what I've heard, he is a man of steel, steady hands, doesn't get rattled or panic. I just left the hospital. When I get to my office, I'll text you his number and give him a call to expect you."

The woman is amazing, Jake thought. Without any details, with only a mention of a neurosurgeon, she knew what was needed.

"We're already on our way up to speak with him," Jo said. "Your endorsement means the world to me, Stace."

"What did the MRA show?"

"Two operable aneurysms, one a bit tricky, so my neurologist suggested Dr. Dunn."

"Have you ever met him?"

"No, not a lot of brain surgery in the ER," Jo laughed.

"His reputation is excellent."

"That's comforting."

"Let me know what he says."

"As soon as I know I'll call you."

"Call the office number, I'll be with patients, so my cell will be off."

"Will do Stace, talk to you later."

Traffic was light, so Jake handed Jo his cell. "Go to contacts and scroll down to Chief Brendler," he requested. "Let's see if a fireman agrees with the doctors."

Jo did as instructed; shortly after that the Chief was on the line. She gave a quick explanation and the Chief confirmed that from all he had heard, Dr. Dunn was exceptional, but he had never seen him. From Dr. Dunn's reputation, the Chief said he would be comfortable with him. With that issue covered, they settled into a quiet ride to Newark.

When they arrived at the hospital, Jill and Mark were waiting.

"Kevin and Kate got off okay last night?" Mark asked Jake.

"Yeah, they did," Jake answered. "They got to fly over the eastern half of the country on the night of Independence Day. Must have enjoyed a dozen different fireworks displays viewing from above. The kids missed it. They're here for another week. We should try that sometime."

"So, they don't know about Jo's diagnosis yet?" Mark asked.

"No, talked to Stacey and the Chief about the doctor we're going to see. That's it. The kids don't even know."

"Okay," Jo said. "Let's go get some answers for the questions they'll have."

Dr. Dunn's office was almost Spartan compared to the suburban medical buildings to which they were accustomed. After filling out forms and handing the insurance card in to be copied, they sat down in the small waiting room. Before they could settle in and discuss Jo's options, the receptionist called Jo's name.

"I don't think the office is going to be any larger than out here," Jill said. "So, we'll wait here, keep our fingers crossed, and say a little prayer."

Jo smiled, turned with Jake, and went to talk with a possible savior.

"Hello Jo," Dr. Dunn smiled. "My phone has been ringing off the hook with calls for you."

"Oh, I'm sorry, doctor," Jo said looking embarrassed. "I just called a couple of friends for advice. It was never meant to bother you."

"No bother at all," the doctor laughed. "People with caring family and friends always have better outcomes."

"This is my husband Jake," Jo said. "We're here as a team and you're the coach."

The doctor laughed at that. "Nice to meet you, Jake," he said. "I understand you're a retired Newark firefighter. Ever come here? My father told me, back in the day they had a wayward alarm system that was set off when the heat came on."

Jake did his best to appear positive, realizing the doctor had a short time to create a working relationship with Jo's "team." He didn't feel very jovial.

The most important person in his life was about to be told whether this doctor was going to cut a hole in her skull and tie off some weak blood vessels. Party time this was not, but he would act the part for Jo's sake. "I was on the engine company that was first due on the south side of the hospital and second due on the north side. We spent many a morning coming here for malfunctions. I also spent too much time in the ER after getting knocked down at fires. That's where we met."

"Really? In the ER?" Dr. Dunn asked.

"I was an ER nurse for years, doc," Jo joined in. "He came in one hot day looking like a drowned rat. Ended up under an air conditioning outlet and was too young and dumb to move."

She and the doctor laughed. Jake smiled at the memory and his wife's resilience. You would think they were here for a routine physical. How long could she maintain her composure? Jake didn't want her to get too emotional

219

after what happened to her sister.

"So, let's get down to business," Dr. Dunn said. "I've reviewed your MRA. You have two aneurysms that need to be attended to. Fortunately, they're in the same area. There are two ways to treat these. Smaller one can be treated with what we call coils. These are inserted with minimally invasive surgery. Unfortunately, one is too large for it to be treated that way. That one is going to require a clip be inserted which means opening the skull. How soon do you want to do this?"

"Doctor, I don't want to walk around with a ticking bomb in my head any longer than I have to. My sister was in the same situation. A week before her scheduled surgery the aneurysm burst and killed her. If you tell me to walk down to the operation theater now, I'll do it."

Jake was shocked. He wasn't ready yet. If this guy says okay, let's do it, how would he react? The very thought terrified him. A working fire was much easier to face. He sat helplessly as a spectator waiting for his fate to be pronounced.

The doctor was no longer smiling. Instead, he was wearing a stern, professional look.

"I have an unexpected opening in my surgery schedule two days from now."

"Unexpected?" Jo asked.

"Yes, a gentleman with a similar condition was scheduled, but he passed away yesterday. If you want it, I'll set it up."

This appeared to hit Jo hard. To Jake it was a physical blow to the head. The implications of what the doctor said added an urgency that had not existed a moment before. Jo's jaw tightened as she looked directly into the doctor's eyes and said, "Okay, doc, when do I check in?"

"We have to do some prep work," he said. "Can you come back tomorrow for the pre-operation checkup and tests?"

"When should I be here?"

"First, can I speak with you frankly?"

"Please do, doctor."

"Do you have a living will?"

"Yes."

"All of your papers are in order?"

"We confirmed it all with our lawyer."

"Okay, then the receptionist will give you the instructions. We can proceed in two days. I've done many of these. Not that brain surgery is routine, but this is as close as it gets. I think you'll do fine."

With that, the consultation was over. When they walked out of the office, Jake felt as numb as Jo appeared. Thank God Jill and Mark were waiting for them.

Chapter Forty-two

Jo rested very calmly on the gurney, ready to be wheeled into the operating room. Jake looked down at her and smiled.

"Lady, you going to stay around and watch me grow old?"

"You're already old," she laughed. "Don't be so dramatic. The risky part is over. If it pops now, they'll just roll me in a little quicker and set everything right."

He reviewed the last couple of days and marveled at her courage. She just accused him of being dramatic as she waited to be taken to brain surgery. Her confidence in modern medicine was well beyond his. Or was it all a façade? Simply false bravado to mask her concerns. Afterall, they did have brutally frank discussions about end-of-life decisions and what to tell the kids if something went wrong.

Her enthusiasm for the conspiracy had grown exponentially. She had even helped Kevin recruit Kate. Now all the pieces were in place to present to the girls, but he felt no satisfaction. Jo would be in the hospital for at least three days. Not until she was home would he feel right.

A nurse came to wheel her to the operating room, leaving Jake to wait. Mark was coming down to take him to lunch. The operation was supposed to take between three and four hours. Jo had made him promise to eat and get some air. She couldn't abide him sitting in the waiting area four hours with nothing to do but worry.

Mark showed up an hour after Jo went through the doors into the surgery area. He didn't say a word, just walked up to Jake and motioned for him to stand up. The two headed for the exit in silence. When they walked out of the building Mark asked, "What will it be, Italian, Portuguese, a diner, a tavern?"

Jake thought for a second and settled on simple fare. "Let's go to Krug's," he suggested. "I may need a shot before we finish."

"Krug's it is," Mark agreed. "Maybe they'll have fresh ham today."

They reached Mark's car, climbed in, and headed Down Neck. "Jill's coming down a little later," Mark said as they began negotiating through their old first due district. "She thinks you need to talk with guys right now."

Jake shook his head in agreement. "Probably right," he said. "If she were here, I might try to make her feel better."

As they traveled down South Orange Avenue, they pointed out locations where they had memorable fires or experiences. New construction now filled the empty lots. The abandoned buildings and projects were all gone. It was a different world than when they worked together at Six Engine. The city still had its problems, but had been on the upswing for thirty years or more. The progress was evident all around them. Jake was content his home town was mending, but couldn't help feel a lost sense of purpose like they had in the bad old days.

After ordering their sandwiches at Krug's, the two men sat at a table. Jake forced himself to eat, knowing he would need the energy to deal with whatever happened in the next few hours.

"So, Pauli changed her flight?" Mark asked.

"Yeah, she figures Mom isn't going to be up and about for a few days, so someone has to care for Dad."

Mark laughed. "She has a very low opinion of your competence now?"

"No, she didn't mean that," Jake chortled. "She needs an excuse to hang around for her mother. It'll be the perfect opportunity to spring the trap without Liz being exposed. Kevin is best suited to deal with Liz."

"What are you talking about?"

"Oh, sorry. I forgot," Jake answered, "You're not in on the conspiracy yet. Jo knows now, so we don't have to worry about Jill inadvertently telling her."

"Telling Jo what?

Jake gave as concise an explanation as he could.

"And you have everyone in agreement on this?" Mark asked.

"Not everyone," Jake said. "We haven't put it to the girls yet. Jo just agreed. The boys agreed."

"It's brilliant if you get the girls to go along."

"We're working on that," Jake said. "Jo was hesitant at first. Then we saw a doctor who ordered a test that changed our lives. Now she's all in."

Mark shook his head in acknowledgement while taking a bite of his sandwich. The bar was filling with the lunch crowd from the factories and workshops in the area. Men were shouting their orders and laughing with each other while Jake thought of Jo and their life together.

"Mark," he said, finding it unbearable to keep his thoughts inside. "What's going on? First John, then Paul, then Jane, now Jo has a surgeon working on her brain. Where did the time go?"

"The time? Damned if I can tell you Jake," Mark sighed. "Seems we were just twenty-five, sitting in the ER with a little heat and smoke. Then a couple of cute nurses came over to help us. As far as the friends we have lost, that's been going on all along. We were just too young and dumb to notice. Remember, 'It is with deep regret we announce the death of retired firefighter or Captain, or Battalion Chief, or Deputy Chief, even Chief of Department.' Those announcements from dispatch were pretty regular."

"Yeah, you're right," Jake admitted. "It's just different when they're talking about someone you know."

"I remember talking with my father, thirty, maybe thirty-five years ago," Mark said. "He told me when he says goodbye to friends and family, he does it as if he'll never see them again. When I commented that it sounded kind of morbid, he said it wasn't. It was just an acceptance of fact. When you're his age, people who have been in your life for decades start to die."

224

"Is that where we're at now?" Jake asked.

Jake felt the frustration of the past few days boiling over. The questions that had dogged him came tumbling out. "What am I going to do if she doesn't pull through this?" he asked, "She's the best thing that ever happened to me. I'm not ready to let go."

Mark reacted with reassurance. "You're not going to have to let go, Jake. She's in competent hands. It's a little bump in the road."

"God, I hope you're right," Jake sighed. He leaned back and finished his beer, still haunted by questions with no answers. Questions that went beyond mere relevance. "Forty years of marriage and what do we have to show for it? A house, a car, some savings? The house with all that sweat equity I put into it to make it perfect for Jo, some developer's going to come along, buy it out, and knock it down to build a McMansion. The car, in a few years it'll be in a junk yard. The savings will be spent on medical bills and medication."

"Jake," Mark reminded him. "You've got family. You've got friends. Everything else is bullshit."

"And if she dies, what do I have?"

"Two great kids."

Jake looked around at the crowded bar. All these guys were working their asses off for their families. If they knew what kind of life he had last week, they'd probably be jealous. How quickly it all changed. Now they probably wouldn't take his life if he gave it to them. But if she pulled through . . . .

He wanted to run that thought past Mark. "I was just thinking, most of the guys here would not want my life right now."

Mark gave him a quizzical look. "With what's happening today, probably not," Mark agreed.

"But if Jo pulls through," Jake laughed. "They'd kill for it."

Mark laughed. "Who am I to argue with that?"

225

"Okay, you've fulfilled your duty and I did as my lovely wife requested. Lunch is done. Now let's get back and see if we can't just will her out with a prayer or two."

When they got back to the hospital, Pauli and Liz were in the waiting area with Jill, Tim, and Carl. An hour later, Stacey came out still in scrubs to talk with them.

"Dr. Friedrick," Jake greeted. "What are you doing here?"

"I volunteered my nursing services to help Dr. Dunn," Stacey laughed. "Jo appreciated seeing me there."

"How is it going?" Pauli asked.

"Oh, your mom is on the way to post op," Stacey assured them. "Dr. Dunn was extraordinary. You did the right thing in pushing to get this done quickly. The aneurysm burst just after Dr. Dunn clipped it. You couldn't have arrived any later."

Jake felt dizzy. He had almost lost her. It would have been just like Jane. "She's going to be alright, Stace?"

"Yes, Jake. She's going to be fine. Give her a few weeks and she'll be back to her normal self."

"When can we see her?" Tim asked.

"It's going to be a while," Stacey replied reverting back to Dr. Friedrick. "She needs rest and time to get all those drugs out of her system."

"Why don't you kids go eat?" Jake suggested. "And take Aunt Jill with you. We'll stand guard."

As the happy group walked away, Mark commented, "If I hadn't spoken to Jill about your scheme, would you have encouraged her to go with them?"

"Probably not," Jake said. "The security of our conspiracy would have to be considered."

They went to sit in front of the room's television. The news was on, but Jake wasn't interested. He had already received the most important news of the day.

Chapter Forty-three

Tim went to pick up his mother while Jake and Pauli prepared the house. Not that there was much to prepare. The doctor had said she had to rest and recuperate for six to eight weeks. Standard care for a broken bone. Only this bone was her skull and it wasn't broken, they had cut a hole in it. Broken or cut, bone healed at the same rate. Part of her head had also been shaved. That might have been an issue in the winter requiring careful covering of the area exposed to the weather, but it was July. Jersey was in the midst of a heatwave. Jake chuckled remembering the first July heatwave he and Jo had endured together.

"And what are you smiling about?" Pauli asked.

"Who me? Smiling?" Jake replied. "Beside all being right with the world, what made me smile? Remembering the first heatwave your mother and I went through together."

"You're smiling about a heatwave?" Pauli asked. "I'm sorry, I guess I'm a product of my central air conditioning generation. Heatwaves don't make me smile."

"It's not the heat, just the memory of us starting out together," Jake assured her. "The chase lounge is all set in the den?"

"Dad, you and Tim put it there," Pauli reminded him. "Where did you get the idea for one of those and where did you find it? I never even heard of them."

Jake marveled at his daughter's lack of knowledge about this particular type of furniture. He had grown up with one of these in his grandmother's parlor. Apparently, chase lounges had gone the way of breakfronts. Only found in the homes of elderly couples and widows. But it was an ideal piece of furniture for Jo's recuperation period, so she wouldn't have to be restricted to their bedroom the entire six to eight weeks.

"Your great-grandmother had one in her parlor when I was growing up," he explained. "When the doctor told us your mother's restrictions, it came to mind. After that it was a Google search."

"It's lucky you were paying attention, there's no way I could have thought it up," Pauli said.

Bedroom squared away, Jake thought. Den all set. Now to confirm the bath was set. He had one of the guys from Seven Engine install bars in the shower for Jo to use in steadying herself. There was also a seat in the shower now. For the next several weeks, she should be all set.

Able to relax for a few minutes, Jake began to think of how to start one of the most important conversations he would have for the foreseeable future. He decided on an indirect route.

"So, what do you think of Tim and Clare?" he asked.

"Tim and Clare? That's an unexpected question," Pauli commented. "They seem to be getting along. Tim is kind of closed mouth about it, but Clare? Clare seems to be smitten as grandma used to say."

"Any feedback from Liz?"

"Liz seems content with the relationship," Pauli said. "She and Clare go back a long way. And Clare was so helpful with our relationship."

Jake saw this statement as a way to broach the subject of why Clare was helpful and how that might lead to motherhood. Before he could say another word, Pauli began asking him questions.

"Dad, I need a little advice," she began.

Jake reacted instantly, "What kind of advice do you need?"

"Well," Pauli said hesitantly. Jake knew better than to jump in. How many times had he anticipated a question from Jo and gotten it wrong.

"This is a little embarrassing," she tried to start again.

"I'm your father, kid," Jake chuckled. "And an old man, no need to hold anything back. I may not have seen it all, but I've seen more than the average

229

guy."

"It has to do with Clare," she tried one more time. "Or more like the clinic she works in."

"Her father's clinic?"

"Right, and it has to deal with her father," she continued. "You see, we've decided to start a family. We're both a little late to the game, as you would say, so we can't spend a lot of time thinking about it."

Jake couldn't keep the grin off his face. Half the battle was already won.

"My advice would be, as long as your relationship is solid, go for it," Jake said.

"Oh, our relationship is great, but we face challenges other couples don't," Pauli stated the obvious. "And one of those challenges is Clare's father."

Hearing this, Jake made an instantaneous decision to say something for its shock value. "You mean his insistence that a male be involved in the woman's life before he'll perform artificial insemination?"

This stopped Pauli cold. "How do you know that?" she asked in shock.

"Clare told me."

"Clare?"

"Yeah, at the Fourth of July picnic," he said. "We had a heart to heart by the grill while you were enjoying the parade."

"Really?" Pauli said sounding perplexed. "And what did you talk about, revolutionary Morris County?"

Jake chuckled. "No, we talked about Liz and you, Tim and her, and her father's attitude toward fatherhood or at least a father figure in a child's life."

"And how did you end up on that subject?"

"Well, Carl mentioned that Clare had a hand in you and Liz deciding to form a family."

"Carl?"

230

"Yeah, it seems that Clare told Carl he would be a perfect donor at her father's clinic. Clare assured me she meant he was a healthy male without any family history of genetic disorders."

Pauli stood flabbergasted. Jake could see her mind was moving at light speed trying to figure out what was going on.

"Then she told me that her father was conflicted," Jake continued. "When Liz approached him about motherhood, he was sure she would make an excellent mother, but there would be no male in her life. So, Clare and I discussed how to convince her old man to help out."

"You did what?" Pauli asked incredulously. "Is that why Clare has been acting so strange? You put ideas into her head?"

"Ideas?" Jake said trying to slow things down so Pauli could adjust, otherwise she would become her mother's clone and explode.

"Yes, when Liz and I talked with Clare about her father, she began emphasizing his need for a guy to be involved."

"Well, that's basic biology," Jake pointed out.

"You know what I mean, Dad," Pauli shot back.

"So, you started this conversation looking for advice on how to convince Clare's father to help you, right?"

This seemed to slow Pauli down a bit. She backtracked a step and asked, "What's going on here?"

"What do you mean?

"First you asked about Tim and Clare, then you talked about Clare, then her father, then Carl being a perfect donor. I know firemen. You've been talking with Liz's dad too, haven't you?"

"Of course, I talked with Kevin," Jake laughed. "He and his wife were our houseguests."

"That's not what I'm saying and you know it," Pauli snapped. "Not only are

231

you a fireman planning out how to attack a problem, but you're an accountant. Always looking at details to figure out the best way to get all the law allows."

Jake wasn't sure where she was going with this, but it didn't sound good. He kept his mouth shut and let her emotions play out. Before she could go any further, Tim pulled into the driveway.

"Okay," she said. "We'll discuss this after Mom is settled in. Just remember it's Liz and my decision not yours and Kevin's."

Shit, he thought. I didn't even get to present the plan for her to mull over in her mind as she settled her mother in.

Chapter Forty-four

Jo was already climbing out of the car when Pauli reached her. Tim jogged from the driver's side of the car and was right behind his sister.

"I told her to wait," Tim said to Pauli.

"Now I'm 'her'," Jo snapped back. "They fixed the problem without doing harm, like they are supposed to. I'm not crippled, just temporarily on medication."

Tim and Pauli exchanged looks of doubt, but let their mother begin walking toward the house. Her head was wrapped in bandages and covered with a helmet, but there were no other signs she had done anything other than bump into something. Jake walked up and offered his arm.

"My lady," he said. "Would you accept this gentleman's arm as we stroll?"

Jo chuckled and took her husband's arm. Tim grabbed the overnight bag his mother had taken to the hospital and then walked with Pauli behind their parents, ready to jump in if necessary. Jake led his wife into the house at a casual pace, paying attention to every step. As far as he could tell, she was doing fabulously.

"We have arranged the house so you can rest up, but not be stuck upstairs," Jake said, leading Jo into the den.

"What's that?" Jo asked as soon as she saw the chase lounge. "That looks like something out of the pictures of your grandmother's living room."

Jake knew when she said it that the chase lounge would have a short life in their den.

"Just temporary, Jo," he assured her. "So, you can lie here during the day. It so much brighter and more comfortable than staying in the bedroom."

"If you think I'm going to stay in bed for six weeks, you're crazy," Jo stated. "I have my helmet. When I get off the pain meds, we'll go out to celebrate. The doctor did not condemn me to prison, just stay off the ski slopes and the jet ski."

Jake felt a weight lift off his shoulders. She was still Jo. They had dodged the bullet completely.

"Yes, dear," he replied in a quivering voice.

"Don't 'yes dear' me, Jake," Jo laughed. "Nothing has changed other than the time bomb in my head."

"So, what do I tell Kate and Jill?" Jake asked.

"Kate and Jill?" Jo replied. "What about them?"

"They intended to camp out here and tend to your every need," Jake told her.

Jo chuckled, then got choked up. "They don't have to do that, Pauli is here."

Jake hesitated speaking, debating whether to tell Jo about the phone conversation he had with the Moores. He decided it might help with Pauli.

"Pauli being here is the problem as far as they're concerned," he said. "She's here and Liz is in Chicago, so Liz is miserable."

Pauli had an astonished look on her face. Then she turned away to hide her reaction.

Jo looked as shocked as her daughter. Jake waited for the ladies to finish processing his latest revelation. How this would play out was beyond him. His hope had been Pauli would laugh and loosen up so they could have a rational discussion. Pauli pulled it together first.

"Okay, I'm back," she said. "Liz and I discussed this. We consider it an obligation of love. She would do the same thing for her mother and I would certainly accept it. So, we can stop that discussion. I intend to stay until you've recovered, Mom. Think of it as me doing something for my mental health. If I leave, I'll go crazy with worry."

Jo didn't react immediately. She considered the situation thoroughly before saying anything. When she spoke, it was in a slow, deliberate cadence.

"I think it will take a few days to settled into a routine," she said. "Once we're used to the routine, there's no need for anyone other than your father to be here."

"That sounds like we're playing it by ear," Tim said. "Clare was also going to volunteer. I'll tell her thanks, but no need."

Jo reacted to this instantly. "Clare said that? Well, she's a nurse. I can see that."

This took them all by surprise. Jake began to worry immediately. What Jo said was plainly contradictory. Was there something off? He looked around and saw Pauli appeared as confused as he was. But when he looked at Tim, his son was struggling not to smile. Had Jo and Tim had a conversation about Clare that he wasn't privy to? Pauli seemed to pick up on Tim's vibes at the same time. She didn't say a word. Then Jo appeared to come to a decision. She turned to Pauli and said, "Pauli, could you go up to our bedroom and get the envelope in my night stand?"

Envelope in her night stand? Jake thought. What was she talking about?

After Pauli climbed the stairs, Jo turned to Jake and Tim. "Tim knows about the conspiracy, right?" she asked.

Tim smiled and shook his head yes. Jake wasn't expecting to discuss this now. It could lead to an emotional meltdown if there was any miscommunication.

"I think we should start lobbying now," Jo said. "Pauli will be more receptive to my opinion today than she will a week from now."

Jake glanced toward the stairs, all clear for the moment. He took out his phone and began texting Kevin while he spoke.

"We already began a discussion this morning," he told her. "We didn't get beyond the point where she suspects something is going on. You got here before the discussion went any further. Last thing she said was 'We'll discuss it later.'"

"How far did you get?" Jo asked.

"She knows we've been talking about Liz and her problem of conceiving at the clinic."

The sound of Pauli coming down the stairs ended the conversation. At least Jo and Tim knew where things stood. Hopefully, Jo's condition will keep a lid on the emotions that could be unleashed. Jake still had no idea what Pauli was retrieving. When she walked into the room, she appeared upset.

"Just in case, Mom?" Pauli asked as she pointed at the writing on a letter sized envelope.

"It was brain surgery, Pauli." Jo answered. "And the aneurysm burst in the middle of the operation, remember?"

Pauli walked over to her mother and gave her a hug.

"Enough of the what-ifs," Jo laughed. "Why don't you open the envelope and take out the smaller one inside?"

Pauli did as directed. After reading the front of the smaller envelop, she opened it.

"If you're reading this, I'm no longer on this earth. After you say good-bye to me, please give serious consideration to your father's suggestion about the fathers of yours and Liz's children. I know it is an intensely personal and emotional decision, but he has given it considerable thought and will suggest a rational way of choosing that will bind both families and double the love."

Pauli stood transfixed, staring at the paper. "Who's in on this?" she whispered.

"In on what?" Jo asked.

"Dad already told me that Liz's dad, Carl, Clare, and he have been discussing Liz and me starting a family."

"Pauli, that is natural," Jo assured her. "Your grandparents talked about us starting a family at our wedding."

"I understand that," Pauli replied. "But our case is different. Different times, different circumstances."

"You get to choose a father in a rational manner," Jake reminded her.

"A rational manner?" Pauli asked. "What does that mean?"

"It means you can minimize the chances of your child having a heartbreaking genetic problem," Jo said.

"You started to ask me a question this morning about the problem of Clare's father, right?"

"How are you going to overcome that hurtle?" Pauli asked. "Maybe we won't even need to see a doctor to conceive. Pete told me about a case in California in the 80s that could solve that problem."

"Pete?" Tim asked in shock, "He's a lawyer, not a doctor."

Pauli shot him a scathing look. "Are you in on this, too?" she asked then pushed on. "Yes, Pete's a lawyer. When he heard of Clare's father having this rule, he said we could sue. He did some research and found a decision from a California judge who ruled a woman who used a turkey baster to inseminate her partner with her brother's sperm was the child's father."

"And how does Liz feel about that?" Jake asked.

"It doesn't matter," Pauli sighed. "You have a suggestion on how to overcome his resistance?"

Jake took a deep breath and began to lay out his proposal and reasoning for it. Pauli listened calmly. She seemed to go through stages of emotions, but controlled herself. This allowed Jake to present the whole proposition without interruption. When the entire plan was in front of them., they could have a rational discussion.

"So, if Liz and I agree that this is the best way, then you feel Clare's father will go for it?" Pauli asked after Jake finished.

"It fulfills his personal requirements," he pointed out. "Clare seemed to think it would and then said it would create a beautiful and loving family."

"I have to speak with Liz," Pauli said. "Did her folks agree with this idea?"

"Of course," Jake replied. "And Pauli, remember, it's just that. It's an idea. You will be the parents. You will have to make the decisicn. Consider it seriously, that's all we ask. It will make your family blood relatives and as they say, blood is thicker than water."

"I wish it was that simple," Pauli said. "I'll call Liz now and see if we can set up a video conference, a family meeting, with all who are involved. Then Liz and I can discuss it and decide."

She marched out of the room, a woman with a purpose, but appearing not to be happy about it.

Jake quickly pulled out his phone and began texting.

"Who are you texting?" Jo asked.

Jake looked in the direction Pauli had walked, then said, "Kevin, I told him we were talking to Pauli. He sent a text back acknowledging he got it and saying Liz was on her way to them. Now, I'm going to tell him what to expect."

"You two are one hell of a team," Jo chortled.

Chapter Forty-five

The laptop could have easily been moved to the den, but that idea had been rejected outright. Tim was to have the den to himself, attending the video conference on his phone. Pauli would be in her old room on the second floor using her phone. Their parents were assigned to Jake's mancave in the basement. The absurdity of this arrangement was not lost on Jake. Whoever said the internet brought people together had not thought of this. They would be together electronically only. Physical proximity was not allowed. Each had to communicate privately with someone not in Jersey.

Tim intended to get Clare up to speed on the happenings of the past day before the conference began. Pauli and Liz were having a private chat beforehand. That left Jake and Jo joining Kevin and Kate in the waiting room of the video meeting. It was ironic. Even with all the traveling back and forth, somehow it worked out that the Jersey folks were in Jersey and the Chicago folks were in Chicago.

As Jake arranged the room so Jo could sit next to him in front of the laptop camera, it struck him how tonight's video meeting resembled negotiations for a marriage contract five hundred years ago. Not that any of their ancestors were in a position to require a marriage contract. They all descended from arranged marriage/kidnap the bride for six months stock.

"Jo," he shouted up the stairs. "Are you ready? The meeting starts in a few minutes."

"Almost done talking with Clare," she called down.

Talking with Clare, he thought. Wasn't that Tim's gig? Was that part of the evening's plan? He had a feeling that even if Tim decided Clare was not for him, she would be in their life for good as a friend of Jo's. Not that it was a bad thing, just unexpected. He heard Jo at the top of the stairs, so went up to help her come down.

"I'm perfectly capable of going down a flight of stairs, Jake," Jo said. Still, he climbed up a few steps and was ready to catch her if she slipped.

After they got comfortable, Jake turned on the laptop. As the computer did its usual dance to boot up, Jake turned to his wife and asked, "Talking to Clare? Did you ferret out any useful info for tonight's negotiations?"

"Ferret out, Jake?" she laughed. "You make me sound like Sherlock Holmes. There's nothing to ferret out. I was just asking her what she felt Pauli and Liz would decide tonight."

"And she said?"

"She said they would probably go for your plan since Liz had already considered something like it on her own."

Jake was speechless for a short while, then blurted, "Already considered it? Really? That's fantastic."

"Don't start celebrating," Jo cautioned. "Already considered is not decided to do. You're going to have to persuade both of them this is the way to go. They're choosing fathers for their children, not cars."

By now the computer had completed booting up, so Jake clicked the conference icon. After a series of passwords and clicks, the conference screen came up. Officially, he was hosting the meeting, so he had a few more clicks before the picture of Kevin and Kate appeared on the screen.

"There you are," Jake said to Kevin and Kate's image. "Can you see and hear me?"

"Yes," they answered.

"Are you doing this as a family or separately," Jake asked.

"Oh, Carl's at his apartment and Liz is at hers," Kate told him. "We're all in our separate, secret cells so we can confer with our attorney or whomever we need to talk to."

"I know," Jo laughed. "Supersecret stuff."

"So, how are you feeling, Jo?" Kate asked.

"I spend a lot of time on my back," Jo chuckled. "And wear my helmet wherever I go which has been the bedroom and the den. Tonight's an adventure. We're in Jake's office in the basement."

"You're still on medication?"

"Still on the meds."

The computer began signaling someone wanted to join the meeting. Jake clicked yes and Tim popped up. There were three more beeps in rapid succession. Jake admitted the rest into the meeting. With everyone present, Jake started.

"So, I call the Covey-Moore, Moore-Covey meeting to order since it's my account," Jake said. "I'll begin with a quick qualifier. No one should feel pressure to do something they are not comfortable with. We're here to discuss options. Then Liz and Pauli will make a decision, All in agreement?"

There was a minute of noise signifying agreement. Then Liz and Pauli took over.

"First, we want to tell everyone that Pauli and I had our DNA analyzed for any troublesome, recessive genes," Liz said. "And we were told that there were no issues that would cause doubt to our being mothers."

Jake listened with interest. They had gone to a genetic counselor? Not even the Chief had suggested that. But that was only half the story unless they decided to go with his plan.

"The genetic counselor said we would be a perfect match if we were an average couple."

They were inching closer to the answer that was Jake's hope. He felt like shouting halleluiah, but waited. Just because a counselor said they were a good match did not mean the girls were comfortable with his proposal. There were societal factors that could sabotage the whole deal.

"So, now we want to emphasize," Pauli said. "That all decisions will be made by the two of us. And we will be responsible for all expenses. So, medical expenses, transportation costs, lodging, food, etcetera will be covered by us."

There were no objections from Carl or Tim who would be the only ones to which these conditions applied.

"Also," Liz stepped in. "We are solely responsible for any children. We will be the parents and will raise our offspring as is required of all parents. Tim and Carl will be known solely as uncles, at least while the children are young. Once they reach an age where they begin to reason and question, we'll need to explain more. But that's Pauli's and my responsibility. Are we all in agreement on that?"

All answered in the affirmative. Jake had a feeling that Pete was behind the questions, at least the phrasing of them.

"If the counselor said you and Pauli are a perfect match," Carl asked. "Does that translate to Tim and me being perfect also?"

"Being perfect?" Liz laughed. "No, not perfect; just being good matches as donors."

"Are you going the turkey baster route?" Jake asked. "Or will it be Clare's clinic?"

"I'm not chancing it to a turkey baster," Liz stated. "I trust Dr. Donahue entirely."

Pauli jumped in to qualify her partner's statement. "If at all possible, we're going through the clinic. A turkey baster doesn't deliver babies."

"Just spoke with Clare," Tim interjected. "She spoke with her father and explained the proposal. He has no problem with our arrangement. So, you can take that concern off the table."

Pauli and Liz smile broadly when they heard this news. Jake couldn't believe the meeting was going so smoothly.

"So, we all in agreement?" Kevin asked.

"Slow down," Pauli insisted. "Just reconfirming, the children will be our responsibility and we have complete authority and final say in all decisions."

Jake, Jo, Kevin, and Kate gave a subdued agreement because they knew the need for this confirmation was not addressed at them. They would be the grandparents who had the right to love and spoil, but no responsibility. The boys would be the fathers. There was case law concerning their position which Jake was sure Pete had told the girls.

"We'll help out if one of you has a boy," Carl said. "But only as any uncle would."

"Yeah," Tim agreed. "We'll take him fishing and give him a talking to if need be."

"You can take a girl fishing too, you know," Pauli teased.

"Sounds like fun," Carl agreed.

The meeting was flowing now, Jake noticed, with the younger generation setting the parameters. That was appropriate since neither Kevin nor he could say how many years they would be around for their grandchildren.

"How about future wives?" Liz asked.

Tim picked up this question. "Can't say for sure since we don't know who those wives would be," he said. "But talking with our current interests, there doesn't seem to be a problem. The children would be nieces and nephews."

"And when they eventually begin to question?" Pauli asked.

"Well, we will be in their lives all along," Carl pointed out. "So, I think they'll be okay with it."

There was a pause in the conversation. Jake waited a beat, then asked for a final agreement.

"All are in agreement that this is the way to go?"

They all said yes, with Kate and Jo looking exceptionally happy about the outcome.

"That's as far as we can go," Kevin said. "Now it's up to Liz and Pauli."

"Liz will be the first to try," Pauli said. "Since she has seniority."

"Why don't you try together?" Kate asked.

"No way!" both Liz and Pauli shouted.

"Two at once," Liz said "Without full support? It doesn't matter how hard these two try. They can't do it all because they won't be living with the children. From what I've seen, motherhood is a twenty-four/seven occupation. Two infants at one time would exhaust us."

"You can always give your mothers a call," Jo said.

Everyone laughed, but all knew there would be no "twins". With that the conference accomplished its goals and they signed off.

Jake reviewed the past months. It was a well fought campaign. They had unexpected allies in Clare and her father. It would have been touch and go without them.

The thought of Clare brought another consideration to mind. What if Tim and Clare clicked? There was the possibility that Tim would move to Chicago also. Then Clare's involvement would become a double-edged sword, leaving him and Jo in Jersey and the kids and grandkids in Chicago. How relevant would he be as a grandfather eight hundred miles away? Would Jo want to move? He doubted it. Their base was in Jersey, but they could video chat over the internet. This was not his grandfather's world. If that problem arose, it would be the best kind of problem. He shut off the computer and helped Jo up the stairs.

Chapter Forty-six

Jake looked out at the Atlantic Ocean. The sun was still close to the horizon. He was setting up his pole for the first cast. Carl came over to see how things were going before he did the same.

"At least Tim can fish in peace now," Carl said. "That first day must have been frustrating."

Jake chuckled at the memory. "We've been doing this for four seasons now," he pointed out. "Did Tim mention frustration to you?"

"No," Carl replied. "That's pure speculation on my part."

"I would think he enjoyed himself that first day," Jake said. "He got in on every fish we caught."

He finished his set up, but delayed casting. The conversations on the beach were what made these trips worth it.

"Did he ever mention missing his surf fishing club when he's in Chicago?" Jake asked.

Carl chuckled. "No, not a word, but when he hits the beach here you can see how much he misses it."

"Not much surf fishing on Lake Michigan," Jake said. "He should move back to Jersey so he can enjoy his chosen sport."

Carl shook his head. "Clare is not going anywhere, not in her condition."

"She's here now, isn't she?"

"She's not due for another four months," Carl reminded the grandfather. "Until she has all the children she wants, she's not leaving the vicinity of that clinic. Wants grandpa to deliver her children."

Jake took a deep breath of ocean air and sighed. Clare had turned into that double-edged sword. Now both his children and his granddaughter as well as his two soon to be born grandsons all lived or would live in Chicago. The challenge was to fly to the Midwest enough to satisfy his need to be relevant in his grandchildren's lives without being a pain in the ass for his children. It would be a delicate balancing act. At least he had these two weeks each summer. Two weeks of sun, surf fishing, and Broadway is how he put it.

When Liz gave birth grandpa decided to claim dibs on the Fourth of July. Every year since that first year, the Coveys and the Moores had vacationed on Long Beach Island in the same place Tim had rented that year. Every Fourth of July they went to Florham Park for Mark's cook out. This year was especially satisfying because both Clare and Pauli were pregnant. By next year they would have two little boys, "Tim's terrors" is what Jake was already calling them, to match Mark's "Terry's terrors".

"Whoa, what's that in your ear?" Carl asked.

Jake laughed. Carl finally noticed his newest acquiescence to aging.

"Hearing aids," he said. "The wife got tired of talking loudly and still not being heard. Too many bells, too many sirens, too many airhorns, then throw in an explosion here and an implosion there and the hearing gets screwed up. Occupational hazard."

"Implosion?"

"Yeah, back in the day before thin screen televisions, we had picture tubes, which are just huge vacuum tubes. Sometimes you'd push into a room and the water would hit the heated glass of the picture tube, the glass would crack, and there'd be a loud boom. One time it was right next to my ear. Talk about ringing in your ear. But the glass didn't fly out. It was a vacuum, so everything got sucked in. Still loud as hell and right next to the ear, kind of like going to a rock concert with the amps cranked to the max. You turn sixty and start paying for all the insults to your ears. So, now I have these."

Carl chuckle and shook his head. "Greatest job in the world you say?"

"Unless you experience it, you can't understand. Now, you better get set

246

up," Jake said. "Won't catch anything without a line in the water."

"We've got time," Carl chuckled. "The sun's just up; the sky's blue; it's only the four of us again. Why rush things?"

Jake smiled. "Now you're a philosopher? What happened to data science?"

"Ha,' Carl said. "I wouldn't call it philosophy, more like we're-on-vacation-thought."

Jake shook his head in agreement.

"So, you've decided to take the plunge with Marie, have you?"

"Time to grow up and take a wife, wouldn't you say?" Carl asked.

"Your folks are happy for you," Jake said. "Between your mother's and Jo's worries, the consensus was you had one last shot at a good woman."

"I go that impression," Carl said. "But it was more the 'Three years of dating and no ring? You think I'm staying around forever without a commitment?' that did it."

"That works most of the time," Jake chuckled. "But the man has to be ready to settle down. If he's still restless, he'll bolt. The ladies can usually tell."

With that he glanced over at Kevin and Tim. They were also taking their time getting lines into the ocean surf. It was a laidback morning at the beach for all, allowing Jake to review the past few years.

Jo took advantage of the miracle modern surgery had given her and began volunteering for the MS Society with Kathy Stanley and Chief Brendler. It was her way of giving back to the neurosurgeon who had saved her life. She had received an award for all her efforts at the annual meeting of the Society in May. Kathy had been the inspiration. With their children grown, volunteering also gave relevance to her life. Would that change after the birth of two more grandchildren? Jake doubted it. Afterall, he had always divided relevance into life's work and family.

His own battle for relevance had reached its apex when he stepped in to help

247

Jane's husband Gary negotiate his way out of a possible jail sentence. They had sat down with Gary's partners and come up with a way to repay any missing funds. Of course, Gary had to pledge attendance at Gamblers Anonymous sessions, but thoughts of prison proved to be a tremendous motivator. In the end, Pete had stepped in to help, but he drew up a contract before doing so. It was humbling to Gary that the reason Pete insisted on the contract was his parents had taught him to take responsibility for his actions.

When he thought of Kevin and Kate, he chuckled to himself. Of all the members of the conspiracy, they had come out the best. Liz had given birth to a healthy, happy, adorable little girl. She had been named after Clare for her contribution to Liz and Pauli's marriage and decision to have children and for Jo's sister Jane. This little gift lived fifteen minutes from the Moores. In four months all three of the grandchildren shared by the Coveys and Moores would live within shouting distance of Kevin. Jake would never admit it openly, but he was a bit jealous of his co-conspirator. He had half-heartedly suggested to Jo that they move out there, but was quickly rejected. Their life was still centered in Jersey. So, it was an occasional trip to Chicago instead.

"Time to get a line in the water," he said to Carl after his review. "We only have so much free time before the ladies wake up and demand our attention. If we want to have a fish fry tonight, we'll have to work now."

Carl smiled at the wisdom of Jake's statement and walked back to his pole. Jake strolled to the water's edge and cast out. They had been through a year of hell followed by three years of recovery. Thinking through his present predicament, he realized his problems now were of the positive variety. He looked forward to picking the right time to see the grandkids.

The sun was shining, the ocean breeze was refreshing, and the fish were calling. Life was good. Time to get a line in the water. That's what John, Paul, and Jane would want. As he cast his line out, Jake realized this is what being relevant after sixty felt like.

www.ingramcontent.com/pod-product-compliance
Lightning Source LLC
Chambersburg PA
CBHW031923060726
47496CB00002BB/639